BREYTEN BREYTENBACH

MOUROIR

MIRRORNOTES OF A NOVEL

archipelago books

First Archipelago Books Edition, 2009

Library of Congress Cataloging-in-Publication Data
Breytenbach, Breyten.
[Mouroir. English]
Mouroir / by Breyten Breytenbach.
p. cm.
Includes index.
ISBN 978-0-9800330-7-6
1. South Africa – Fiction. I. Title.
PT6592.12.R4M613 2009
839.3'635 – dc22   2008050229

Archipelago Books
232 Third Street, Suite A111
Brooklyn, NY 11215
www.archipelagobooks.com

Distributed by Consortium Book Sales and Distribution
www.cbsd.com

Printed in Canada

Cover art: Mark Rothko

This publication was made possible with support from Lannan Foundation,
the National Endowment for the Arts, and the New York State
Council on the Arts, a state agency.

All we are is the result of what we thought.
BUDDHA, *The Dhammapada*

Every individual does penance for [his] separation
from the boundless. . . .
ANAXIMANDER

Contents

G? 13

Wiederholen 25

The God Eating 40

The Other Ship 45

The Double Dying of an Ordinary Criminal 50

The Temptation in Rome 68

The Man with the Head 74

Hanging on to Life 77

The Day of the Falling of the Stars and
Searching for the Original Face 88

No, Baba 95

The Oasis 109

The Shoes 114

Max Sec (Beverly Hills) 117

The Break 120

And Move 129

Flight Aid   *136*

The Execution   *139*

Departure   *154*

And Then   *159*

Forefinger   *167*

The Redemption of the Image   *175*

This Little Flea   *177*

Book, a Mirror   *179*

"Tuesday"   *196*

Birds   *201*

Re: Certain Papers Left in My Possession   *204*

The Hat Which Didn't Make It to Heaven   *212*

Leftovers   *216*

Know Thyself   *220*

The Collapse   *222*

Short Story   *235*

A Pattern of Bullets   *237*

On the Way to Ku   *251*

Shadows Break through the Mind   *254*

Bump in the Night   *257*

The Self-Death   *262*

The Key   *269*

Index   *273*

Song of the Masters

if you put the lion out to graze
he might well eat the tulip-bird
the sun will upear in a daze
and I be stuck for a rimy word

Caesar is born and I don care
Hitler is born and I don care
Nixon is born and I don care
all masters gong away

the buildings in their water rend
big bave soldiers bleed the turd
die evy day with doth to blend
an' I shall ride the runny word

Stalin is die and I mot scare
Franco is die and I mot scare
Vorster is die and I mot scare
All deaftlife will be may

MOUROIR

G?

*Japan has many reasons to be sad, and elephants are
almost unknown there, I don't know why.*
Nehru

Now, in retrospect, it is difficult to remember exactly how or precisely when it happened. You should be like the elephant, the animal which can remember all its earlier lives in visions, which stands there contemplating without moving, and then chews the cud: grass, all grass. A life is the metamorphosis of the earlier one(s). A clever man has said – if civilizations can survive only through metamorphosis then the world consists of that which has been forgotten. (But another sly one objected that the living constitute the memory – event and thought – of the dead.) I'd love to see and to recognize a black elephant. Black he must be, but not rubbery. Rather more like silk. Silk that by candlelight has a silvery skin as if of frozen dew when day breaks over the dunes. And its eyes must be huge and dark, and mild, a concentration of the night, the night bumped; and with long eyelashes.

When we lived in Wellington, when I was only a pipsqueak as high as a lap, in the house by the railway tracks close to the station, but the embankment upon which the lines were laid – the beams and the shiny rods especially like protracted silver notes which ought, thus you thought, to vibrate into eternity – this embankment was higher than the house itself so that the trains were in heaven at night, there I was sitting one day on the edge of the small cement reservoir, the dam being in the yard under a tall bluegum tree and the shadow of the tree was as birds, no, more like finely notched wet stains on the earth and against the grey walls, petticoats of black lace stripped from the bodies there – you might have seen it in this way if it hadn't been that the soil itself was already shiny and black from the coal-dust and the soot; I was holding something in my hand and turned it upside down so that a liquid at first squirted over the wall and then flowered. A long golden jet over the wall. The stream, the gold, a snake or a hose or an intestine or perhaps even more intimate – it remained suspended like that: thick and alive. I felt that it was something come forth from my own nebulosity and even so from outside myself. Something which may be my protection. If I could only pin it down! In a manner of speaking, of course. A godliness? A god? But it also left me thinner and more empty. Can that which exhausts you nevertheless take you under its wings? (Maybe this incident was not during the day; perhaps it was already towards nightfall "when you can see three stars at a glance"; the stars like the illuminated windows of a train, and the fair napkins, decanters of wine, silver cutlery. . . .)

A second time I saw that original house when I passed by there many years later, this time in a train with my wife, and I pointed it all out to her. The house was deserted and ordinary. (Against one wall the bleached signboard for "Joko Tea".) How did the building, with the flip of a wrist, get to be so ugly? The wire gauze around the back porch was full of holes. So the flies at last obtained entry – by gnawing? Plunderers! (What we in our hurry see as shadows is in fact a liquid chucked out by the light, all the dirt which light hides behind objects in order the cleanse the eye. It is this wetness which is transformed into flies. Shadows are widows of the light. Death too is a widow.) All about the house the grass grew tall. The front, that side which looked away from the rail embankment over the marshes and further along the dark nick of Port Jacksons on the river banks – the river of a silver trunk, and slightly higher upstream to the left was a favourite bathing pool where brown water used to be dammed behind a floodgate for use by the distillery on the bank, the manager of the distillery was a small fellow with wrinkles, dark hair and a big voice and he had pretty daughters on bicycles, I remember N. Bok with the tits, the thighs twitching whitely under the shortish school skirt – that front of the house was built of wood, an enclosed veranda and a few rooms on either side, and the whole caboodle was rickety now, an old beast with the hindquarters a-drag, the wood most likely mouldy and musty, greyish green from the years which are no longer there. There was still the cement dam in the anthracite back yard, empty now, a dusty glass eye. There also, look, was the bluegum tree full of dust – and without monkeys! (The then house was similarly under dust, and at times it moved from top to bottom, a war widow dreaming the hands of a lover, a servant believing ghost stories; and at regular intervals it used to be filled – pierced – by a fierce whistle as when my cousin Kowie the toothless driver came steaming by in his gleaming locomotive: a pig poked; waving of black neckerchief in white hand-palm and rosy shells of gums.) Also the row of plane trees running parallel to the tracks. Then, between the houses and the marshes, the enclosure where grazed the donkey bought for half a crown from the pound when we were small still. And, unexpectedly, a pomegranate bush, flowering crimson in the hedge around the enclosure. But the train flashed as fast as a photo past all this. Lickety-spit.

In that dilapidated section of the house, the wooden part, we sat down in crocked chairs and knobby armchairs. (This, the third occasion to broach the house.) My father, my mother, my wife, I. And the sieur Vlilv. The house is as seedy inside as, so long ago, it seemed to be from the outside. An underground network, a sunken graveyard, a slovenly aquarium full of dust, the lack behind a glass eye. In this room with the fusty wooden walls there are but a few pieces of furniture, grey eyes for windows, and a thick carpet of dust covers the glyphs and the horizontal planes. It's stuffy. As if the house keeps captive a greyish light. We came here especially from the past for our appointment with the sieur Vlilv but he doesn't live here either; the house is now occupied by brown prostitutes, night butterflies, and one of them used to be in our service, she worked in the kitchen, early mornings when light was still opaque like train smoke she brought tea and rusks. They allowed us to use their house for our rendez-vous. We hear the grousing of the bed in the next room, of how there are many sighs and whispers and giggles, how someone (or two persons?) then jump(s) up with brusque movements, the irascible footsteps over a floor of a woman without underwear, the swish of a cotton dress over naked buttocks, and then a voice outside in the yard, sharp: "Home! Go home, you! Viola-a-a, he tricked me! Viola-a-a, dammit, I say he tricked me!" A train rumbles past, higher than the roof ridge and higher than the tip of the bluegum; the house quakes. My mother goes to fetch coffee in the kitchen where there's a stove with a glowing red surface and she pours from the coffee pot's spout a thick jet of steaming black coffee in a cup, but in one way or another the coffee reaches her hands and she exclaims her pain, hands in the air, the hand-palms like little red bootees for a baby. It's been many years since cousin Kowie ended up under the wheels of a train engine.

The sieur Vlilv has a long yellow face, deeply bruised by age, notched and chopped, crocheted in downhill creases. Above the forehead his hair waves, dead as winter's grass covered with hoar frost. He holds his two hands with the knuckle-fingers stretched so that the tips, interlaced, touch lightly, the two indexes resting on the chin. His fingers a slender spire. (Many years ago, in another country, I knew him as Alberto Giacometti. Evenings, at dinnertime, he sat sketching figures around a glass of red wine, over and over, the more lines he added the more elongated they became, disappearing into the paper napkin over the table. And then he went away with the cancer.) We have a weighty problem which we want to discuss with him, concerning which we need to obtain his advice. His eyes are burning quiet and yellow in the slanted light. He sits there, deeply withdrawn in the labile armchair.

"Why did you wish to see me?"

I hem and slide forward on my dusty chair. My father places both hands on his knees, he too leans forward, the eyes black swallows in the orbits, looks intently, looks small nests; on his pinky glows a ruby set in a broad golden ring. The coffee cups are still empty; just now, when the train puffed by, they were tinkling in the saucers with the pattern of blue flowers. Dust whirled and settled again. Against the gauze of the back porch the whisper of flies, the whirr of shadows.

"We have a weighty problem we want to discuss with you," I say, "concerning which we'd like to have your advice."

A voice in the yard screams: "Out of my sight! Fuck off! Viola-a-a, he tricked me!"

And then more remote (with a sob?): "I don't screw around with goats. . . ."

Because this is what had happened in the meantime: In Paname we, my wife and I, had a lodger, a household god, so we thought, protecting us – for me, in fact, it was the same god of which I'd become conscious when young, something or someone issuing from me and yet not part of me, something or someone bleeding me white and therefore revitalizing me (a rumbling, a blinding flash, a shaft of light, a wetness) – Rab was his name and he was most sad and timid with a hollow yet soothing voice. He was big, taller than I, more solidly built too, and absolutely black. His body – up to the shoulders – was that of a human man, the flowing lines of a youth at home in his body like an animal in its own physicality, black and with pleasing proportions; his head was that of a bull, oblong and sleek and black and agreeable to the touch, and huge pitch-black eyes with extraordinarily long silky lashes. The lines from forehead over the raised eyebrowcrest and thence to the muzzle – which was damp, and of the same dark pigmentation as the hide – could only be described as noble. Below the broad lips and lower than the ridge of jaws the heavy dewlap swung in folds and dimples. (From side to side when he moved.) It was ever a joy for my wife to caress Rab's dewlap, to grasp hold of a slim fistful.

Often Rab stood in the hallway, just this side of the half-open front door, from where he could observe the happenings on the street, the wet sidewalks with their superficial glistening of lights. There the transparent glimmer of coloured glass panes set into the door fell over him, the Rouault blue, the wine rosé, the evening ochre – and was reflected in his eyes so that, between the lashes, these seemed to have small windows. And he appeared melancholic and lonely: someone from a totally different civilization longing for a mate which probably never existed: and still he was too shy to risk it outside. Sometimes we suspected that he stood there listening for something – perhaps the sound of the shepherd's flute when the sinking sun clothes the bamboo groves in a downy blond gold, or the shinily hissing wheels of a train at night during the winter, or the white rustling of a lady filing her nails in a blue bed in a room overlooking the sea, or the ping-ping and the clackety-clack of steel balls on a pin-table, or the slow tearing sound (like orgasm) of a mirror breaking with the likeness still captive in it; or the movement of an articulation in a linen sleeve still protruding above the earth when the rest of the body is long since buried – something, a noise, a belief, something beyond our hearing.

He was meek and without defects. At night the three of us sat around the table. On the table was laid a glistening white tablecloth crackling with light. Then there was nourishment put on the tablecloth but of that we (I at least) were hardly aware. We sat waiting for the light of the room to be a full ruby red pulsating in our wine glasses. Rab at the head of the table with a snowy white serviette by his left hand, straight, unmoving, both his hands lightly fisted on the table, his aristocratic head with an expression of silence. Later I would not remember if our hands ever really moved, although there was the clicking of silver shoots. When my wife had cleared the table, but the glasses were still deep with wine (and after having gently rubbed one hand over his dewlap, or sometimes both, when she put the dishes and plates to one side), we placed the chesspieces on the board and started playing. Rab was very keen on the so-called Polish opening (the one to which Rutger refers as the 'orang-utan') and in my riposte I always attempted to lure his queen forward as rapidly as possible and then to trap her. I wanted to annihilate the queen and thus disrupt the rhythm. Between my middle finger and the index a cheroot burned its thin tendril of smoke. Then Rab silently and deeply looked into my eyes until I entered the domain, the moon-shadowed gardens, the empty palace in the night, the dormitories of sleep without ever knowing exactly when the line separating flying from falling was crossed. When I then stretched out on the bed next to my wife, her body under the nightdress smelled of carnation.

One evening, the sidewalks and the streets were wet like new black coins, Rab asked if he might borrow my car. But of course. My wife and I still accompanied him outside to where the automobile was parked in the stained shadow patterns of a street tree. He got in behind the wheel, started up the engine, and left. The tyres swooshed over the wet surface. Many hours later, when he did not return, my wife – and I too – became very anxious. With a crease between the eyebrows she decided to go look for him outside, and after phoning and commandeering her brother, Pip, to keep her company, she left the house with a yellow raincoat. Before the chessboard I sat listening to rain murmuring on the roof. I moved the pieces, move and counter-move, but without an opponent it was a sterile and schizophrenic game which I was fated to lose and to win. Each individual drop I could hear plopping on the rooftiles. When later on it was very late, and night soft and secretive, I went to take up a position in the hallway by the half-open front door, Rab's favourite vantage point; his odour still lingered there and I could insert myself in the area of this aroma to stand there in nearly the same way as he was accustomed to do – in the illusory wholeness! I was the stranger at the masked ball. My heart was clear, translucent, brittle glass.

And still later, I don't know what time it was since the night started drifting, I saw my wife and her brother, Pip, returning home. When she was just outside the door I could see the raindrops touching her, meandering over her face and the collar of her coat. The drops were big and slow like oil, like dying moths ending up in oil, like worms crawling through oil. (Just like that it had been earlier in the evening when we escorted Rab to the car and when I closed the car door behind him and leaned forward with one hand on the windscreen, the finger-marks under my fingers were grey against the glass and with fine concentric labyrinth lines. Silver the drops were on the glass, the light beaded in the globules only, no reflection of my face, hard behind the windscreen and draped in these luminescent beads Rab's dark head looking straight ahead, a moment before the wipers would come into action with a *swosh-swush* and a light spray.)

In the entrance hall of our house I took my wife's wrists in my hands. Cold entered my fingers, the knuckles. This is what she told me while I was caressing her pulse:

"Down below by the crossing of boulevard Saint-Moche where the red lights are, Pip and I placed ourselves. There wasn't much traffic."

"Ah!" I say.

"The lights regularly changed from red to green to a yellow colour rather like amber, then red again, again green, and so on. I thought, if he comes by, if our motor car passes, I shall see him, I shall recognize it."

And I: "Ah!"

"Perhaps he got lost. . . . Perhaps he's looking for us. . . . The traffic flow became even less as it got later. . . . When it is late the streets are more present, more *street*. . . . And then I noticed it – our car – dark and wet and shiny with rain, just like a new black coin. I don't know if the traffic lights were red or green. It came by along the sidewalk where we stood and the tyres made a swishing noise on the wet tar, you know how, and how the droplets then splash in arcs."

And I: "Ah!"

She: "I lifted my hand, this one" – she twists the one wrist between my fingers so that the right hand lies palm up, a baby bootee washed up in a gutter, a wrinkled fish – "so that Rab may see me, may see my hand, and a rivulet of water ran down my sleeve all along the arm. . . . But he didn't see me. . . . I don't know if he saw me. And then I suddenly realized that he was not alone in the car. By the glow of the street lamps and the late night café on the corner I noticed *Rab is not alone in our motor car.* In fact, he's not the one driving it. Behind the wheel there's someone else, a black man wearing a coat looking like a clown's costume, such a big blocked pattern. A smartly dressed fellow. And he wears a hat with a feather stuck in the band. Duck. His face shone and his lips were slightly parted and puffed so that one could see the whiteness of his teeth – just as if he were humming a tune through the nose. Both his hands were posed on the steering wheel higher than the dashboard. Black hands – broken-winged ravens. Rab sat next to him. He looked directly in front of him. His head was dark. The dewlap. . . . I saw it all in such a hurry and yet I keep on seeing it still. Oh. . . . I know. . . . I don't know anymore. The car disappeared. It doesn't stop. Neither does it return, no, never again. Oh. . . ."

And "Ah," I then said.

Light failed. (It was a sad affair.) The sieur Vlilv never budged; only the fires in his eyes smouldered. (Tomorrow, one thought, the flaked ash will fleck his withered cheekbones.)

After the explanation and the silence it was clear that the moment for taking back the sieur Vlilv had been broken open. I propose to do so and my father acquiesces with dark eyes; the sieur Vlilv says it's most decent of us, considerate et cetera, but that it will be quite sufficient if we could take him as far as the station; he has a return ticket to his destination. We walk down to the enclosure where the captive donkey used to graze, long ago. We find a carriage there, a tame one. We get in and I drive. We must remain standing with our eyes closed to slits for it would seem that at earlier times the carriage transported hay, and bits of chaff were now blowing all over. There is the sharp tang of long-gone life. We drive over the bumpy ground under the grass, out on to the gravel road and further to where it catches the asphalt. The sieur Vlilv's hair is swept upwards by the wind; among the curls one sees the glistening of the chaff's faded gold; the backs of his hands, the knuckles, are pale with the effort of clinging to the carriage's edge. Evening sky is of tin; the colour and the heat of day burnt away.

The carriage is awkward to handle, not so easy to swivel – with the result that I'm forced to choose the way where I can best control the vehicle.

Nearer to the station the town begins, the first tall buildings with man-high marks of rubbing and scraping against the whitewashed walls. The streets are gorges of twilight, up high among the inclining balconies (canopies) with their empty washing lines the first three stars; bats speed in low parabolas through the weak sky, with the sound of mirrors crackling and splintering, the squeaky noises of radar in orgasm. Despite my best intentions we get caught up in a labyrinth of blue clots – the narrow and sombre and twisting lanes; I no longer know in which direction the station is situated. The high and soundless buildings exclude the heavens. Had there been more space, perhaps a horizon, one might still have oriented oneself by the smoke-flags of some train engine, but already it is too late and too dark and day lies smouldering, finished: the smoke is everywhere. We end up among a procession of refuse lorries descending, just like us, in concentric circles through the network of narrow thoroughfares – and on all sides, scraping behind the buildings, are other lanes, again buildings and streets once more, like the grainy pattern of a fingertip, falling lower, so that we hear the rising of hubbub and clanking, how it washes against the façades, flows under the arches and in the tunnels. The dust lorries are closed in, with long spouts on the bodies, like threshing-machines. These spouts eject a yellow liquid, golden in the dusk, up into heaven. It splashes all over us, the thick jets, the big dark drops; I see the stickiness in the sieur Vlilv's hair; my father closes his eyes so that his spectacles are emptied; soaked-through bats plunge down, fall into the carriage where they lie fluttering – blue cots in the greener obscurity.

And I think back on something which the sieur Vlilv pronounced in a very tranquil tone of voice earlier in the afternoon, a citation it was from the *Bhagavad-Gita*, namely a dialogue between Arjuna going forth in his war chariot to do battle (the two enemy armies are in position for the confrontation), keening now with the futility of all this, bewailing all the people, kings and soldiers, friends and relatives and antagonists (the king on the opposing side is blind already) who will have to bite the dust, die (and why?) and Krishna, disguised, of course, but still, as ever, a reincarnation of Vishnu, with him in the war chariot; and Krishna saying:

> *Your words are wise, Arjuna, but your sorrow is for nothing.*
> *The truly wise mourn neither for the living nor the dead.*
> *There never was a time when I did not exist, nor you, nor any*
>   *of these kings.*
> *Nor is there any future in which we shall cease to be. . . .*
>
> *Realize that pleasure and pain, gain and loss, victory*
> *And defeat, are all the same: then go into battle. . . .*

Wiederholen

La cendre c'est la maladie du cigare.
BENJAMIN PÉRET

When we were young we often had the fancy to go camping or holidaying for a few days further than the dunes where the land flattens again. Now, looking back, I no longer remember the details exactly and it may well be that one of our group lived there permanently so that the rest of us just went to visit from time to time. The land was terrible, sublime, massive, majestic in its absolute barrenness. Stretched out it lay around you: to both sides and to the hinterland it was unending and apparently smooth – just here and there like a guileless pattern of reef, a crinkle or a seam – until that too curbs away into the perspective, in the haziness of the no-more-see; to the front – in my memory I now view the world from the veranda of the house where we usually sojourned – there was at first a firmament of nothingness, for the skyline is the distance which you always carry near you, inside you, but then further along where it starts descending to sea level it was more indented, there were, scanty at first and gradually with deeper contrasts, the waves of dunes as the land washed against the sea and crumbled there, there were fissures and gaps in the walls of the land, chasms with high walls trapping the shadows and causing them to be more or less intense, and through which pass serpentined, places where the ground suddenly disappeared under your feet, so suddenly that involuntarily your stomach was squeezed higher, rather as if there were landslides or a centuries-long erosion of catastrophic magnitude testifying to – relatively speaking – telescoped cataclysms. Purple it was then, brownish at times, depending on the cracking of the day or the twilight of the evening – but the dominant colour scheme of this naked world was grey, a hundred different shades of grey, starting with the wet ashen colour deep under the wings of a broody speckled hen, passing through the nearly transparent silver of falling rain to the hard glitter of a blue-grey rock ledge in the sun, and stone reefs and harshness were the most common characteristics of this area, but despite the nudity it wasn't cruel or sore: all these hues of grey surged and heaved, a gigantic play of aloof light and shade washing over the expanses to give contour and nearness and a sombreness, a depth, a mystery, a surfaceless mirror. And yet there was no chiaroscuro alternation of frisk-light and sucking-shadow: the summits of heaven were cloudless and limpid and blue with maybe just the slightest haze of limitless distances or the trembling, nearly like smoke, when there is a play in temperature shortly prior to the piercing of the sun or immediately afterwards. The sun, fearsome horseman with a robe of glistening blood, ah! Except for the falling away of the land in the direction of the sea there was neither hill nor abrupt rock formation nor disintegration of terrain, nor sand windblown in heaps even, to project fervent stains. No vegetation worth mentioning – be it tree or shrub – which might have brought the colour of differentiation, even if that were just a needle-line or a knife-notch or a small hairy fist. No, all these tones of grey were indigenous to the environment – but there was change nevertheless, movement. That which created the illusion of a succession of cooler blots and inaccessibility was indeed part of a much larger context, the impersonal rocking of the sun-planet through a space which could never be plumbed and is perhaps therefore, with our limited definitions, not space at all, always expanding, bigger and more illimitable; it was, seen closer to us, maybe the languorous round of seasons: but in these quarters there were no noticeable seasons and no climate to speak of. Or does the soil have its own climate? Where the dunes start rolling and the ravines and gullies sink away to a lower area, there at least other colours may be found: the dove-grey with violet tints of the sand, gold maybe from a reverberation of light between cliff faces or beams skimming over crests, the flicker and sparkle sometimes of a glow – like movement – being splashed off anthracite or quartz, a curve of greenery and nearly the appearance of grass or very ancient dappled glass and verdigris where an aperture opens up in the earth. At certain times of the day there were blue sections not related to anything at all, immanent, unreal, except that the eye could perceive them. And by night there were horrible dark hollows, knots in the grain of darkness usually so grey and so smooth, sluice-chambers in the horizon, a mothiness, a leprosy, the opening up of vertical caverns – which, when you stared at it from miles away, from the yard of the house, when you tried to feel it with your brain, down and down, caused the skin of you forearms to pucker from a cool satisfaction. The land softens, the land caves in, the land unravels, the land screams with a gurgle becoming dust once more of a black liquid in the holes and the splits.

Somewhere in that high country was the house where we would stay. So far back it is now that I no longer remember how much time we whiled away there: maybe only a few days, maybe months on end. Time had no constitution then, no skin or cells or pattern or feeling. Time was a cold crystal, transparent, a spectrum, a stalactite or a growth with every century a single drop. My realization of time silted up. But now, much later, it is a physical pleasure to fetch it from somewhere within the unknown folds of the self, to find the thread and to start reading, to dredge the self's receptacles. A curettage. The house was built of weathered grey planks long since gnawed at by the darkening of all things passing, by the finest hardly visible particles of mica which when whipped up over the flats by winds had to be hurtled against something in the end, by the corrosion of saltiness in the condensation of the night. A dilapidated stoop, knocked together from planks in the same fashion, provided a kind of platform to one side of the house. Over this small stage there was a lean-to propped up by four wooden pillars not really very solid any more. From the stoop the drawing room could be reached and the two windows giving on to the front were laced with curtains. These two curtains might have been white once upon a time but now they were barely a lighter shade of grey than the tremendous world outside. They were the only windows so endowed; peradventure they were the only two windows in the house. Around the house then was the area designated by us as the "yard", but who could ever tell where its limits were, where the yard stopped and the waste land began? "Yard" was a "convention", an "agreement" – an oval-shaped imagined zone around the house with its outer boundary never more than twenty-five yards away, perchance a little more tamped down than the rest, and indicated as "living space" by garbage and implements – mirrors, cardboard boxes, chains – which at times could be found there all strewn about. The only other compromise towards the taming of the farmstead was that which we planted there and which never grew – flowering shrubs, bushes, even trees. With enormous trouble we transported grown trees, for instance, from the coast to the house – along the way the leaves and fruit dragged in the dust: it was the abduction of an exotic princess from a far-off empire; we then dug a deep hole and made the tree to stand upright in it. Occasionally it took several weeks, months even, before the transplanted tree shrivelled up entirely and had to be unearthed – that is, if it hadn't tilted over all by itself in the meantime – eventually for firewood. But never it took root. Trees or brushwood, anything that could capture the wind and give it sound, is so always needed around a house. Because otherwise you lose all memory of yourself and are gobbled up by nothingness to become part of the night.

On the flat area before the veranda we had erected a target for shooting practice, a plate on which was painted a man. We had one pistol, very sacred to us, which we guarded jealously. Above our heads the sun traversed the blueness like a gigantic jet seemingly moving slowly only because it is flying so incredibly high. Everywhere about us the reach and the shuddering of the silver landscape. No shadows at all except for our own, the house's cape, shards and blotches from the transplanted trees. But their leaves were already wilted and dust-coated – as corpses planted up to the waist in corruption they were decomposing in leaves and twigs. We took turns aiming at the target. Tjak was always the one enjoying the shooting the most. "Aber es freut mich!" or sometimes also: "Dennoch freue ich mich daran!" he called out time and again. I became aware that my eye was out, or alternatively that the sight of the pistol was not adjusted to my eye. Although I could group all my shots in a small circle – we had pasted white sheets of paper over the painted man's vulnerable parts to in this way establish our acumen – they were for ever too low, too far to the left. Purposefully I tried to adapt by taking a bead on the top right-hand corner, hoping to place my shots in the desired bull's-eye. I was, with one eye closed to a slit, still busy trying to elucidate this aberration to my comrades when I became aware of their not paying any notice to my explanation. Something else had a priority claim on their attention. Alarm! They were silent, the heads rapt and alert as those of birds all turned in a certain direction. I lowered the arm with the cocked pistol and followed the attraction point of their eyes with mine, attempting to make out what it was they were staring at so distractedly: over the floor of the grey plateau a group of men moved, and evidently on their way to us. Far away we could hear small bells throbbing. There are no fixed routes over this vast highland, no paths or true crossings, and I have never yet seen a company of travelers trekking over its rims. Nevertheless it had to be possible, it had probably even occurred, that people all through the ages journeyed here. Who could deny or affirm that vegetation flourished in these parts long ago, that there were yurts or farmsteads or even inns here and, who knows, perhaps cities with canals filled with lapping water. Dust. All dust now. Passed and extinct. Or had it always been thus? Nothing, no indication or track could ever prove the hypothesis or its refutation. Still, these two extremes were reconcilable, eventually one: the nothingness contains traces of what was – aren't we all, and everything around us, finally the wind-blurred drawings of the structure of decay? But this troupe now, although still quite a way off, clearly carried threatening implications for us.

"Mensch, was ist denn los jetzt?" Tjak murmured.

The purpose of the visit of the observed group wasn't clear except that it contained no promise of good for us, and we therefore thought it wiser to take certain precautions because they were numerous – far more so than us. We entrusted Tjak with our pistol and with the instruction that he must make himself scarce: our intention, in so doing, was to safeguard our only weapon and property of value. Within a few hours evening would fall and under the cloak of the night, for there was no moon, Tjak would have had a chance to reach a safe haven with the pistol, or at least the protection of distance. In the meantime we would attempt to occupy the unwelcome intruders and to hold them back.

Our uneasiness had good grounds, our fears were realized. It turned out to be Albert and his gang, and faced with their superior numbers we were soon powerless. Without too much bother they took over everything and held us captive in the living room while they searched the house from floor to loft. For us time no longer mattered. But gradually it became night and, as was often the case at that hour, an evening breeze started blowing; the grey curtains fluttered slightly. The wind – experience had taught me this – would become stronger towards midnight, a veritable sighing, and the tarrying heat would as always make way for the pure-skinned lucidity of the night and then for the merciless cold of the small hours, for the sharp reflection of starlight on stones, like ice pellets. Albert apparently surmised – or did he know? – that one of us had eluded him, that our firearm had slipped through his fingers: he delegated members of his gang to go over the surroundings within a radius of one and a half kilometres with a fine-tooth comb. It became dark.

When the gloom had settled in completely we all heard the crack of three pistol shots in the distance, two near together and after a pause of what must have been three seconds a single last one. Afterwards nothing. All lifted their heads and listened to the silence with ears pricked up. Nothing more. Nobody talked. No one referred to the strange detonations. Later too, as far as I remember, no explanation was offered and it was never discussed. In the course of the first quarter of the night the search parties returned – whether all or just some of them wasn't clear and neither do I know whether they reported on their doings. We became drowsy. Now and then you could hear someone groaning in his

31

sleep. Albert sat in one corner on a chair, his heavy head bowed, chin on chest; it was no foregone conclusion that his eyes were still open or, on the other hand, closed. In any event, he asked no questions, gave not a single order, didn't try to start any conversation; just hunched there without budging, peering down into his private night.

When it was already quite late I got up to go and smoke a cigar outside under the naked heavens. It was an old habit of mine to do so, even under otherwise normal circumstances: to slowly contemplate the fantastic pageant of the galaxy, all those beasts and formations and images and petrified ice fields and remote fluttering fires and to see how they rock by, to see how blanched they are; I know of no better solution for oppressive thoughts: the I is liquidated. The wind came from far away, noiseless, and encountered no resistance until it came pushing against the house with a soft, burbling sound. The wind smelled of unknown mosses and contused moulds, of crystals and of dust. The wind was also with a rustling in the loose leaves of the tree. The clatter was so muffled that one could presume, had you not known any better, that it wasn't caused by the wind's goings-on but perhaps by the slight and gradual fall-go of the stars overhead. It passed through my mind that the leaves will not be on the tree for much longer, that they will come loose as they've always done before and that the trunk and branches will be parched and grey, without sap of vegetative faculty. I also absorbed the notion that all come to nothing and fall away in this way, so, just like the grey ash of my cigar; and I furthermore thought of the white eyes in the bottomless abyss above my head, of the little clumps of bones, the white almond blossoms on invisible branches, the fluttering of pale wings. When I looked around me I was, alas, once again brought to the realization that our "yard" would never be transformed into a "garden".

And all at once, under the rather deeper blackness of the leaves' whispering, I became aware of something, or someone – of a presence, a barely noticeable change of position. I never moved an inch. From under the cover of dying or already dead leaves he stepped forward, laughing softly with shimmering teeth. Tjak. Or really – this too I immediately and intuitively sensed although he uttered not a word with reference to himself – actually not Tjak the way you and I would normally mean when talking about Tjak, or about Murphy or Giovanni or C—— or Glassface or Tuchverderber or Nefesh or Fremdkörper, but his . . . what? His spirit? His memory? His momentary mirroring in the grey matter? His remains? The power field of words around him? Very close to me he came and softly he enquired whether he may finish off my cigar. I handed it to him, the smoke-flowing little grey stump notched by my fingernail at the one end, and deeply he sucked on it and for an instant the smoke lingered blueish grey between us before being carried away by the wind. When the cigar tip glowed clearer at short intervals, I could observe the large dark and wet stain on his chest: nearly as a shield protecting the body very intimately it was, or the ever-spreading blood puddle in the sand under the young doe giving birth whilst dying, or like a submerged rose it was of colour and to the touch – and it had an odd odour, the dank and yet distant smell of a wing. "Aber weisst du, ich habe mich damals so unauslegbar viel gefreut. . . . Wenn ich das unbedingt mal erklären könnte. . . ." he still whispered nearly inaudibly soft with the wind among his words and starshine on his teeth, and then he was gone. Gone, irrevocably gone before my eyes. With my fingertips I stroked the paper sheet over this afternoon's target and felt that it was sticky.

Many years went by. I don't believe I ever again visited the house of grey planks and certainly it no longer exists, but became – as others before it? – one with the grey, the brownish and the purplish environment, just like the trees in exile and the exotic scorched flowering shrubs and little bushes one by one. Or does this house in reality still exist? I use the stirrup-word "reality"– knowing that it contains no conception – with aversion and reluctant lips. Is it not true, friend, that nothing finally gets lost in us? That the house, now that we discussed it, still lies somewhere in a huge grey landscape, a landscape alternatively becoming more sombre or brighter without shadows or boundaries being cast over it? I don't believe I ever again penetrated the upland as deeply; steep-climbing gorges and canyons in the passes coiling higher along slopes where tons of gravel had come sliding down, at times cutting the route or burying it – but certainly no further. Occasionally I did visit the coast. The coastal strip itself, the fence running down into the sea was an area we were not allowed to enter. I knew – I no longer know how – that an ultra-modern camp had been constructed beyond that frontier on the slightly greenish hills and the yellow dunes, with the very best facilities: cinema halls, restaurants, drugstores, even a landing strip with a well-equipped control tower. Once I tried to explain it all to my mother. She was with me on holiday there – outside the fence – or she had come to visit me while I was holidaying there by myself, and we decided to go swimming. My mother was then already very old but her face and her body were fat and without wrinkles; with the hair tucked under a bathing cap and without her glasses she was quite white and blind. We watched a child – a little girl with red flames at the throat – playing in the water, and I tried to interpret to my mother the fugitive images on her retina. It was low tide, although stormy, and the girl clearly had the intention to obviate the barrier and to get, from the sea, to the enclosed zone. Despite the low tide the coast of that forbidden area was most dangerous with edged rocks, pools where the waves frothed, and a sea bottom descending rapidly and sharply. My mother was worried about the little girl and couldn't understand why she insisted upon reaching that particularly treacherous beach; even from afar we saw the blood on her feet and legs, we noticed the water at her feet being coloured and foaming like a crocodile, and still she continued laughing with a shrill, hysterical voice while stubbornly attempting to reach the side. I explained to my mother that that camp, out of bounds to the little girl, was a veritable heaven on earth for children, and I described the wonderful luxuries to her in detail. But, when I wanted to point these out to her, there was nothing to be seen beyond the fence except for a few grey buildings, very low and smooth like bunkers just about entirely buried in the sand. Just seams; only bumps and reefs. I had to point out to my mother – though I was now blindly entering an unknown terrain – that the much vaunted wealth was probably installed in a subterranean way, yes, even the landing strip of the airfield. But that it had to be there, of that I was sure!

Along the coast the weather was continually fair. Above the blue space, below the sea blue or black at times, and like weathered gates maybe giving access to the deep land above and beyond were the brown sandcrests and hilltops along which the paths climbed; roads of an origin and a purpose and of the people using them – dealers? agents? recruiters? *izigijima*? – fallen into oblivion. The sun in the hollows of the heavens was a silvered beetle at the hem of a sky-blue robe – but blue is just black seen from close up or grey seen from afar – or, you can express it this way too – the sun was the phosphorescent skeleton of a rider having to roam like an unsatiated and restless spirit through all times and all spaces even though the flesh has long since become blue dust. My heart wasn't with the lips of sea and strand. Besides, on the side of the demarcation where people like me could move uninhibitedly, there was nothing – no asylum or hideaway or night club or public toilet or workshop or quay or church hall, no bus stop or road sign or cigar factory or drawings in the sand or birds' nests. My heart stayed elsewhere, where it's higher and clearer and more healthy, where the landscape is so insignificant that time's passages could leave no mark and where time therefore does not exist, where there are no emotions or desires or memories to cling to. Perhaps my heart was only a sheet of paper with a number of holes, glued to the rough and by now nearly indistinguishable silhouette of a man traced as target on a metal plate. I couldn't absorb my restlessness: there was a hole in my chest. The sun is at last a heart. Whenever I could I attempted ascending with one of the twisting and climbing paths, but never succeeded: so many of the passes were dead ends or had fallen in desuetude or had silted up or become eroded or were never intended to lead anywhere. On one such occasion – it was not yet noon and in my imagination I saw how the sky and the sun and even the stars, which by day also travel clothed in blue, become lost in the grey of the high plateaux somewhere above me until there would be just a soft shimmering over the earth, heaven and earth one imperishable because already gone – on one such an occasion when my imagination had like a bird flown up from my body to go and scout far ahead, I was obliged to stand off to one side, tightly pressed against a rock ledge to make way for a convoy approaching from ahead in orange-coloured dust clouds, on their way to the lowlands. There were a few camels heavily laden with grey baggage, a rider with expressionless eyes on a horse – maybe he was blind – and mostly donkeys with pack saddles, driven and accompanied by men with long headcloths wrapped around their heads and mouths and noses so that the light points of dust in their eyebrows were very evident. These men held, like lepers, small tinkling bells in their hands. I watched them coming by, and how they took no notice whatsoever of me, how they disappeared out of sight lower down around a bend of the pass. And I was on the point of continuing my journey, the dust raised by donkeys' hooves had settled again, the sun was a vulture high up in the air and I considered that this caravan must definitely be coming from somewhere and that they therefore could indicate the route to the highland – or one of the routes – on condition that I remain on their tracks – but in spite of the dust the soil was hard and it was difficult to retrace the fresh marks on the rocky parts; there were too the millions of slits and small hollows and little riffs of old precedent tracks retained intact through the centuries, tracks forking off and disappearing in all directions so that one got the image, knowing it to be true, of a whole world consisting of layer upon layer of tracks – when I heard someone calling behind me. "Murphy! Murphy!" the one voice bawled, followed directly by a choir of further voices. What now? What could have happened? Were these the intonations and incantations of a midday prayer? But *Murphy* then? Or are they calling me? I turned around and ran back. A hundred yards from where I last lost sight of the caravan they were now motionless in the twelve o'clock heat. The beasts of burden were not unsaddled but just stood there, quiet, with lowered heads and the reins trailing in the dust; a camel or two stood ruminating with the funny cut-and-hash lip movements so peculiar to them. The drivers were all off to one side of the road, crowded around something on the ground there – here the area along the track was flat for a short distance. They no longer called out but rang their little bells with a sort of absent concentration. I rushed there. Over the skyline, not from the road but from further away, from behind a hill, a man appeared wearing a white shirt and leggings. When he came nearer I could see his blond hair and his blue eyes. Even if he were much older now than years back I still recognized him instantly. It was Murphy. Indeed. Ah, I turned to him and now also remembered – or did one of the caravan drivers inform me of this? I cannot recollect – that Murphy was a frontier guard, that it was his duty to patrol the wire obstacle stretching from here somewhere – no one knows exactly where – inland in a straight line ever higher through the gullies and over the hummocks. I didn't know in whose service he was, whether it was to prevent the inhabitants and authorities from the other side from breaking out towards us or to restrain our people from penetrating the closed-off strip. He carried a little whip. Together we pushed our way through the crowds with their bells to see what the focal point of their restrained excitement could be. The men in the inner circle stood grouped around a rubbish heap. How did it happen, so my thoughts went, that in my ascent I never noticed this ash heap – it is after all something remarkable in such desolate surroundings! And from when does this garbage date? What does it speak of? Whose was it? Was it exposed by a recent or more ancient sliding of the soil? Was it always here then – and I so sunken in the endless wandering of my searches, which could never reach a destination, that I knew deep in my soul – that I never saw this remarkable aberration? I can't remember even having heard a suspicious rumbling. . . . The men were intent on a cadaver lying among the ash, the petrified garbage, the broken-legged or splay-backed chairs, the burst mirrors, the cardboard boxes, the grey planks, the blue rusted chains, the rests of tree trunks from distant kingdoms. It was the corpse of a brown boy, so fresh in appearance that he could scarcely have died earlier than that very morning if it hadn't been for the rigid, tooth-fixed smile between lips forced open, on his back there as if only to rest for a wee while with the uncovered face and the limpid eyes turned to the unending blue nothing-ness. His shirt was still clean, unbuttoned to the belly – excepting one dark and damp stain. Over the swarthy skin of the chest I could see a bird tattooed in a dark red line of dots reminding one of a string of shiny rubies. His one arm was bent at the elbow so that the hand pointed straight up. In this hand he held a pistol and the still flexible index finger was neatly and exactly folded around the trigger. From the barrel emerged, stiff and silent, a jet of grey smoke just like the tendril of a creeper or the heart attack of a tree.

The remainder of my narrative is not much and can be accounted for in a few sentences. Murphy, with an embittered grimace, took me through the fences to the forbidden territory. We betook ourselves to the terminus for air travellers; we were to take a flight, off and gone. It was a modern structure full of people also sitting there, waiting for their respective flights to be called. Murphy told me a long story which it is not in my power to repeat here. Part of it however concerned the clothes which Albert had stolen – or borrowed – that time, some of Murphy's also in the lot, and had handed in here at the lost property office where it was kept all these years, and that he, Murphy, come hell or high water, now had the intention of retaking possession of same. We ordered drinks. The cocktails were of a rusty red colour. The waitress wore a black dress with an oval-shaped white apron. Her calves and thighs were most smooth and shiny and well formed and when she bent down over the other tables to serve the passengers-to-be, we could see the white leg as far as the elastic, and a dark shadow higher into the moist folds of the imagination. The other travellers all sat leafing through magazines which they held high in front of their noses so that we could not identify their faces. All the magazines had covers of a bright orange colour. We learnt from the waitress that the lost property office was to be found on the last floor and that a signboard with "Damen und Herren" would indicate it to us. But, she said, we were to wait: at the apposite moment we would be sent for.

The God Eating

Quando fiam uti chelidon.
DANTE

In this way one comes down into the desert. It is grey all around the eye, grey and barren and dry as if from some ancient and unlifted curse. Scattered about dimly observed in the myopia are darker objects. One is not certain whether they are alive or living only in the black stultifying flame of death. The curse is a flame. These perceptions may well be cacti or cactaceous rocks, all clarity damped off, daubed with a minute immobility now and dark with the colour of damson. Dark with the colour of damnation? One is not sure. Yet one senses the heterosis, the hybrid vigour of things unpleasant to the imagination because the eye is too shy to concentrate.

He focuses – that is, he allows his vision to grow on the grey sand. A fly is scribbling minute tracks of immobility where he looks. The fly has a blue metallic weight, fur-powdered legs, two hairy protuberances which must be eyes, two transparent wings folded back. The nun wears a veil over her bearded face. Where the fly has imprinted the earth seems freshly disturbed though frozen. And so he decides to dig, hoping perhaps to uncover a flame. He sifts the sand through his hands. He feels the grittiness under his nails. He has the pattern of walking the excretion of the fly's tracks under his nails. When he has dug a shallow grave he comes upon something of a lighter colour. It may be a placenta, the interred afterbirth of a long-gone pilgrim. But no, he sees; it is a newspaper still slightly damp. He remembers that he has heard a newspaper referred to as a kite. Over the creased and flamelike surface signs are sutured. Words. Yet one senses the heterosis, the hybrid vigour of things unpleasant to the realization because the eye is too shy to concentrate. He deciphers a sign: "EYEGO".

Other people have passed through these regions then. Perhaps they understood the way in which one comes to the desert. Perhaps they even lingered on, attempting to stay. Perhaps too all of this was not always as stripped and as captured as it now appears. A little higher up where the skimming eye scans the bulk of a horizon it notices what he understands to be ruins. The humbled leftovers of long-gone inhabitants. These sombre greyish and crumbled walls have become part of the hillside, tracks, an exposed labyrinth of departed life. The hue is that of rocks. Or cacti seen against the sun when one is near-sighted. Spiky words in a lost tongue.

And when he climbs to where that settlement once was he finds that it is not deserted after all. Some nomads must have decided to stop there for the winter. At the highest spot of this former town around what must once have been the central square a few of the buildings still seem intact. There the tribe of travellers has found refuge. It could also be that they simply had a breakdown of transport. He sees their cars and caravans eroded by weather, as colourless as inferior metal, broken down, half hidden in the gullies or deflated upon their axles when out in the open along one side of the square. The whisper of smoke curling out of the airholes of one of the dull forts.

He comes upon the band of runagates and puts a hand on his heart to introduce himself. An old man looks him over with cool fingers. The old man has a long grey beard moved by the wind. Like oily smoke. He wears also a long greyish coat and high boots which are very smooth and polished. All the other members of this group appear to be women. But of that he cannot be sure for there are children too and even though the greybeard with the boots may still be very vigorous it would be unlikely, he thinks, that they are all his offspring. The women are covered by long colourless dresses. Their heads are shadowed by hoods. Deep within the darkness of the hoods the eyes are watching him, shiny and pinpointed flies.

He comes upon the group of vagabonds and introduces himself. "My name is Nefesj" – this he says to the old man – "and I am the foreigner." The old man laughs at him. The many women and the children look at him with the broken flies of their eyes and some of the children laugh also. They allow him to stay. Rather: they don't chase him away with stones and songs.

Often now he wanders through the hulk of this long-lost town. Apparently no restrictions are imposed on his movements. He sleeps in the lee of one of the disintegrating walls where the stars aren't quite as glittering, as hard. At times he imagines insects or tiny animals among the stones, lepidopterous flitting, lizards, leporine shapes leaping away through murk and crack. The labyrinthine walls of alley and outhouse merge with the rocks. The winter has come. He climbs away from the ruins. Out here he is aware of distances, greyish, the cool fingers of the piano – except that all his silences are engulfed by a greater silence. And now he notices patches of snow as if dirty beards had been put out to dry. Bleeding from the soil. Fluttering above ground. Marked in the snow then he observes tracks, coals, immobile passage. A flame may have dribbled. But the signs are left by a horse learning to write these surroundings, ostensibly belonging to the old man with the boots. The grey horse lives around the settlement. In some way it must be inseparable from the fortunes of the stranded travellers. An obbligato.

In the dead village itself – among the buildings changing in nature without ever really changing their nature – and the rotting snow-dusted vehicles, there sounds do not lift off the ground. The furry jar is never cracked open, the kite never secretes. But he is convinced that there must be other males in the community. Behind the walls where it is darker even if there are no roofs he fancies the succulent swishing and whispered ah-ing of copulation. And sometimes he hears the guttural coughing of male chests coming from one or another of the caravans. Nothing is demanded of him. He attends of his own free will the ceremonies taking place in the largest inhabitable house bordering on the square. These gatherings, he decides, must be of a religious nature, but although he doesn't remember the days of the week he knows that they take place regularly. Always they are of the same pattern. Always he finds patterns and symmetry and repetitions which are rhythms which he cannot grasp. The old man sits on a low wooden bench facing the wall in the largest room. His boots reflect a dull glow in the half light. Greedy the boots are, monopolizing the light. His beard is grey upon his coat and his eyes are tiny blue wings. On either side and ranged behind him on similar benches the women sit. Nothing happens for a long time. On occasion the patriarch may erupt in laughter. Or attempt singing a very serious but tuneless song. No other men are ever present except for the beard and Nefesj. Then a brazier containing smoking coals is brought into the room. The acrid smoke stings the eyes. Over the meagre heat the old man usually warms a chunk of meat. He then passes the meat around and everybody present bites off a piece and chews it. The meat is grey and old. Sometimes it is alive with maggots. Or flies. It is the meat of a grey horse. It is not always heated.

Like seeing it grows darker and less clear. Too dark to read the wounds in the newspaper. In this way one comes down into the desert. The maggots in the meat are lighter in colour. They are blind and minute. Wingless pale fat flies. A foetus. Immobility. Behind the walls he perceives women giggling. Among the crumbled remains of the long-gone outpost he comes across some carvings. These are the leftovers, dark, hybrid, one would expect to find in a burial place. They flake to the touch. They are faceless, defaced. Defeated perhaps? Blind as defecation. He notices that in the cold the cars are plundered. The annealed vehicles still sport aerials, the feelers of an arachnid, useless as *armes blanches* in a battle lost and buried in a dream. He decides to no longer attend the religious meetings. He has seen the grey horse with the wind a cold flame in its mane.

Also the meetings are no longer conducted in the big house up by the square. The laughing old man with the mirrored boots has retired to his caravan. There in conclusion the private ceremony will be enacted. Yet one senses the metamorphosis and the heterosis. In this way it will be done. Like news. Wires. A kite of dust. Word goes through the corrupted pattern of the once-existent town: the old man pronounces the word behind the sagging partitions of his greyish caravan. "We never had a horse" – this he says – "so go and fetch the man called Nefesj. The one who is said to be the foreigner."

The Other Ship

He'd expected death to be a newsflash of coded images, or maybe the sudden opening and unfolding of core impressions absorbed over the space of a lifetime, the hobo's wealth of rags and tatters, but with the awakening he heard just a rhythmic thumping: like a heart without circumference. At first it reminded him of a ship, of the enormous pistons driving the propellers. And when he propped himself up, stiff in body and insipid of thought, then it was indeed so, for he found that he was in a smallish cabin. But the throbbing proceeded from the cabin (or ring) just next to his. There, lifting himself up on his toes, he observed sailors tamping down the earthen floor tightly with pneumatic rammers. Lounging against the walls, officers or nurses in white overcoats oversaw the labour and when they noticed his presence they smiled ever so slightly their thin purplish smiles. Their teeth weren't as white as the cloth of their protective garments. Perhaps it was their intention to be friendly or to manifest sympathy.

Where had he been in the dark interlude? Did he sleep? For such an eternity? Was he absent merely, elsewhere, so occupied by other matters that this time-stretch must perforce seem black to him, this in-between? Or could it be a crumbling instance of amnesia? After all, everyone is sickening for black-out.

Maybe he himself was ill, bruised by this cataclysm which had overtaken his family. Family yes, but he couldn't be sure that it concerned his family only – didn't it hit all of mankind? Or, fear above all fears, the simplest explanation was probably that he, Lamourt Lasarus, is dead; that the imperceptible gurgling of time, just like the structures of cause and effect and the vibrating of life into death, can no longer hold any sense or relevance for him. . . . The cabin is empty. Over the tamped-down soil messages and squiggled calculations can now be finger-traced, carpets may be spread, furniture placed. The sleeping space may once again serve as the temporary living quarters of time-fattened voyagers. There and back the boat may sail tacking about with the breezes, or in one straight line without ever again entering a port or dropping the hook in the mouth of a delta, protected by cove or inlet, and with time their bodies will be eaten, fermenting, skeletons, dust – and thus find a permanent abode. Will be shaken as life-matter is rocked in the egg.

And more he remembers. Before this dark time they were surely somewhere on the shallow land. A great mishap occurred in that place. His father with the round-shaped grey head had died there already. They scooped up the leftovers and put it on board when they departed and this relic is somewhere in the hold packed in ice. With hands folded over the chest and with a grey expression where the face used to be, the body lies somewhere behind partitions among ice blocks like the wreck of a winter ship aground on mountains of white glass. Will they bury him also in one of the cabins? No – when they came aboard his mother and his sister were still alive. It was during the obliterating voyage they died and that is precisely why they had to be laid away *in situ*. Nothing must upset the pre-arranged projects.

He also is reminded that the inmates of that shallow land with the few slopes then looked at him half in pity and partly with distaste. He was never very popular with them. Something he must have done to provoke the disapproval. Would it be that the catastrophe which plunged them all into obscurity could be ascribed to him or his actions and positions? Was he to be held responsible for the Great Flood and the never-come-again? There is no ending to the wretchedness. His younger brother's darling cat, the house cat, Cat Ashcoat, was also killed during the same events. From this blow his brother went soft in the head. Or maybe he too was affected by the mysterious happening and the pollution. The cat was never very big, with long orange-coloured fur. Later, much later – he would remember – when already aboard this ship, his little brother still sat cradling the small carcass in his lap all the while humming softly. He wore his pyjamas. There was an inconvenient smell. And in this intense and autistic isolation his brother sat pulling fistfuls of fur from the cat's corpse. It came away easily. Over the white material of his outfit the orange pelt glittered.

And now he tried all along the corridor to reach the upper deck. He considered it strange to move so slowly, so uncertainly, so *deadened*, and that it must perhaps be ascribed to the vessel's kicking and sliding and mating movements, but he never felt seasick. On either side of the long passage all the dark cabins. At times he could hear slow noises through the partitions. He was looking for light now, an illumination of the dark time sequence behind him during which, so it would appear, everything took place and form, also the transformations; he wants to situate himself again; he, Fagotin Fremdkörper, needed a clarification of his own condition, a focal point, an I, a departure. In the dining saloon, by a long table together with some other passengers clad in formal evening garb, he comes upon his two elder brothers upright in their chairs. They are wearing black tuxedos with black bow ties knotted at the throat. His eldest brother's face is all caved in, is as grey as a dried-up waterfall, but still the face tries to look at him in an ironic way. There is neither victuals nor cutlery nor crockery nor crumbs nor custard stains on the white table linen. His second brother's face is very grey and stiff and scarred and callous with undigested wounds. The face is too dry to be nodded in his direction. There is neither food nor silver implements nor rice grains nor the blotches of faulty pouring on the white table linen. Opposite them at the table the women are seated, bent slightly forward over the napkins on the flat surface so that the enclosed white breasts may be seen darkly, lollipop tits, rancid maybe, a shimmering of lacquer over the exposed skin. The inlaid eyes of the ladies are dark and their mouths a little ajar and these orifices are deep and pulsating and warm red from within, just like glasses filled with wine. Just like bowls full of blood. These females did not turn their heads, neither did they lift their hands. There is only the swelling and the folding of the mating broody breasts. And the extended and luxurious dining space filled with a golden glow from the mirrors lining the walls is similarly rising and falling rhythmically. But he dares not sit down with the others, he is not correctly dressed, his heart is fluttering too painfully in his throat, and judging by the way they are looking or not looking at him it is evident that his presence is unwelcome. He was absent already. People are raising crooked smiles to him. People have mouths full of toothlike reflections.

He walks out on the afterdeck, turns his face aft. He wants to see the screws breaking frothily from the groan-waves. He particularly wishes to see which flag is pinned to this vessel, under what nationality they may be sailing, desiring to ascertain in this fashion perhaps their port of origin, their ultimate destination. High, lowing aloft, sputtering like a dying breath, there is this wind, higher than the rigging of the masts and the throbbing sea-black queendom of stars. High in the breath-hollows is the fluttering, the shuddering heart. A little hill-bird blown away over the wavetops now attempts to hide in the moving stillness. The deck is slippery.

Then only does he see, low in the night on the sea, quite close in the dark here, not much further than a scream away, rising in their wake, screw-thud by screw-thud exactly duplicated, *the other ship*.

The Double Dying of
an Ordinary Criminal

Carpe diem, quam minimum credula postero . . .

(i)

It is an unapproachable, ungrateful country. Along the coast, in an undulating green strip between the indigo sea and the ribbed, foaming mountain chain, the climate is tropical. There are sharks in the ocean and other fish large and small, dark coloured or of silver or ivory. On the land flamboyant trees grow, trees with shiny green fleshy leaves and violent outbursts of flowers: banana, palm, mango, the blossomy downpour of the bougainvillaea, the star-wounds of the poinsettia, the hibiscus with hairy dark ants most likely looking with sticky legs for sweetness in the calyx, canna, Ceylon rose. Nights the humid darkness is scented with the secretive magnolia, the camellia, the gardenia. The fruit are often fibrous, glutinous and soft. The trees – such as the guava – are enclosed by their particular smell, the heavy perfume of a full-bodied woman who has perspired a lot. The heat and the high humidity cause the milk to turn sour instantly, grow mould on the clothes strung on wires or kept in wardrobes, rot the wood while steel and iron are devoured by oxidation. To the north and west stretch the swelling sugar-cane plantations, the cane is cultivated and chopped by people of a dark race, people with large sombre eyes and smooth black hair. These people are sometimes called "sea kaffirs". Here and there among the rippling and sharply whispering sugar-cane they erected rudimentary single-roomed temples for their gods, the inner walls decorated with bright representations: often the swarthy mother god, Kali, she who also at times assumes the aspect of Parvati or Sarasvati on the winged throne of a swan, or that of Shakti – the bride, companion and *alter ego* of Shiva the destroyer. On these plantations as also in the cultivated forests further removed from the ocean, where lumberjacks cut and saw the yellow and red trees, and elsewhere too, there is the constant flashing of many kinds of birds, butterflies, large insects with shimmering black bodies. As well as snakes. The cities service the ships which come to trade here, and the holiday-makers and pleasure-seekers come to relax on the guava-coloured beaches and to bathe in the tepid waves within the protection of the shark nets. When the barriers are raised the stuck sharks are there like white torpedoes. In the streets one encounters the many fumes of decomposition and dismantling, of viscosity and dry rot and sweetness; occasionally also the harsher tang of spices and seasoning herbs. There are night clubs and taxis and rickshaws. People smoke or use in other ways a rank stupefier commonly called *dagga*; other names heard are *bhang*, "real rice", *gunja*, *jane*, "Maryjay", "rooney", "DP", "green stuff", "weed", "grass", "dope", "popeye", "wheat", "Tree of Knowledge", *insangu*. It makes the eyes darker from within and red around the lids and it lies like a curly smokiness on the voice. It analyses the sense of time the way one would eat a fish morsel by morsel off the bone. It entices the appetite.

The Coast is separated from the Heartland by a chain of mountains which seem blue from afar, the mountains of the Dragon, hundreds of miles long, like the great wall of China with its watchtowers. The colours of the sun remain entangled mostly in the structure of the mountains. But some of this citadel's summits are so high that they've lost all colour; they are dusted with a sparkle which could be snow or ice.

Beyond the mountains the Heartland commences, an inhospitable region, a semi-desert which further and deeper will silt up in a true desert of brown and grey dunes; unresting dunes. It is a high plateau with hardly any diversity and little vegetation apart from the grass which grows tall and becomes white like a bleached photo during the winter. Now and then there are crevices or denser ravines in the folds of the high country, something which can be held darkly in the hollow of the hand, or more elevated ledges, ridges and mesas. When summer comes gigantic cloud constructions wash over the land, are piled up, unchain in thunderstorms of a prehistoric force with coiling swords of electricity and smoking arrows of light, until the clouds crack and tear, the bottom gives way and flood waters are poured over the ochre earth. The people of this land are hard and obtuse and doughty – but cunning – as the earth and its climate require of them. Their eyes lie waiting deep and unflinching in the heads, robed in wrinkles under thick eyebrows, and when they lose their teeth quite early on, as happens often, the jaw muscles are tough and bitter. They cultivate the topsoil. They sow and reap maize with big red-painted tractors, ploughs and other farm implements. They keep numerous herds and flocks, Brahmans with awkward humps, or earth-red oxen with white horns spread very wide on either side of the head – Nguni or Afrikaners by name. These beasts constitute practically the only heritage left by an ancient yellowish race of humans with Asiatic features who wandered over these wastes in days of yore. The real wealth of the

Heartland is hoarded under the earth's crust where, when the earth still moved, layers and veins of gold were deposited, and copper, and further south also buried volcanoes, pipes and alluvial soil full of diamonds. Over these riches the people built their cities: glass, concrete, steel – rising from the desert to sometimes be split and obliterated again by fulminations from above. In the streets the long flat automobiles crawl, flashing the sun like heliographs; inside the vehicles are people who have absorbed too much food, with fantastic coiffures or moustaches pearling perspiration, and with knees spread wide. The other people without means of transport are of a darker hue and they trot along the sidewalks with long rhythmically flapping coat-tails, passing by the enormous shop windows. From these cities are ruled and administered the Coast, the South, the Mountain Fastnesses, the Old-Land, the Gap, the Middle State, the Frontier, the Reserves, the Desert, and other colonies and possessions.

He was born in the country of Coast and grew up there. Little has been documented concerning his juvenile years and not much touching on his adult life. His mother became very old and started wearing a black dress with thick woolen stockings. Her back was bent high between the shoulder blades. He was a tall and sturdy fellow with brown hair, slightly oily, falling straight over the forehead. His legs were hairy and when he deigned to smile only the left side of his mouth was tilted upwards with a minimal contraction of muscles. We don't know whether he was interested in any sport. There is talk of a work he was supposed to have had, and of a wife; even children are mentioned. He was still young. Twenty-eight years old.

Hell doesn't exist. It *comes into being*, each moment it is created relentlessly, and then it is strictly personal and individual, that is, proper to each individual – which doesn't necessarily imply that others aren't touched or concerned by it. As tubes of light the hells burst in the heavens and illuminate, alter, the area within their reach. The act, the misdemeanour then, a fraction in time, causes a chain reaction, a mutation eventually flowering in the fated echo or the obverse of it; a clandestine bleeding. Each crime contains the hell befitting it. The snake's skin fits without any crease or pucker over the snake. When the felony is committed the hell opens up on the spot; when it at last – and often in public – bursts forth, it is redeemed. The one is an utterance of the other. The one eliminates the other.

He became a bum – nobody quite knows why or how. He met up with a woman, much older, a companion and an *alter ego*, a person like him dwelling in the dark mazes of the city. As much and as often as they could afford to they smoked and they drank. Nights they then slept in empty plots by smouldering rubbish heaps, or in condemned buildings due for demolition. Sometimes they lay in water furrows. They also danced.

The old woman tried to tempt drifters with her poor body – boozers, sailors, blokes ostensibly gentlemen with problems sneaking through the streets late at night (late in the blossoming of life, already in the dropping of death). She was the bait. He was the hook. Also the tackle, rod, gaff and cudgel. When she managed to seduce an unsuspecting customer with an obscene caricature of hip swaying and the slimy dark tongue as clotted bleeding between the more tropical red of the lips, the edges of the wound, leading him to a sheltered or deserted spot, then *he* jumped on the greedy or shaky one from behind. With a stick or a knife, sometimes with a length of piano wire twisted in a noose. Always the purpose was to break the subject open, to murder; three times at least it is known that he succeeded. Some victims were chopped up and chucked piecemeal in a sewer. Robbery, it would seem, was not the motive. Perhaps it was a perverse form of sexual satisfaction or the foreplay thereof. One night the prey was a blind jeweller, who could understand the facets of gems or the shivery internal working of watches with sensitive fingertips. It may also be that the jeweller's blindness is an injury resulting from the assault.

Without too much trouble they are trapped by the police. During the subsequent trial they are both found guilty and sentenced: she with tearing mouth to an insane asylum, he to the death cell. The expression is: he got the rope. They would top him. His life was to be reeled in with a cord.

He is transferred to a cell in a building of red bricks in one of the ruling cities of the Heartland. His appeal against the death sentence is rejected. The request for mercy likewise. The long wake has started. Altogether a year and a half passed.

The Monday the hangman came to inform him that the next Tuesday would be it – hardly a week then. Together with him in the pot there were five more "condemns", Unwhites, people with sallow hides and of diverse crimes. They would go up together but were not to swing simultaneously. Maybe the Unlife up there would make them equal. A folded sheet of paper with a black border, where his dying day is announced, is handed to him. The hangman weighs him, measures his height and the circumference of his neck. With these data the length of the rope et cetera are calculated in an approximately scientific approximation. It was a Monday during the summer and each day of that season the clouds were a thundering sea battle above the hard, cracked earth.

Some people are dead before they even come to die. When the Unwhites are informed (when the countdown starts), they directly open up in song, they break and let the words erupt. There is a pulsating urgency about the singing, as if one can hear how scorchingly alive their voices are. All the other prisoners – in any event only awaiting their turn – help them from that instant on: the basses, the tenors, the harmonizers, the choir. Every flight of the prospective voyagers' voices is supported and sustained by those of the others. As if a stick is suddenly poked into an antheap. The sound of the voices is like that of cattle at the abattoir, the lowing of beasts smelling the blood and knowing that nothing can save them now. Perhaps the Jews too, had they been a singing people, would have hummed thus in the chambers where the gas was turned on. Maybe they did? This making of noises with the mouths continues day and night, erases night and day, till those who must depart go up in the morning, at seven o'clock. The best flying is done in the morning. For that last stretch those who leave will sing alone. Day in day out it continues and in the early hours it is a low mumbling, the murmuring sound of the sea which never sleeps but only turns on to the other hip. In this fashion, during the final week, that which is fear and pain and anguish and life is gradually pushed out of the mouth. A narcotic. And so they move with the ultimate daybreak through the corridor as if in a mirror, rhythmic but in a trance, not as a men alone but as a song in movement. They are no longer there; just the breaths flow unceasingly and warm and humid over the lips. (The opposite may be alleged too: that this delicious and fleeting life is purified and sharpened over the last week by song to a shriek of limpid knowing.)

For him there is no such grace because his like – the fellow condemns in his section, in his part of the prison, the pale ones, the Uncoloureds, people from the ruling class – don't sing easily. Nor can he, like the others in the pot, be put in a communal cell – of course there are far more Unwhite candidates than Uncoloured ones. *He* must pray death (or life) all the way out of himself. The pastor is there to assist and to show him the words, for words are holes in which you must stick death. He will die in another way before he is dead. He becomes his own ghost. The eyes are deep and bright in the sockets. It gives his head the

56

appearance of a skull. His quiff falls lank over the forehead. He sneers without any fear of the warders. Like the other seasoned prisoners – those who know the ropes – he wears his shoes without socks.

> *All hope is lost*
> *Of my reception into grace; what worse?*
> *For where no hope is left, is left no fear!*
> (blind Milton)

The minister. In fact a chaplain, and with a rank in the service. He is a small chap with an absolutely naked scalp, dressed in a modish tailored suit and shirted in flowers branching out over ribs, belly and the small of the back. He has red puffy bags under the eyes and, so one imagines, folds of white flesh around the midriff and in the groin. It is his task to prepare the soul, to make it robust, to extract the soul and wash and iron it, and then to let it be acquiescent. It requires a fine ingenuity because the soul is like smoke and so easily slips through the fingers. He spends much time on his knees and it is not good for the pants. He prays and emits suffocated sounds. Some vowels are stretched beyond measure, are pronounced in a placatory way as when a little child tries to make a big animal change its mind. When he prays he closes his eyes and holds the hand of the convicted. With eyes closed, when talking aloud, you move on another level. That which is there is not there. That which isn't there is there perchance. Heaven grows behind closed eyelids. His order is a tall one. During the last week something crystallizes from the doomed, surreptitiously, and comes to cleave to the clergyman. It is the soul wishing to remain among the familiar living when the soma comes to nothing. Like a snail it is searching for a new shell. So the body becomes lighter. . . .

The executioner (bailiff, hangman, topper, rope expert, death artist) is a tall man in the sombre weeds of pious neutrality and with a melancholy countenance. His post or position is private and part-time. When, through resignation or death, a vacancy occurs, anyone – a pensioner for instance, or the father of numerous sickly children who needs a little extra income – can submit his application to the magistrate. He then tenders for so much or so much per head (at present, before devaluation, it is seven rands) for he is remunerated by the head. He must see to it, together with his assistant (if any), that the gallows remain in good well-oiled working order, for they are often made use of. When the pot is pointed out it is his duty to be the announcer and to make the necessary preparations. He is the tailor who will fit you out in a new life. On the fateful morning he is there bright and early. He reposes his head on interlaced fingers against the bars as if he were praying or dozing off. When the candidates are brought in under escort he makes them take up their indicated positions – warders are keeping them upright – and adjusts the nooses around the necks below the ears until they fit just right. Then he closes the eye-flaps of their hoods and presses with a pale finger the button activating the trapdoor. They then plunge twice their own height. The complete procedure seldom takes more than seven seconds. Up to seven persons can thus be served simultaneously, standing in line like bridegrooms before an altar. After the thrashing about the corpses remain hanging for ten minutes in the well. What has not snapped will be throttled. Thereafter the still warm and very heavy (because deadweight) corpses are pulleyed in, the handcuffs taken off, they are undressed, and lowered again. If the correct results were not obtained the whole process is repeated. When shudders and convulsions are no longer observed the limp cadavers are deposited in washing troughs and the doctor on duty makes an incision in the neck to establish which vertebra was broken – this information must be entered in duplicate. Bloodstains have penetrated the metal of the wash-basins. Bloodstains, crud, snot splotches also on the ropes and the hoods, and the cupboard where the coiled ropes are kept stinks of stale effluence. The burial takes place within a few hours. The clothes of the deceased are brought back into circulation in the gaol. After all, it's state property. If for some or other reason a dead body must be preserved, there are modern shiny iceboxes for that purpose in the autopsy room. As all of this happens during the fresh and innocent hours, the vocation of hangman need not interfere with any other job; your executioner could be a teacher, a psychiatrist, a politician, a chicken farmer, publisher, or unemployed.

The gibbets. In other ages the pillory was erected prominently in a square or on a hilltop, and the complete ceremony was public and a joy for the birds, not so much for its deterrent effect but because it was such an intimate part of everyday life and death, and a rude form of amusement. We live in *these* days and no longer frequent or know one another. No longer are we animals with the snouts in the trough of death. Also, civilization has come over us. In our time the place of execution is a privileged one, where it is dark, behind walls, through passages, in the heart of the labyrinth. Few people know when the seeker has found it. It is there like some bashful god, like the blind and deaf and self-satisfied idol of a tiny group of initiates, for the satisfaction of an obscure tradition. And that which is intimate, like defecation, must be kept hidden from prying eyes. The artificial gloss of an insouciant existence must be safeguarded. Usually there is no trouble or unpleasantness during the execution. But it has happened that some of the damned refuse to fit the pattern and that they then, that last morning when the cell door was unlocked, threw a blanket over the officer's head and tried to smash him against the wall, head first like a battering ram – so that he had to live for months afterwards with his neck in traction. And it has also happened that one flappie,* in that fraction of a second when the trapdoor falls open, timed the moment exactly, and jumped on to the back of the man in front of him so that his fall was broken and he had to be hoisted back up, kicking, to die all over again. The blind shaft is as inevitable as the sunrise; the ritual leaves no room for any deflection or improvising. The last route is secure and actually no longer part of the personal hell.

The pilgrim, the candidate, is accompanied to the preparation room by a spiritual comforter and the officers. This place is called "the last room", the departure hall. The nauseating sweet smell of death is already all-pervasive. Here he is handcuffed and a white hood is placed over his head. The flap above the eyes remains open until he has taken up his position below the gallows. Exceptionally it may happen that the spine and the neck break completely at the instant when the earth falls away below his feet and that the head becomes separated from the body, that the head alone remains suspended there. But that just happens in the case of candidates who are rotten with syphilis, and then mostly with female Unwhites. For this negligible probability, seen statistically, one can hardly provide in advance, in a scientific way, a solution. What occurs more frequently is that the male reprobate at the critical crossover reaches a benevolent, jetting orgasm. To beget a child is thus always a form of dying. What's more, this final poke in the dark is fulfillment, at last a total embrace of the mother god. An influx and an unfolding. It is said: to die by the neck is to

*Flap – long-tailed widow-bird, sakabula; common name for Black prisoner.

sodomize the night. . . . Precautionary measures are however taken with female executees. They get watertight rubber bloomers and the dress is taken in around the knees and sewn up. Nor will she afterwards be undressed like the men to be hosed down, but she'll be buried just the way she is in her clothes. The reason being that the female parts – uterus, ovaries – are spilled with the shock of falling down the shaft.

At times a doomed one may attempt during the last days and nights to take his own death. He will for instance try to crush his head against the cell wall or to dive head first from the bed to the floor and thus be rid of his thoughts on the cement, as of a hard rain. But it is not allowed; after all, it's not a sacrifice which is demanded but an execution which concerns others too and in which each one must play his ascribed part. It is a matter of mutual responsibility. Steps are therefore taken to prevent the suicide of the weak-hearted. Those whose lives in reality ceased existing with the death sentence are kept alive in bright cells permanently lit, and day and night a warder keeps watch through the barred aperture in the door. There are days and there are nights. . . . Once the candidate has been chosen his person and his cell are frisked for any concealed weapon or means of release. But apart from that he lives his last days like a king. The meal of the convicted may be ordered to taste, even fried chicken.

He swore that they'll never string him up alive, that he will do himself in. His cell is searched. In the ink vein of his ballpoint pen they find a hidden needle. A dark needle, blue at present, which was to be introduced into the upper arm from where, theoretically, it could accomplish the short trip to the heart where with a flashing snake of pain it would perforate that organ-organism the way the god Krishna (an incarnation of Vishnu) long ago pinned down the snake Kaliya with his lance: a short ultimate journey. He doesn't know that his needle has been discovered so that he retains the illusion that he himself may freely decide when to abrogate his life during the fatal week. Perhaps it doesn't matter. He will die in another way before the final sunrise.

It would however have been better and more effective had he smuggled in a razorblade at the beginning. He could have done so with the pretence that he wanted to cut out pictures to stick them on a sheet of paper. He could then spend such an inordinately long time doing so that the guardian will end up forgetting about the blade. This little silver-fish he should then break in two, washing the one half down the toilet bowl; the other part he hides on his body at all times. The last evening he wishes all the warders a good night and lies down in his bunk with an extra blanket over him and his back to the door. He has one hand under his head on the pillow and pulls the blanket up to his chin. Then he would have to work quickly, for the convicted is not allowed to sleep with his hands below the blankets during the last week. With the broken blade he slices through the large vein in the crook of the arm, in the valley of the shoulder, in the armpit; a clean cut several centimetres long. His hand stays under the ear; the arm thus remains flexed so that the wound, the bearded and sighing mouth, may peacefully continue bleeding under the blanket – like the mysterious, sweetish smell of a tropical flower in the night. He rests with his body to the wall so that the blood may gather on the floor between the bed and the wall. When they arrive then the next morning to wake him for the final exercise, the body is already all of marble. . . . Or – an alternative – he could have pulled with the fingers, his tongue as far as it would go, closed his teeth over it, and then have tapped lightly with one hand against the lower jaw. In this way the lower teeth break through the tongue close to its roots. Nothing can save you from that blooming. Or he might even have swallowed the tongue. Fool!

From the land of Coast his mother arrives with her grey hair and her black back. Together with the preacher she visits him daily – but she of course is behind a glass partition since contact visits are not permitted. Death is contagious. When she prays, her hands, the knuckles and the joints, are so tightly clasped that it must be a tiny god indeed who finds asylum in such hand-space, a god like an idea worn away over the years, rubbed small, like a seed.

He stands in his cell under the bulb-eye from the ceiling, talking to his warders. One warder expects him to make shit at the last because he caught him doing exercises that final night. The pointing day is a silver-fish in a big bowl of liquid as murky as blood, in a dark house where night yet resides.

Monday comes with a cold persistent drizzle, an unheard-of way of raining in the Heartland in the summer. But apparently, so it is speculated, strong winds were blowing over the ocean from the Coast and a penetrating rain fell there. This strange weather is brought to the Heartland by the wind from the east – from the Coast therefore.

His last wish is that his eyes should be donated to the blind jeweller. His eyes are of a shiny green colour, like the stones jewellers sometimes mount on silver for a bangle or a gorget. It is not known whether eyes too have memories – who can say for sure where sensory memories are situated? When one leaves one's eyes to someone, doesn't it in a way mean the grafting of one person on another? But an eye cannot be grafted – only the cornea under favourable circumstances. And, in any event, his last wish cannot be honoured since there is not sufficient time to comply with the required formalities in duplicate and triplicate.

When the day comes he is up early. He will not see the dawn because the forbidden place where fruit will be hung on the trees of knowledge of good and of evil is in the very same building. Neither the knife of day nor the cape

63

of night are known there. Some detectives come to enquire whether he might not be amenable, for old times' sake, to admitting his culpability for a series of unsolved murders. He pretends to be exclusive – as if each man were an exception. He will take many dead with him to the rot-hole. It is suspected that he may have polished off up to fifteen victims. . . . He is led down the tunnels by officers and a soul-stroker. The song has already taken the Unwhites up, through the same corridors, ahead of him. At last, after whiling away so many months in the waiting rooms and the outer sanctums, purified and prepared, he will now enter the secret and sacred circle. Another hell is to be wiped out; a new one may be opened. Cause and effect continue. But he is no longer the man he was eighteen months ago.

In the preparatory room he greets the warders one by one by hand. The lines in the hand-palms are laid over one another; there is a touching, a crossing, a knotting of fingers. Night-flies meeting, parting. He claims he will meet them all again "up there". Here there is the aroma of sweetness although the night is icy-cold. He is given his blood and shackles. Now he is the minotaur.

The mother is already waiting on her knees in the undertaker's hall where the box with the rests, the shell of the sacrifice of atonement, will be brought: at her request the family will take care of the burial. What the gods don't wish to eat will be fed to the earth. There is no more room between her hands. From her body something like a bleeding bubbles up, the reminiscence of a foetus, and breaks in her throat like the dark cooing of a dove.

He stands underneath the tree. Upwards, higher than the ceiling and than the roof ridge, is heaven; peace blue; stars have been incinerated by the light. A fish mirrors. The hangman, who has been leaning his head on folded hands, comes to adjust the rope, the umbilical cord. Exactly behind the ear the knot must lie, where the marrow, consciousness, the wire of light, grows into the skull. He follows to the last the cool movements of the executioner. The eye-flap is turned down. It is dark.

It is dark.

The trapdoor opened with a shudder running through the entire building. A door closing. A flame of lightning through a cloud. A knife slipping into the fatty layer below the ribcage. One heartbeat through all the tentacles, nets of silence, equilibrium-sticks and vein-sides of the body when you are shaken awake from the dark.

Outside the day. The sky a deep blue, purple nearly, the way it looks when seen through the porthole of a high-altitude aircraft or above very high silver-clean mountain peaks. The sun is a blinding thing, so ardent that you daren't look at it to establish its shape. In the air nothing, no substance which may deflect the sword strokes. A sharp and clear cold, crumbly and yet glass hard. Breaths hang in limp tufty cloudlets from the lips. Somewhere snow or hail must have fallen, surely in the mountains, and that in summer.

(ii)

Once upon a time
not so long ago. . . .

One is loath to write too soon about something like the foregoing. You let the days pass you by although you're aware of the fact that you'll have to open the thing sooner or later. You allow the days to go hard in your throat. For it is like a contusion around the neck: first too tender to the touch, swollen with blood compressed in the capillaries; later the swelling goes down and the injured region becomes bluish purple; still later a yellowish blue and then a lighter yellow when it starts itching. Afterwards it is for a while still a scratchy place in the memory. And yet the matter must be disembowelled because we are the mirrors and mirrors have their own lives. Mirrors have a life too and that which gets caught in them continues existing there. Reality is a version of the mirror image. It is a literary phenomenon I'd like to point out to my colleagues: the ritual must be completed in us also. Before death points? Does death depend on us?

> *you hang the life*
> *tied to death*
> *until it dies*

> *you drop life*
> *gibbeted to death:*
> *until death is.*

Even though something can be inserted easily enough into the mirror, none of us knows precisely how and when it can be taken out again. Do mirrors have looking-glasses too, deeper layers, echoes perhaps incessantly sounding the fathomless? This is the result: the eye and the hand (the description) embroider the version of an event, the anti-reality without which reality never could exist – description is experiencing – I am part of the ritual. The pen twists the rope. From the pen he is hanged. . . . He hangs in the mirror. But where in reality he is separated – conceivable in spirit or vision and growth of flesh draped over humid bone – hanged, taken down, ploughed under – each of these steps remains preserved in the mirror. The mirror mummifies each consecutive instant, apparently never runs over, but ignores as far as we know all decay and knows for sure no time. (A mutation, yes. . . .) He thus keeps on hanging and kicking in the remembrance. You only need to close the eyelids to see each detail before the eyes. And the writer just as the reader (because the reader is a mirror to the writer) can seemingly make nothing undone. He cannot reopen the earth, cannot set the snapped neck, cannot stuff the spirit back into the flesh and the light of life in the lusterless eyes full of sand, cannot straighten the mother's back, cannot raise the assassinated, cannot reduce the man to a seed in the woman's loins while a hot wind streams over the Coast.

Or can he?

Is that the second death?

(Shiva, as Nutaraya – King of the Dancers – has in his one right hand a drum which indicates sound as the first element of the unfolding/budding universe; the uppermost left hand holds a fire-tongue, element of the world's final destruction: the soil is fire devouring the body to ashes, and brings repose, till the next time. The other arms represent the eternal rhythmical balance between life and death. The one foot rests on the devil of "Forgetfulness", the other treads in the void, as is usual when dancing, and depicts, according to Heinrich Zimmer, "the never-ending flow of consciousness in and out of the state of ignorance". Shiva, god of destruction, god of creation, et cetera. The heart is a mirror/The mirror is a heart.)

The Temptation in Rome

People on the mountains don't worry about
mosquitoes in the plains, nor do the inhabitants
of Egypt about umbrellas.
SAUL BELLOW

When the new pope was elected, when smoke fluttered miraculously white above the chimneys near the Sistine Chapel, when the huddled masses on the enormous square before St Peter's with its imposing dome by Michelangelo had stopped holding their breaths and mumbling, had cheered and wept and recited the prayers, were blessed by straggly hands in wide white sleeves, when the sun had lain down red as blood and had risen blood-red (despite Galileo), but it did not stand still in the heavens since that wasn't called for, even then the College of Cardinals had not yet realized clearly on what a rare bird they'd imposed the mitre and crown, exactly whose finger they slipped the fish ring on and who they got to sit on the fisherman's chair. That they were still to find out. With heartfelt regret and communal self-reproach, beating fists on the chest, yes, oh woe. Later, when regret comes too late. For Giovanni XXXV was an intransparent man. Gentle but a thorough worker, so he would be summed up by the majority of mankind. Gifted young priest he had been (from Flemish workers' city), punctual, loyal; quickly making headway to bishop, to the *Curia*, subtle jurist charged with the elucidation of ecclesiastical disputes, *nonce apostolique* in Beijing at a stage when that crucible of the world started progressing beyond Communism as had been foreseen so much earlier by Mao, discreetly the purple of cardinal, and then – Papa! And nobody caught even a whiff of his idiosyncrasies. Perhaps, supposing they did know, it wouldn't have mattered much, as the Church had after all been immunized to some extent against her more flamboyant and eccentric characters who, from the time of the Borgias and Farneses at least, were woven like gold embroidery through the history of the ages. But, had they in their wise counsel been able to see ahead, they would have made other provisions, or asked the Providence to provide for different arrangements.

Three whims especially Giovanni XXXV had, and these were well camouflaged until he attained the exalted position of infallibility: he was an epicure, a gourmet with wide and unbiased and truly cultivated tastes who had partaken of every renowned dish on this earth excepting always the meat of the anteater, and then not just that of any old aardvark or ant-bear or armadillo, no, it absolutely had to be the marinated tail of the pangolin, prepared *à l'azanienne* – during his patient and excellent service he all along searched for this culinary curiosity to this day unobtainable so that the finding and experiencing of same came over the years to be a barely controllable obsession; in the second place he dreamed every night of heaven as a bulging black cloud above his head, as the baldachin of a fourposter, menacing, and because of this he gradually lost first all interest and then any keenness and in due time his faith in heaven and its attributes – and at last, alas, also in its resplendent inhabitants and janitors, for who looks forward to disappearing, sucked up in a dark vault? And only the habit of abnegation and the external forms still aided him in maintaining the requisite appearance of piety; but particularly, in the last place especially – he couldn't abide Satan. This cock drove him up the wall. It was the custom since God knows how many popes already that a black cock be kept on a tiny balcony next to the living quarters of the highest authority, and that the name of this disturber of the peace should be Satan. Where and why this thorn-in-the-flesh practice originated the devil alone will know. The present panicled beast, a braggart, a bully, a big bugger, a temperamental tempter, a ruffled ruffian – he exasperated two of Giovanni XXXV's predecessors, outlived them, probably even helped them into heaven – the present crier was a true windbag. His Holiness couldn't stand it any more – the defiant shrill crowing before dawn, twice, up to three times, so that hearing and seeing are shaken awake with a shock as of ice, and the raw sense of shame and disaster is laid bare, as also that ancient longing; that this anachronism had to subsist in the twenty-first century, and that *he*, Infallible Authority, had to move in a bare cock-stride away from the virago's scaffolding!

Within the space of a few short weeks the old man's condition started worsening irrevocably. Of what use is it to be the pope if no one, but exactly nobody – delegate, ambassador, plenipotentiary, chargé d'affaires, missionary, seminarist, chaplain, inquisitor, abbot, monk, nun, Franciscan or even Jesuit – could get hold of that one fierily desired dish? Why come and lick the amethyst of his ring to then tell him with downcast eyes that the scaly anteater has long since become extinct? What does it matter to him? Of everything he had eaten, from the similarly extinct elephant's phlegm-tender trunk to the undone blue heart of the Korean sepia to the unearthly concoctions of the most distant satellite, but now he was sure: for ever since he can remember he had been yearning for that lost republic in Africa's carapaced anteater's pulpy-soft tail floating white up in a Roman sauce. . . . And what does it count to be pope, disenchanted, forfeited from fear and all further ferreting forsaken, when you still have to hallucinate at night, see the bulging black canopy descending to enfold you, trying by force to swallow you up in dark oblivion? But then! At the last moment on the ultimate lip of the wine-dark night, to be woken like old weak meat by the prehistoric roar of the bone-beak!

He lifts his hand laboriously – they have become thin and translucent and timid in the wide folds of the white sleeves of his robes of office – his mind has started swimming, red and warm, but he reasons just unerringly enough to have noticed the scavengers commencing to circle around him – and beckons to his secretary to come closer. Monsignor Pierolo Woulololo the latter is called – "a name like a turd", the old pope reflects cynically, but also (he realizes with a sense of heaviness) one of those wanting to direct and manipulate me now that my hours are running out. "Any news from our spier?" (thus he expresses himself, in an archaic fashion) he asks with soft tongue. A slow shaking of the head and a mournful eye (the Pharisee!) are the only answers.

Ah, was he dreaming then? A rumour had been reported to him about how, somewhere in Trastevere in the very shadow of the Santa Maria church, so close by really, an exile from that distant lost land is supposed to be living and that this rumoured man, conserving an interest for antique species is said to have a tame pangolin "for purposes of research into suspected eating habits". But even the most subtle investigation of a special Swiss Guard brought nothing to light concerning animal or man. People live so unobtrusively, so invisibly in our day.

He sighs, drools something in Latin. Another language which nobody understands any more, not even the ecclesiastics. There is a flare-up of fire in him. It grows darker outside. A little muzzy from the atavistic hunger he looks through the window but the nightly fireworks display of space vehicles departing for and returning from far-off colonies can no longer amuse or distract him. (And man's history is speeding by, fugitive colours shooting into the void. The Chinese devise the first rocket and use it in raising the Mongolian siege of Kai-Fung-Fu in the year AD 1232. The Babylonians decide that Mars must be a planet. In the year 160 of Our Lord, Lucianus of Samosata already visits the moon in a story. Ditto old Nicholas Copernicus in his *Of the Revolution of Celestial Bodies* in 1543. Ditto Johann Kepler's *Concerning the Movements of Mars* in 1609, although based on the earlier observations of Tycho Brahe. And Galileo Galilei – poor Galileo, we made you a heretic – comes in 1610 with his *Messenger from the Stars*. And William Congreave with his crazy experiments, trying to turn rockets into weapons. Jules Verne's *Voyage to the Moon* already in 1865. Then Hermann Ganswindt with his projectile-impelled vehicles. Yes, the Germans, the Boches, the Tedeschi, their Gesellschaft – Association of Space Travellers, and later von Braun and the others of Peenemünde with the VI and the VII, and how soon afterwards they helped projecting the Amis, the Americans, into the tolling depths of space aboard their Mercury, Gemini, Apollo, and suddenly all manner of laboratoria, artificial planets, fleets to other galaxies. And meanwhile the other thinkers and dreamers and world conquerors, the Rumanian Hermann Oberth, the Russian Constantin Tsiolkovski who as early 1903 postulates the colonization of other planets, Yuri Gagarin the first hand mirror spinning around the globe, mirror in which mankind suddenly discovered a new resemblance, the dogs, the monkeys, the rats, Titov with the light hair, Soyuz, Neil Armstrong like a diver on the moon. . . . How far we've come since then. Every square centimetre of this space ark of ours under surveillance. Wipe-out a million kilometres away. Distances cancelled. Wars. Rays of destruction. Plasm and ectoplasm. Fires of discovery. Always more profoundly into the never-ending. Nothing is now invisible or our own. . . . How man's furthest reaching dreams have been given shape and existence! Surely it *must* be possible to find the anteater. . . !)

He sleeps. With a smack-a-muttermunch of lips. All his confused being purified now and one-pointed to the single last desire. He dreams. Is he really dreaming? In the volcanic mind he leafs back still through archives' yellowed annals of vanished civilizations, the volumes researched over the years, and all at once remembers – since how long already obscured and put out of thought? – lines of a sonnet from that annoying country: something . . . something . . . about "life which is only a line of ants", of "soldiers yet serving the blind queen". . . and "how sweet it must be on the anteater's tongue". Cloud? Antheap? Tongue? No . . . no . . . NO!

They heard something like a flutter and an anguished slobbering noise. Succeeded by silence, they claimed afterwards. No. No one had sat up with him, not even the ambitious secretary of the thick greenish name. When they came across him outside on the balcony he was already gone. With blood flecks on the white nightshift. Ants – weird how suddenly they appeared from nowhere in this sterilized century in *this* building! – were already active on the fragile corpse. Just as black – only smaller and more granular – as the clutch of feathers in the gaping mouth which stifled him at birth. And the humid prints in the wide-open eyes were not even dry yet. Were these then, after all, tears of joy?

The Man with the Head

Will the dead
Hold up his mirror and affirm
To the four winds the smell
And flash of his authority?
ROBERT LOWELL

There was a man, whether from Japhet or from Novgorod I do now know; and
he was very sad. Pee–too–wee! Pee–too–wee! The man said out of sadness there
where he sat by the window and watched thick blue rain falling from the sky
so much so that all the blueness had fallen from heaven and the pee–too–wee
he groaned again dejectedly for there was no gaol in his county. That is why
he was so sad. There were old people and there was no prison to put them in;
there were fat people and clever people and people with glasses and knotty veins
and half-dead people and some all humid with cancer and property owners and
people with skirts and corns and real people and nowhere a gaol to lock them
up. There weren't any black people in his country but nevertheless not even the
smallest or cheapest little old gaol or boop or slammer or calabuso or ballon

or clink or taule or cooler wherever and however to keep them separated. *Pee-too-wee* the man sighed and from pure desperation put his hands to his face and stated pulling. He tugged and pulled and suddenly his face gave way and quite coolly remained sitting in his hands, shivering. The man laid the face in his lap and the two of them stared at their mutual lameness. *Pee-too-wee*! Squeaked the man at his wits' end as he doesn't quite know what else to say. And *wee-too-pee* his crocked face answers all plucky. Who are you to *pee-wee-too me*? asks the man very angry highly upset all of a sudden the hell in. I shall curse thee – I'll say "dammit" to you. And also dammit and buggerit and fie and whoreson and forsooth and without munching my words a powerful mammit. The man didn't know all that many curses and the others which he did know he dared not employ for if he started sounding off and got himself arrested for private disturbance of the peace there would have been no gaol to punish him. Now I am properly right up to the nostrils in the whatsit, the man thinks. And *who-pee-too* taunts his face with the thick blue tears in the eyes. Just you wait a little while, my china, said the man as he put his face on the table most careful not to crumple the eyelashes, I'll show you who the master is around here the cock on the dung-hill; and through the window he climbed out into the rain with the intention of going to the shop owner across the road to buy a cocked mirror with which to confront the cocky face. But when he had his back turned the face immediately saw its chance and took the gap *moving* from the table to the floor through the front door over the veranda down the street ears in the neck. The shopkeeper asked the man and who do I have the honour to be serving? and the man became as red as blood with anger because he had since long been a faithful customer. And mirror I do have, the shopkeeper murmured thoughtfully, but oh my dear they seem to be all empty. Thereupon the shopkeeper happened to look through his shop window and clapped his hands and started crowing with the giggles – that is to say that the hand-clapping frightened the laughter-crow in his belly to life – and he shrieked whose face is running there then? First the man wanted to curse but he reconsidered remembering that he had already packed out all his usable curses in the house across the street; so he jumped up and started running down his face huffing and puffing. In front the face runs and then the man follows and they run and run and run; only, it is more difficult for the face to move because the man is not bothered by running tears in the eyes. Well, my friends, had there been, as it behoves a proper country, gaols down there, these events would never have taken place. And if I'd known whether the man hailed from Japhet or from Novgorod or perhaps from Windverlaat, I just might have been in the position to complete the story to all our satisfaction.

They're probably still running now *pee–too–wee wu–wu–sho*.

Hanging on to Life

It took place in London and it must have been after the war since a soft wind, tepid, warm nearly, was now sweeping over everything and curving the grass-plumes. The grass was not yet dry. There was just a touch, a whiff, of melancholy in the air. Blue-glass sky. Actually incomprehensible toppling over into the void of course. My wife and I, in the company of K and his family, approached the city from the west in his powerful car. During the autumn you enter the city by a highway nosing all along the hem of the ocean and which at times has to hang on to breathtaking high bridges connecting the crests above the chasms. Hanging above the cracking of seabirds and the tinkle of wavelets against the rocks. The bridges are the skeletons of rotted-away hills. Down below in the lie of the gorges then the brilliant flash of water in the fiords. Within the city walls too you may from such an elevated bridge squint down a declining crevasse to a floor covered with bushes, tall grass, shrubs without berries. (Dry now, because inside the circle of walls.) Seen from up high the few houses isolated down there are the doll constructions of children, the excrescences of the imagination, faults in glass. Near those vague houses (neglect has taken over) are parked the cabs and the caravans of gypsies with padded leather jerkins, of fortune-hunters and fortune-tellers, of cattle farmers with gaiters who camp there when they have to bring their animals for slaughter to the city's abattoirs. To that place the couples who have entered upon a short-lived agreement will come then for hasty intercourse with casual implications of the flesh (the dryish barking coughs, the stainless-steel tongues), probably assuming that down in the coppice and *virtually on top of the garbage dumps* they will be invisible to the eye of the traffic. And who cares. Yet, everything is very evident from up here, revealed like the sweaty lifeline of the hand: the brown jackets with turned-up collars of men with black side-whiskers, the rusted mudguards of some obsolete lorries, pantyhose like a love letter on a bent twig, the naked buttocks competing half moons in the grass where tails and tracks have already been trodden and a whitish substance forms a crystalline crust over the stalks.

All along the ridge of the hill blocking off one end of the valley the city is strung. Cream? Froth. In the first rank the buildings stand precariously on the very lip of the abyss. Crumbling away. There are palaces with broad paved terraces receiving the sun like some luxurious inundation, the sun a benevolent torrent, streaming from the glass-blue jar, and steps leading to vaulted porches with decorations and flourishes moulded in the stucco. There are other buildings with multiple storeys, the cream layers of a cake; and some are sober of colour and of others only the posturing façades remain. Here, in the central circle, an exclusive quarter of the city, the front doors have keys of solid gold, there is a structure of grey concrete like a bunker or a fort sunk into the protecting red earth. Over the walls and ramparts showing above ground, plants and tussocks of grass started growing. The semblance accorded by green creepers, by trails – the appearance of dilapidation (watch out!) is deceptive however, and in fact it is intended only to allow this ultra-modern complex to blend with its background in such a fashion as not to disturb the historical atmosphere.

From close up you see the extensive glass windows, and behind those panels full of clouds American tourists with binoculars and cameras bobbing on the extravagantly stained bellies and with highballs in their hands slowly cruise hither and yonder, flipping their tails. Sharks' teeth snigger. Shark people. "Hi there!" One knows too that there are subterranean swimming pools and the most up-to-date recreation facilities, massage parlours, cocktail bars, quivering dance floors, one-armed bandits, an artificial cherry orchard vibrating a wind, whorestalls, exchange offices, turntables, map readers, *chemin de fer* and other bagatelles, as also counters for airlines (including that of Nomansland). It is in reality a hotel from where the plebeians – with low profiles, it is true – may have a peek at the aristocrats. On the one grey wall are fixed discreetly the letters: BUCKINGHAM PARK. Conspicuously different and as if pushed aside, there is, in the last line of the circle of buildings, a simple single-roomed farmhouse with a roof of sods – but this house is so situated that it has an unimpeded view on the west where in the fading light the folds and the heights of a distant green land (a medal) can be seen to be glowing like wave-crests. (Deeper in the city, on a more intimate square, I later see in the display window of an art gallery a painted reproduction – 40cm x 75cm, canvas on stretcher, in a gilded frame, origin guaranteed – of this same little house, stark now in simplified lines and volumes, but imbued with a tremendous light – one may say a searchlight – pouring forth from the heart of the structure through its windows, and with underneath a caption, on a copper plate, reading: "From this house the light was switched off over Ireland during the last war". There was something heroic – shall I say manful? – and at the same time tragic about the painting as also about the dark and uninhabited house. But I suspected that this was a circumstance we could sense and yet not elucidate to our satisfaction. Like listening to the mournful song of a survivor from an earlier generation, ancient and with blunt teeth: a life-wrecked person. And in the language of that generation – with alternative forms, other types of diphthongs, whistling w-sounds, constructions foreign to the ear, contaminations, an upwelling: "voor wat meer coper ende tabacq als andere hottentoos genieten".) (I have many suspicions.)

Deeper inside the city we decided to fortify the inner man in a restaurant (situated in a tower) noted for its delicate dishes, the clusters of crystal grapes in small bowls of ice water, the steamed napkins impregnated with the odour of myrrh, its stock of Nuits-Saint-Georges Grand Cru. This tower, encircled by a rank growth of shadow trees and gardens beautiful as if trimmed with velvet set out on several levels, this tower then was on a rather steep slope so that the diner with the spoon in the right hand (a feeling of silver under the fingertips) could look through the window over the bay with its babbling little waves, could sink away in his own ruminations, a thread of angel's hair stuck to his lower lip. Now the environment has been rendered desolate and the brown varnish of the tower has started peeling away in strips and curls, the rooftiles have become lustreless. Perhaps a dead pigeon in a gutter somewhere. (Watch out!) There was the unseasonly pollen of dust in the trees. And the tower's doors were barred. We still knocked against the wooden panel. Knock knock knock. After some minutes the latch was lifted and the door pulled open from the inside by an elderly man dressed in the somewhat slovenly clothes of a head waiter, maybe even a maître d'hôtel, and with a dark blue apron reaching to just above the shoe-caps. On the forehead, hard above the bridge of his nose, he had a rose-coloured birthmark like a blossom pressed between the pages of a complete encyclopaedia. Next to his left eye was a mole. He let us in and invited us to sit at a large table in one of the rooms off to the side. In the distance a canonnshot puffs. Like a heavy bell broken loose from its beams and ropes would plunge down the campanile. We are the only guests in the eating place, it would seem. The panes are full of bee tracks. Below us a schooner walked in a stately fashion over the water to the security of a cove or a bay – who will know? – with the evening sun's book of flames in the sails a crimson contrast with the green shiver of the sea. It is a delegation of burning trees – the light a thin layer of snow or silver fur over the yards and the rigging and a shiny dampness in the water as also from the pendulum of the bow – all of this in an inexplicable way continuing to burn in the water – it is a delegation bringing the light of civilization to a dark region. The old man with the birth-flower came to lay the table with utensils of the finest silver. We are served several kinds of salad. (That which I missed so badly in prison.) Water pellets like fishscales glistening in the fleshiness of the leaves, and the walls of the room were tinted red by the silent flame-tower far below us on the sea. Only the crepitation of dry twigs being broken somewhere in the hills. The old man has one very slow foot. A flapping sole maybe? There's no ice-cream on the menu: always a bad omen. I think the glasses were crystal.

High up, against the neck of the hummock where the twisting ground track ends and runs to earth, K waited for me. We pulled up our pants a little higher, considered the possibility of sticking the trouser legs in the tops of our socks. Then we climbed further up the incline to a part of the hill with denser vegetation, away from the growl of the city, and we were glad to be out of the sun's shuddering under the coolth of trees. Partly in shadow and partly in the sun an ancient milk cart stood as if it would never get going again, an emaciated nag slumping listlessly between the draught poles, the hide too thin and the bone structure etched, a pitiful old bag; also the driver with frayed waistcoat, ostensibly out of heart, he had a tin with tobacco in his trouser pocket and a knuckly hand on the lump formed by the tin in the pocket on the thin leg. A ridge-backed rock lizard lies breathing in the heat. Round the mouth line of the driver there is the blue of inkstains and a mobile hairiness, a fudged drawing, a nib stuttered stuck in the blotting paper. Sharply defined lie the shadows on the earth under the horse and the cart, under those parts which catch the sun, haunch and splashboard and nodules and belly and spokes and tail; the shadow Indian blue and lame and ungainly with clusters of meatflies, innards which burst open are splashed over the soil, anchoring the vehicle and its passenger now. At first there were only cypresses with dark ink blotches around the trunks but gradually the roof of leaves above our heads became denser and in places the narrow alleys were overgrown with ferns, thistles, sorrel. At once we are in a part of the forest where the ground is most uneven, strewn with rough boulders. First we notice nothing else, nothing remarkable, nothing out of the ordinary. Then, as with those games in the newspaper where you have to look closely at the drawing to suddenly descry all kinds of figures camouflaged in the thickets, then there are all around us among the trees and the shrubs or half hidden by rocks a great number of very old horses. Some are already paralysed and can barely move the heads ever so slowly, heads with skin stretched drumtight over the bones so that you may read the outline of the skulls quite clearly, an archaic alphabet. Others try again and again to stumble to their legs. Many have a red mucid moustachiness about the lips; a thin film of foam. It is as if they are transparent, of an ancient type of glass, pale rose and pale violet are the dominant colours, but inside the yawn-thin carcasses there is nearly nothing to see except, now and then, the absent-minded peristalsis of entrails. Some still attempt to eat of the grass and the leaves. When they try to move it is a most painful and clumsy struggle. It hurts you to watch. The eyes are opaque and white and infirm like things suffering even in the subdued green sheen of the forest; around the rims in the corners of the eyes, there is a white crust, an excretion, and minuscule white scrawlers gnawing at the very eyeballs. Maggots? Where the sun penetrates and floats down like a leaf, a pale flash, an eye is sometimes a mirror throwing back a dumb whiteness. Above and below the eyes the hollows of the sunken sockets are bruised and dark, as broad and as deep as the hand of a man. We were in the secret place where decrepit horses come to pass away but cannot; they can't ever die because here everything is in a state of waiting. There were practically no sounds; occasionally the snap of a branch when one horse trying to get up flounders against another tired animal. Above, through the treetops, there was also at times the softly gnashing flight of a sea breeze. Those among the beasts which were already lying down tried stretching the heads, heavier than undeciphered hieroglyphs, as far as possible away from the bodies in order to catch some air, and then there was a thin trickle of ants, a crumbling black snottiness, from some hole in the ground to the nostrils. The broken attempts at breathing moved the grass blades. Over all of this there was the sweet clove-like smell of dying, the old odour of hairless horsehides, perhaps too the swooning scent of live decomposition. But not of death. *Graviora quaedam sunt remedia periculis.*

(After he tried for six years to attain enlightenment by living the life of an ascetic and by subjecting his body to all sorts of deprivations, the Buddha says – as written down in the *Majjhima Nikāya*, Sutta 36, that is in *The Sayings of Medium Length:*

Because I ate so little my limbs became like the joints of dried-up creepers . . . my buttocks were the hooves of a bull: my protruding spine like a string of balls. . . . my ribcage the crazy rafters of a tumbled-down barn . . . the pupils of my eyes looked as if they were lying low and deep . . . my very scalp was wrinkled and shrunken as a white calabash cut off before it could ripen is shrunken and wrinkled by a warm wind. When I think: "I shall touch the skin of my stomach" then it was my spine I took hold of. The skin of my stomach clung to my back. When I think: "I shall obey my natural needs", then I fell over on my face just there. . . . When I . . . stroked my limbs with my hand, the hairs, rotten at the roots, came away from my body.)

A while further we came to an opening in the ground down which we clambered, first K and then I. It is cool inside this labyrinth but very dangerous too because in places the passage is not only more restricted than the waist of a man but furthermore with a swivel or a crinkle in the narrowest section. It is not entirely in obscurity however and sometimes there's a little more space so that one can stand bent over to remove the powder and the bits of wood from your knees and sleeves and then there are stalactites and stalagmites of a pearl-grey or a moth-white colour. The sides of the tunnel glimmer and are smooth as coral to the touch of the hand. The hand-palms are unsociable like toothless parliamentarians. Glass, you think, glass and alabaster; sweetness and thrashing. Often it was too alarming to breathe. Higher we crawled on our stomachs through the bowels and the belly of the hill – it is inevitable that I should use this image which is entirely symbolic of course – until we arrived again in a larger hall, spacious enough, and hewn from the living rock itself.

Here we could hear water flowing. One wall of this space is blocked off by a curtain hanging from the vaulted roof to the floor. The curtain is suspended by rings from a curtain rod which stretches from one end of the hall to the other so that one can easily slip the cloth open. From behind the partition we hear the lamenting of several pale voices, how they rise and disappear. In the hall, on a chair behind a desk sits a woman. When we enter she gets up. Her hair is as grey as sweet water in a dirty glass and the fire-resistant plastic frame of her spectacles is blue like that of an American tourist. It will be far-fetched and unreal and indecent to think that her breasts too might long ago have been blossoms (the firefree plastic), for now there is an ungainly bosom, an enormous goitre, a monstrous soft fruit, and adipose. Stains show under the arms. The lady invites us to return for a conducted tour of her catacombic domain whenever it may suit us. Outside the hall we found ourselves once again against the opposite slope of the traversed hill, in the parking lot under the coolness-trees of the flaking tower. Our wives and K's children were there waiting for us. High in the tower, through a half-closed shutter, one sees fleetingly the visage of an aged person with a morose expression and a lighter-coloured fungus or spot – nearly luminous – slightly higher than the eyebrow; against the wall or the ceiling of the room behind the shutter one suspects the ruddy wash of glass-like or burning reflections; but the perceived person is immersed in old thoughts of his own, staring in another direction, towards the interior of the country, perhaps over a sudden depression in the earth where accumulated junk and discarded contracts turn in the wind, where farmers squat to scratch with twigs the encrusted cow dung from their gaiters, where women with thick lower limbs lie in the cool protection of a shrub, naked from the knee to the hip and the skin of the buttocks all puckered. We can smell the sea. It smells of rotten eggs.

The lady with the bosom which hangs twitching from her neck and shoulders, like a calf just born, too weak still to climb to its legs but already alive with awkward movements, sweet, thrashing – the lady, our guide – pulls aside the curtain covering one wall of the hall of stones. The space between curtain and wall is divided in separate cells. The grey curtain's folds glisten with a phosphorescent sliminess where the eyes of moths watered, it brings to mind the veins in old glass, and the guide moves it to one side. In the first section there is a trough or a manger and in this crib lies an old woman. Her hair is curly and her face wrinkled and red and humid like that of an infant who has just been writhing and crying. She wears a home-knitted sweater, buttoned to just below the chin. Her gown is pushed up to above the hips. Her bare thighs like the skin of an old naked hen. On her one foot, the right one, there is a silk stocking. Through the stocking one may see that the foot is dark, as if exceptionally contused. But it is also shiny and smooth and from close up it is clear then that the foot, up to the ankle, is entirely covered (overgrown) with long, rough, thick, black hairs. The woman lay on her back, the eyes closed and her hands balled to fists, and she kept on repeating in a weeping voice: "Look at my foot, my foot. It's all hairy. It's the hair of the fairy. Look at my foot, my foot. . . ."

In the other units, separated by wooden partitions, there was a bed here and a cradle there. And in each of these, under grey covers there were human figures stuffed into the rags of blankets and counterpanes, everyone wailing or lamenting with particular intensity at his or her own pitch. Watch out! They were all old, sometimes grey, sometimes without clothes. The eyes were either shut tight or staring blindly (staring at blindness) or else veiled by glassy tears – and a white matter in the corners of the eyes, around the lids. Where some of them have kicked away the bedcovers, as writhing babies sometimes do, you can see how smudged the thickly applied make-up has become, how fudged are the rouge and the corpse-white powder and the black accentuations. You will also notice the clown clothes, the costumes of fools, of augusts, of pierrots – blocked, striped, with dots, patched, too voluminous or too tight. Under the blankets, on the mattresses, there was sawdust – humid, mouldy, with insects. They were the weak of mind, those who have become children, the droolers, the Irish terrorists, the moribund members of a dismantled circus who washed up here, the orphan people, those who were rendered anonymous by war, gypsies without a fatherland, earlier clients of the eating tower which is now spoilt, retired police spies – all of them now in the care (or safekeeping? under observation?) of the lady with the glasses of fireproof blue plastic. Or were these tatters and folds the standard outfit for all admitted to this institution?

We continue inspecting and then decide to go down the maze again, to crawl on our bellies to the other exit, to the live burial ground of the horses. It is still autumn. I notice how the person crawling ahead of me gets stuck in a narrowing of the pipe and how she can neither advance nor retreat. I can look down her dress further than the hips. And I thought: by means of our bones the flesh clings to life, or, by means of the skeleton does the flesh adhere to life.

The Day of the Falling
of the Stars and Searching
for the Original Face

Nobody knew the origin of his history, of how he happened to be there. One could only speculate. Perhaps – so the theories went – he had been abandoned by some passing fugitives. It could be that he was the offspring of pioneers who had moved through these barren regions, tried to settle, and perished, overcome by the hostile environment. Or else that he had been kidnapped while still very young and then left for dead somewhere among the dun-coloured dunes by gangsters who'd lost their gamble and fallen out with one another. It would be tempting to think that he was a young prince, illegitimate for sure, left to die there because of palace intrigues. It would be even more tempting to imagine that he'd had some choice in the matter, that he had escaped to this paradise – the paradise of neither knowing nor questioning. What if – sacrilegious thought! – he were some weird mutation, dropped by one of the creatures among which he now lived? But nobody really knew and no one would ever know how to solve the riddle. (And even so he could never be lost. Is it not written in the Book that He is closer to us than the artery in the neck?)

Neither was it ever made clear how his presence among the wandering herd of gazelles was first observed. People later claimed that an old tramp, or a schnorrer crossing the desert to a far-off marketplace to flog his trinkets and his rags, first saw him. Others maintained that it must have been nomads. Or explorers. (Though we do not read that either Livingstone or von Humboldt or Burton or Speke or Scott or Saint-Exupéry or Münchhausen ever passed over these wastes.) Or tax collectors then. Or ash-tongued missionaries with embers in the eye sockets. Or mapmakers. Or American tourists. Or game-thieves.... The first inkling of his existence became as obscure as his very origins. Time is a desert. The minds of men sift away with the sand. Winds flow over the sands, erasing tracks. Factors are obfuscated. But in this expanse, white and treacherous as a page slowly being eroded by words, facts serve no function in any event. Horizons are too abstract here. It is recounted that some clan leader in the dusty past had moved his eyes above the fluttering veil over the illimitable nothingness, that he had squinted at various points along the edge of his vision and that he had named these, rather lyrically, Abd el Kadel, Mesrour, Ahmed Madrali, Israfel, Al Sirat, Nour ed Deen.

A place once named is not afterwards supposed to move again. Naming is taming. It is casting the arbitrary over the unknown. It may well be that these name-places took root in man's mind, became reference points, barriers to the boundless. However it may be, it would seem that they constituted roughly the points of the star over which the herd and its adopted human lived. It was the birthplace and the lair of the sirocco, and other fever-laden winds shooting forth their rustling tongues to insatiably lick up any moisture or coolness. Distances were hazy from a lack of obstacles. Around the rim the sky was cemented to the earth by a thinnish grout of greyness. Water was a pittance always to be searched for all over again. Flora was scarce, nondescript: in good years a meagre crop of frutescent growths to sustain the earth, and strewn across the floor of a wadi some pots of small shade perhaps sprouting a rare miniature cyclamen. Fauna was even more rare: lizards and ants living off ants, the odd sand-tinted jackal harbouring incongruously the human wail, at times the grosbeak and the poult. But through this landscape, light, speckled, free, the gazelles in their fugacity. And with them the boy on all fours, naked, as rapid as his companions, nibbling grass, of the same smell and the same destiny, unburdened by any knowing.

Poachers probably first brought the rumours of this strange deer to the dwelling places of man. And from these outposts the rumours spread until they eventually reached the ears of the Academy. It is the function of the Academy to raise questions and then to run these to ground. How, the Academy asked, could this be possible? How could any human – for by all accounts it, the boy, was said to be of the *Homo* species – how could he survive in such frugal surroundings? and what ought to be done? Must he be captured and brought back, introduced to society? Some argued in favour of this step, others against – as it is the custom of an Academy to disagree. The rumours of the existence of the culturally unclassifiable creature were confirmed. A party had gone out on horseback and through their binoculars they had managed to observe (after a search of many days over this uncharted region) the fugal movements of the gazelles and the boy. The boy, they reported (continuing to refer to him as Boy even though they could glimpse that he had a beard), even acted as a sort of fugleman, leading the high-stepping herd in their flight.

The question of cruelty had to be considered too. What would be the most efficacious way to apprehend this unique hart? For the Academy by its very nature decided the need *to know* to be paramount: they felt that it was the destiny of man to advance. Or, as some secretly knew, that man must inevitably be brought to fall from grace. One leader stood up in the assembly and justified the general decision by quoting from the Book:

> *I died from the plant and reappeared in an animal;*
> *I died from the animal and became a man;*
> *Wherefore then should I fear?*
> *When did I grow less by dying?*
> *Next time I shall die from the man,*
> *That I may grow the wings of angels.*
> *From the angel too must I advance;*
> ALL THINGS SHALL PERISH SAVE HIS FACE.

An expedition was fitted out with nets and gaffs and set out to capture Boy. For days they criss-crossed the rufous labyrinth without walls, with scouts flung out far ahead of the main party. Dust caked their moustaches and their goatees and whitened their garments of fustian and gaberdine. At night the stars whispered of winds and a lone predatory jackal mocked them with the disembodied howl of a knowing human. They succeeded in sighting the gazelles and although it was repeatedly attempted to cordon the herd off or to drive it into some convoluted canyon, they failed. They failed and they saw the rippling fugue of movement as the deer disappeared through cracks between earth and heaven.

And Boy the boy? Will anyone ever know what impressions entered by his senses and what kind of mind these constituted? He reacted to these foreign animals as a deer would. But did he not sense, issuing from some atavistic instinct, the unavoidable defeat brought by these creatures encroaching upon his unknown existence which he knew so exclusively? Of course, like all gazelles, he had come across one of the strangers at some place in the past, fallen in the sand, dead and infested by flies. He had recognized no affinity between himself and such an object. It held no attraction for him. It was inedible and not even moist. It stank, and not just with the familiar putrid smell of decomposition. It was in no way like him, sleek and pure as a buck with a light fuzz over the skin. No, it had had other loose skins around it, fusty and frumpish, a strip around the neck, a glittering string across its paunch, so that its body had been divided into darkened because covered private parts and exposed and thus obscene public parts.

Then – but "then", time in sequence, could have no contour or contents for Boy in his unmapped being with its fixed edges of nothingness – then these creatures had multiplied like invaders and were now returning, ever after them, perched high on other four-legged beasts with the appearance of bigger horn-less deer, each carrying also an upright and sometimes reverberating object. How could he know that these frightening things were fusils, employed to herd them into some cul-de-sac?

What rippled through his consciousness? Perhaps the disintegration of the unquestioned. Perhaps now, to retain some security – if he knew the slithering security of the naming of parts, and by that desire it was already contaminated and being sacrificed for ever – perhaps now he would have named them Abd el Kadel, Mesrour, Ahmed Madrali, Israfel, Al Sirat, Nour ed Deen, had he known the tongue of man and its corridors. He would have sensed the magic incantations of the arbitrary. And it could not save him or preserve his integration.

It had been a bluish morning. First light had come to the towns of men, shoving under every door a blue slice of incandescence. The Academy had sat the whole night, creaking in their clothes. They had looked into the labyrinths of themselves and they had come up with the solution. What was needed they now knew, was for Boy *to see himself* and in this way to see the relatedness between himself and those wishing to capture him. And in this way to become alienated from his mates. The whole must be shattered. Their plans were laid. They twirled their moustaches absent-mindedly between thumb and index. Knowledge is self-knowledge, self-abasement. Nothing must be allowed to prevent that terrible destruction, that slipping into the twisting courts of uncertainty and not-belonging. Belonging to not-belonging, belonging to brokenness – can man achieve a more beautiful and more painful integration? They fingered and stroked the mirrors they had acquired, occasionally filling the silvery surfaces with fleeting visions of mortality.

It was a dark morning over the desert. Clouds were cliffs and cascades in the sky. Maybe the rainy season was at last at hand. And juicy grasses would sprout up in its wake. And there would be the traces of insects and other small beasts in the damp crust of an early daybreak. Then the wind scattered the tumbling structures, leaving tracery, a *poult-de-soie*.

It was finally, once the star was traced in the sand of the mind, not all that difficult to hedge off the herd of buck with Boy still in their midsts. They were backed into a cwm. Did Boy then comprehend the folding in and the blacking out of his horizon? The small herd stood trembling, rolling the eyes, listening with their very hides. The Academicians got off their prancing horses. The ill-smelling beasts with the flapping skins descended from the prancing beasts with the things attached to their bodies. The Academicians took out their mirrors and flashed them, flashed the authority of death which is the reflection of loneliness. The sun was flooding the vast untamed speckled space and pinpointing, burning with heatless flames the instruments of demise.

Boy saw. He advanced and he observed in these surfaces the deer he had always seen, but so distant and small now. He also perceived among the gazelles something, a being, a creature resembling those standing behind the surfaces looking at him and making hawking noises. He saw as if seeing the stars broken from their flight and firmament, and flung falling on the earth, flickering, hurting now so much deeper than the eyes. He saw the cracks and advanced toward the pools of water held aloft as if by magic. He didn't realize that he was looking behind reality. He didn't know that these tongues could never be lapped up or integrated. He was not aware that he was to forgo for ever the taste of water.

No, Baba

Time, he then says, must move ahead although it has no destination. (There is no time. Only we ourselves who run smash into dismantling, and try to force the regulating correlative "time" in an attempt to measure, comprehend, excuse.) But still we need it as a catalyst of life; it is only in the searchlight of time that there is life. Life is in the present, in the now. (Commonplace!) That which lies behind is death and ahead is death. Like the view from an aeroplane – when that would be time – flying over an immeasurable landscape, thus is life. That which sharp-immediately sweeps by under the wings and that which the eye up here may frame, are alive. Unpredictable, involuntary, unprejudiced it crawls forth from under the wings, is unrolled. (Cover, flyleaves, title-page, text, end-paper.) Once you have moved over it, it is swallowed by distance; the further back it is the quicker it disappears, becomes that and then imagination. It is like a page of written words falling in the changeable water (when trees lose their manuscripts) – the letters run and change their language, the paper will be part of the water and the water in the end will be clear. Theoretically such a craft should be able to return and to quiver over the already stroked surface, but it can never be the same terrain because in the dark, in the past sense, certain shafts and funnels and towers and neutral zones decay and crumble faster than others, are changed, become stains or even nothing, so that a hypothetical second passage would reveal a modified landscape. (Behind your back everything grows to hell.) Quicker, always quicker they sink; the further you are the faster they go. The future, that which may not yet be illuminated by time and thus by life, is similarly subject to change, tearing and careening, birth and decline, mutation and syncretism and bastardization, destruction and slaughter (frost over the yard), which we will never be aware of because it takes place in the penumbra. It is only the clear light of time-at-work, that fleeting moment and tangent point of relationships, people, objects, dreams, which generates the illusion that we may grasp and hold something existing and immutable. The environment is perpetually changeable changing death. The difference between life and death is that there is actually no difference; it is the play between illusion and reality. . . . Life is that which in the twinkling of an eye is lit up in a never-ending, pulsating and crackling darkness. (Isolated in the temporary.)

Naturally one also realizes it from within, he thereupon says. Or you think that you experience it from inside. There is the internal cohesion of the momentary which is not sudden, at least, that is not the way you live it. You experience it as something growing inside – let's project it as the inner form of a bird solidifying in you. But which then rises in flight and disappears or which is plucked from you or is flushed and frightened off before you could even observe its description. It flies away and vanishes in the dark because you could neither recognize nor follow it with the senses, and totality is never completed. If it were to be completed you wouldn't know it since you were part thereof. You never knew the outlines etched clearly. Thus the witnessing is for you like the inwardness of a bird departing from you or put up before it could decently take on shape, and in the nature of things you don't realize that it was the "self" of the moment which has been displaced. Emptiness is form and form is empti-ness. And emptiness is loneliness. Without emotional connotations. You add on two letters when you wish to transform the moment into a monument: NU – that's naked. Monakedment.

The memory too, storeroom of experience, is subject to the same process: time/life is a lighting up of death, the spotlight picking out a grain of sand – and everything occurs in that grainy look – if the universe were a beach. Try to imag-ine what lies beyond the universe: you on the thrumming, eroding edge; to one side the sea with what it contains, its watery secrets, its sunken civilizations, its shells carrying the echo of absence on the dry land; on the other side the interior which had to come from the sea via the beach, with its wounds, its journeys and its trips, its spotted animals, its mountain roads, cities and deserts. In the con-volutions of that storeroom the experienced, the shapeless birds, the full birds – since we cannot take in the concept "emptiness" – are stocked, to such an extent that they become entangled with the roots of the mind because we must assume that the mind, primordial shape, houses the memory, primeval void. And like the unspeakable black land of death – of which it is a component, which it has part of – it mates and twitches and dies and changes without tracing the con-sciousness. Back of your mind everything laughs to hell. No wonder then that the mind is so fertile. And it is clear why it should have such a bad smell when opened. Here and there, selectively, we cling to something in that memory, small mirrors mostly, thinking (as if thinking isn't dissolution!) that these are immutable, more or less on the principle that that which momentarily we close our eyes to will stop playing tricks on us; that which I do not let live in my seeing is fixed for ever, is dead and thus immortalized in life. But everywhere behind us the mirrors are growing deaf. Or pulling their own faces. When the image is gone, the mirror reigns. And that lying furthest wastes away the soonest, in the same way as that waiting ahead the most distantly will approach the fastest; they depart and mutate the most and we notice no change. We live – what we envisage as living – based on the images in departing mirrors without being able to observe the measure of deformation, even without any consciousness thereof. Yes, sometimes only on the afterglow of an image as reflected in another polished surface. But it is of little importance. I, he says, am us. We are the aviaries of birds without amplitude which have smashed into mirrors because they/we wanted to be aeroplanes. Thus we live in death. The black traces in the glass. And in this way life is a growing death. There is only one tense. The dead season. Isolated in the temporal.

What happened the furthest back was that he had something to do with boats. Perhaps he had been, in his tender youth, a cabin boy on board a three-master sailing with bulging cloth the trade routes between continents, perhaps particularly towards the Orient and there from one island to the following, mornings when the sun in an aureola broke through the fogbanks above the oil-grey sea or else came to dip the tips of slender palm trees in bloody luminosity; evenings when a baked wind from the land propelled the hint of spices, particularly cloves, over the waves, and also the rancid stench of villages which as yet knew nothing of modern drainage systems. Hamlets on mouldy stilts, their roots in the rotting. Perhaps he had been a galley slave on one of the Phoenician longboats in the Mare Anticum, and perhaps they travelled all along the vague coast of North Africa where the sea, in places, is light green and very shallow with sandbanks, and under these ridges some skeletons and cuirass pieces remain preserved, with the drum beats in his ear like the heart's nibbling in his chest and the lashes of a whip over shoulders and back. Perhaps he jumped without outer garment from a dhow to dive for coral in the Red Sea and slapped his hands on the water to scare off the sharks. Or perhaps he trawled for sardines with his mates while the sea was very stormy and blue-black like the fear of an ink-fish, and ice, several centimetres thick, blossomed on the boat deck and the handrails; but once the catch flip-flopped over the planks like handfuls of living coins, then they could return to Björnholm or one of the other Baltic islands where grey winds eddy in the shrieking of mews to drown a fortnight's cares and joys in drink.

However and wherever it might have been, a feeling of betrayal clings to the memory. Something like a blue line. A blue line over salt-encrusted planks. But also over the people. Or in him too? Shipwreck? He doesn't think so. He had a rank taste in the mouth. The faces of fellow travellers by the lantern's light, bobbing shadows over nose-bridges and cheekbones, and shards or sparks in the suspicious and furious eyes? He sat leaning his back against the wooden ribs and could sense the sea lapping at that creaking partition against his spine. And a blue beam. The other men talked about it.

Later he was on a beach at low tide. At ebb the sea withdraws a long way, like a huge thirst, and exposes an area of black sand. The force of the currents and spring tide along these parts washes benches and ridges in the sand so that fingers of water shine in all directions over the laid-bare territory. In places there are naked rocks which, with different tides, would be covered by water and foam. There is a stench – the damp sand, the gullies, the rocks – as strings of seaweed and bamboo, half-digested crabs, putrid prawns, debris and floatage of every kind and origin are strewn all over. Also many empty plastic bags, containers, condoms. The cloacae of a nearby town probably run into the water here. Although a wind is gathering speed it in no way upsets the gnats and the sandflies hovering over the waste and the oozing rubbish. They are vibrating questions in the air, questions which will strip everything bare if only they were given time and tide to do so.

He is here with the prince. Off to one side of the beach, just about where it runs into a steep rock cliff, he finds three hats which, miraculously, are brand new and still dry. The wind is slightly cut off here but when it capriciously grabs hold of one of the headgear to send it spinning like a wheel over the sand, the booty is very nearly lost. But then he succeeds in retrieving and keeping all three. From far away the prince espies the loot and comes running with pale ankles to claim his share, the part of a prince, this, the best hat which with smooth fur is practically a mirror in the sun.

He is enraged but obliged to satisfy his lordship. He has to content himself with the smallest hat, a brownish porker with a very narrow brim, limp and with not even a feather. He pulls the little hat right down to his ears so that the crown may fit deep and tight over his hair. Then he sees how the prince, Albert, drops his watch in the dark sand and vengefully he puts his foot over it to push it even deeper into the stickiness so that just the glass over the dial protrudes like the one eye of a pair of glasses squinting into the sun. Albert stands at the foot of the rock barrier, crying with one hand fisted before his eyes and with the other holding down his new hat, crying because of the watch he lost. Through his tears Albert sobs that he wishes to return home.

Now he pities Albert; and besides, he is afraid of what might happen if the prince were to start sulking angrily. Thus he runs back to the hidden watch and digs it up with long finger and index. He holds it up in one hand, swinging by the strap, nearly a tacked-on wrist, and jumps up and down. Shouts against the wind at Albert standing diminutive by the rocks: "Look what I found! I have it!

I have it!" In the immediate vicinity he discovers four more timepieces which he stuffs in his pocket although not one of them ticks as swanky as the prince's; in fact, two are pumping rather irregularly with little spastic leaps. He also finds, partially silted up under a stone, something which at first he doesn't recognize. Upon closer inspection it turns out to be a long string of jewels, little ones with in-between sapphires as big as beetles with light bulbs in the bowels. Then he realizes that it must be a rosary since a small image dangles at one end, carved most likely from ivory, of the Christ with pulled-up legs on the cross. The nails gave him cramps. No bigger than a locust and just as leggy. The legs so twisted that they might be artificial, and the cross a wee crutch. He thinks that the carving will fit well in his slightly cupped palm, like a dead locust. The string too he surreptitiously pockets with the intention of cleaning it later and then giving it to his wife as a present. Findings keepings. *Spoliatus ante omnia restituenda est.* Then he jogs to where the prince waits. Long trails of a blubbery substance of dubious origin lie in all shapes on the banks of the furrows washed in the sand. A stickiness clings to his feet. When running he rouses swarms of seabirds – gulls and sandplovers and cormorants – like tatters and tears they wail and call names above his head.

With the prince he climbs up the perpendicular rockface. There are steps and twisting tracks hacked from the façade. Where no other way could be found tunnels and chimneys were cut in the rock itself, higher, ever higher. This road-making – brilliantly conceived and executed – still continues endlessly. From all over there are the sounds and the reverberations of rock drills, small explosions, pickaxes, crowbars, spades and trowels, the squeaking of ropes over pulleys hoisting buckets of gravel and letting down buckets of mortar. The slope with its ledges, niches, rocky outcrops, crannies and holes, is alive with labourers. Simultaneously however it serves as the favourite nesting and breeding place of several kinds of seabird. These birds are incessantly chased off but they remain hanging from the sky above their nests, or where their nests were supposed to be, with gaping beaks and poisonous beady eyes and the gullets full of horrible scissor-cries. It has happened that some workers were attacked. Usually the birds only peck out the eyes of the people. Several day labourers have bandages over their eyes, or dark glasses. Some of them, tougher than most, aren't at all concerned about their appearance; their eye sockets are yawning raw wounds like overripe figs left on the branch for the go-away birds. The workers who can still see lead their blind comrades by the hand to their work stations. Many have been posted here since such a long time and now know the inclines so thoroughly that they can find their way on their own despite their want of sight. The whole scene is flooded by a tremendous din: that of the workers and their tools, the yodelling of the eyeless ones, the gnashing and croaking and hissing of gulls, and above all the lowing of the wind through crags and hollows and alleys and around corners. The workers have a supplementary task too, namely to whitewash the smooth pebbles at the foot of the wall. And this duty must be fulfilled once every twenty-four hours (the small stones of Sisyphus!) as the incoming tide rubs off the paint just as the outgoing ebb will suck in most of the pebbles or bury them under a filthy goo. . . . Day and night the labour continues. At night lamps and torches and lanterns are made to stand in every available hollow or hung from nails and wedges driven into the rock. Then it has the air of a festively decorated pleasure boat struggling to rise above the waves.

For lunch the labourers partake of tomatoes from brown paper bags. When the prince moves up or down the labyrinth all must get out of his way. Like monkeys they scatter up the steepest slopes or go to squat on the ledges; they hate these interruptions and with bared gums they snarl the most awful curses and imprecations at the prince and his retinue. Luckily the contents of their words are entirely blown away by the thundering elements. Some of them moan like birds of the sea.

With difficulty he climbs upwards all behind Albert. In front of them the men clamber out of their path. One worker has large shoulders and jade-black eyes. His name is Angelo Giovanni and he is of Polish descent. Angelo Giovanni glowers at them with eyes like torn-open ant-heaps before climbing nimbly up the rockface along an uncharted route running parallel to the path whilst holding on fast to his bag of tomatoes. When, several metres higher, they emerge from a pot-hole, Angelo is already sitting on his heels on a traverse off to one side and slightly higher, staring at time. The black-eyed labourer takes aim and then throws an overripe tomato very precisely. The missile whistles over Albert's shoulder and explodes in his face where he follows in Albert's steps with bent knees. The red meat and the gluey pips spread over his eye and cheek. Thirty metres along to the right a blind slave with neither headcloth nor blinkers gets up from where he was haunched on an outcrop, thrusts his two clenched fists in the air and crows triumphantly: "Holy! Holy! Thus he got his eye back!" Then, with a graceful plunge, he dives into space, and is smashed to pieces in the dizzy distance on the slimy beach down below. Light, which was a skein over the sand, is now blotched. Immediately the seabirds descend in screeching flocks. From up here they seem to be scarcely bigger than gnats around a scarecrow. White wings flapping over the ragged cadaver. Expression.

Above, on the plateau, it is altogether silent. The wind still strains but since there is nothing opposing it or holding it up there is also no sound. You see nothing except this table-landscape which is flat and limitless and yellow. No mountain chain or cloud-castle, neither smoke-column nor leaf-tree nor any other irregularity: just nothing.

With Albert he sits at a chess table while the wind keeps plucking inaudibly at their clothes and their hair. The chess table is made of clear glass but it has no legs. It is only a transparent block placed on the plateau. They execute their moves with intense concentration, without exchanging a single word. He can feel the watches ticking in his trouser pocket. He imagines that he can sense the little hands moving like a caress over the tender flesh of his inner thighs. A streaming silence. Albert has pinned his watch to the crown of his silver hat where it now shows off like a spare eye to indicate the flow of time. There is no one – neither angel nor bird nor fly nor labyrinth-maker – to look at the time on the face of the watch. Nothing. You would have been able to see the fly-wheels shuddering with movement but not to hear their throbbing. A reduced wrist suspended there, which has not yet deciphered the message that it is dead. A scare-time. When a piece – pawn, bishop, knight or rook – is eliminated, it sinks through the board into the glassy depths of the table. Then it shrinks, slowly at first and gradually ever faster, but it remains part of a game with the other pieces. The two players also are moves in the ritual. Invisible threads of correlation entangle everything. All go down in the game. There are different layers of volatilization amplifying and tied into each other, and all dimensionless. The two contestants are manoeuvred. Arrive at a position of tension or aggression or defence in the relation to the pieces on the board and those again to the pieces moving in the glass depths. From the result of each move hang life and death. A game endlessly renewed. Mate, opening, Polish defence, Berlin counter-attack, check. Smaller and smaller. In this way and at this distance there is no difference between life and death.

Then there was the court case. There they all sit, man and mouse, in the sanctified courtroom. The largish room is paneled in a dark, varnished wood. High up one wall are the stained-glass windows (with vulgar motives, he reflects: vine-leaves, grape-bunches, owls with dead feathers, sheep's heads with glass eyes – the multiple adornments of death; even as those against the walls of the place of ashes outside P – where Wella was cremated long ago, he remembers) which permit coloured light-staves to grope through the musty interior. The judge, an old man with little grey feathers of hair over a shiny skull – the Old One he is called – sits fretfully wrapped in a red gown, cushioned on a kind of enclosed dais built into one wall of the hall. This hierarchical construction resembles a roomy pulpit. It is shadowed by a baldachin similarly decorated with patterns carved in the wood, of the same vulgarity as those of the windows. There the Old One perches, lofty, malicious, as if he could be an auctioneer. The rest of the hall is just the dock. No public, no legal representatives. The accused pack the space from door to doom.

He knows not why he is there. He doesn't know yet of what he will be accused. It may turn out to be of the theft of a string of jewels, of underhandedness in chess-playing, of terrorism or some such nefarious act. Or perhaps because of what he attempted to describe in the first couple of paragraphs. Or because of a blue streak of which he no longer knows the lapsed meaning. For the time being it doesn't really matter either since the group of people amongst whom he finds himself (his *izintanga*?) are seated right at the back of the hall. The benches on which they sit are sunk at various levels into the floor. Some, therefore, can truly be said to be in the well.

Right in front directly underneath the throne of the Old One prisoners are lined up. They are all Unwhite. Among them also an immigrant. He is easily as aged as the Old One, but he wears a big, awkward pair of glasses slipped down to the tip of his nose. His bony face – the head is a bone-riddle – has vaguely the same appearance as that of a pelican. He has only a few very long grey hairs left, combed flat over this domed head. His name is Mister Murphy. Mister Albert Murphy.

Apparently it was his case which was just now disposed of. Two hundred rands is the fine imposed. Upon hearing this Mister Murphy pulls himself up straight with umbrage and starts objecting with violent gestures. His face has taken on the purplish glow of a beet. "Two hundred rands!" he screeches. "Is an insult! At the very least it should have been twenty-one thousand. Who, who do you (seamheads) take *me* for? My name is Mister Murphy. Albert! I am the immigrant, a businessman, and I was in the war, dammit man!" At this he bends down and starts unscrewing his right leg. It is evident that the artificial limb was attached to a stump hardly twenty centimetres long. The stump, enclosed in a blue leather cap, now grotesquely jerks up and down like the severed tip of a tail of a farm hound. Mister Murphy waves the loose limb with the neatly polished shoe about him. Two court orderlies fray their way through the shackled Unwhites and Mister Murphy hands them the leg with the shoe. The defence's exhibit A. The leg with its calf and knee of imitation flesh shines like a largish pink fish in the dusk-light of the court.

Next to him on the last bench right at the back of the hall someone was busy filling a sheet of paper with words and his attention is drawn to it now. The paper is nearly entirely covered with letters and squiggles. It looks like a poem. He can make out the first line: "No, Baba – don't trust the chains on your ankles. . . ." The rest is illegibly entwined in flowery letters and letter-like flowers. All of a dark blue colour. This drawing or description in fact becomes hazy lower down the page. It is only like a written page gradually inserted in water and the ink is dissolved. The lines and arabesques which have remained the longest in the liquid, fade the fastest. The water will become whole again.

Now at last the Old One has found his legs. The hubbub roused him from the swoon or the sleep in which, as is customary, he sank after pronouncing sentence. He lifts his two balled, vengeful firsts to heaven – flabby with age and the momentous weighing of pros and cons, being proposed to and disposing – and cries: "Holy! Holy! Did I not also fight in the war then?" He climbs down from the referee's chair and plods with difficulty to the back of the hall.

Then he notices for the first time the hallstand behind them. And draped over the stand is something . . . something like a birdrobe. It is another gown belonging to the Old One. Under the robe, this he can observe now that the Old One starts manipulating it, there is a hanger. The Old One brings the hanger to light. It is filled from end to end by a row of medals pinned to it. The badges are like ancient watches grown blind and useless. When picking them up and straightening them out, the row of medals on their faded ribbons jingle and quake. Look, the Old One demonstrates, these are for all the skirmishes and battles in which I took part. . . . The Great War with Delville Wood, Passchendaele, Papawerkop, Verdun, Festubert, Vimy, Somme, Etaples, Fort Douaumont, Bapaume, Thermopylae, Tin Hats . . . and the line of words drooling from his mouth becomes ever longer, like jewels strung on a cord with clotsapphires in between. These names, these words, convey an old odour of musty blood and clods mixed with quicklime. . . . "And these here were for the Other War. This is for the relief of Berlin, and that one for the liberation of Paris afterwards." It strikes him as strange that Paris should come after Berlin. He had always thought it the other way around.

"And this here," and the Old One bends down to lift with both hands something which had been lying under the hat rack in the shadow-pool of the gown, "this I picked up more than twenty years ago on the beach of Paris." In his hands he holds a roundish, pale object emitting a horrible rattling noise. It is, so the Old One explains, a bag or a ball made of skin and devoid of any colour – very likely the featherless skin of the older birds themselves – in which the gulls kept their chickens for security and protection when they went out looking for carrion. Indeed, he notices then the smooth, miniature skulls, bone-riddles without clues, and the wide-open beaks of the chickens protruding from the mouth of the purse, and among the other sounds he distinguishes again the cheeping and the hissing. At the bottom of the bag there are some more eggs or maybe even whitewashed pebbles – nobody has ever been in the position to verify – and with the trampling of the chickens ("look, thus") these eggs or these things click against one another, the ball oscillates as anything with a rounded bottom will be wont to do, and this movement causes a noise fit to frighten off any predator or enemy. Suddenly it reeks of rotten eggs, of old-old iodine-saturated sea. And the hall is entirely filled with the ghastly chainlike clack-clack clack-clack.

"In this way there is no distinction between life and death," he then also says.

The Oasis

Quien mucho abarco poco aprieta.

You insist. You wish me to tell you again that old tale about the horses. Why, nobody knows. And besides, it is such a long time ago that memory itself is covered with wrinkles and dust. But since it is what you desire.

It is an old town, the streets more or less depressed through the various quarters so that one is left with the impression that the houses are built on high banks. (The kind of town of which a Yevgeni Zamyatin could have written: "This conversation took place one quiet revolutionary evening, on a bench in Martha's garden. A machinegun gently tick-tocked in the distant hills, calling its mate. A cow sighed bitterly in the shed behind the hedge. . . .") Wistaria thread a wealth of shadows over the stoops. Ceylon roses are planted in tins painted red. And trees, trees. Everywhere trees. There are so many trees in the town that the wind will never accomplish its tasks, will never dispose of enough time to go blow elsewhere also. The wind is breathless, without wind! There is day and there is night and all the pale mysterious hours between day and night, the thrashing of leaves. There is the eternal shiver as of countless hands waving green greetings. It is never still – silver blots before your eyes, the scales of the sky, a mobile catching the light and turning it over, turning it inside out and grasping. And always the ripples streaming through space as if a net filled with reflecting sound is dragged over the town. Wind nesting in the trees of the old professor's courtyard. Wind rubbing a caress over the many trees around the dwelling of the neighbouring girl. Permit me the confession: that must be why I took an interest in horses. Up high from the loft day after day I could look down on the lass horsebacked under the trees – her sharp young body with its stretch-and-hop, hopping and stretching with the trot, sit-sitting with the triple, the coat-tails flapping away from the round buttocks solidly outlined in the corduroy jodhpurs, her stick-straight back ending in curls, the horse's hoofs flop and the leaves rustling their silver. And I am not allowed to go and play with her. It remains an unexplored secret.

I have two horses, two young foals. It's true, there used to be an earlier, older nag in the family: Patanjali. But we hadn't trained him all that well and we later did away with him, rather in the way one would get rid of an illegitimate child. Sometimes I see him moving through the streets with his little cart – we called him Easel for short, because of his long ears – and one may still observe in his movements traces of his education with us. When he wishes to evacuate the bowels he goes down on his haunches. The tan-coloured skin (like a jersey) drops in folds. He struggles with the forelegs, trying to transform his knees into elbows so that he may scratch with a bashful hoof behind the ears. The foldings are left behind in the street. But I take the necessary precautions not to be seen by his shiny eyes.

I have two horses, two young foals, the one a nick bigger than the other. Their names, Savopopo and Savokampi. I keep them in the loft. In front, giving on to the street, the high veranda runs down the loft's west wall. Up the inner staircase in the back of the building I surreptitiously climb. There they are on the veranda, unaware of my presence. They stand whispering, on their toes, the young one with the dark curls and the slightly bigger one with stiff white lips, both totally dedicated to the effort of lifting the peg from the gate closing the veranda off from the outside stairs, intent upon climbing down and absconding. Ah, and they are blood-young. Until they see me and become frightened and covered with shame. Why do they want to run away then, I ask myself. They serenade me in the way I taught them until I can no longer rein in my sorrow and am obliged to turn my sobbing face to the wall so as not to inconvenience them. A man doesn't cry in front of his horses. Then it is time to sleep and I prepare a couch of litter in the warmest corner of the loft. We lie down, Savokampi by Savopopo, and I pressed tight against them, above us the cool hushing of leaves, thousands upon thousands of cards shutter-flickering punching data. Savokampi's dark eyelashes, I notice, are wet with tears.

In the late night I'm sitting in the old professor's house, telling him the tale of my two horses. The room glimmers. The professor has a grey visage. I wrap up my story in words and try to present it in patterns which he may comprehend. Actually I display everything but when I deviate from the truth the grey face becomes quite hidebound and then he wags an admonishing finger to correct the lessons. I always have to report to him, starting from the beginning afresh. Among my words the leaves rustle. When I relate how they sang for me my heart is deeply moved and weeping I have to turn to the blindness of the room's wall.

All of that is so deep in the past. You did want to hear the telling. The whole night through I sat at the table by the window with the night-writing under my fingers. I can see far across this town where we decided to while away the darker hours. It is only a traveller's halt in the desert – perhaps their only income is from the pilgrims interrupting their journey here for the night. On either side of the speedway, quiet now, are three or four rows of hotels; and further still more, up the hillsides. All the windows are dull gleaming squares. There is the same light, barely sombred by the passage of night, in all the many windows, but I can scarcely believe that slumbering or cold people may in fact be stretched out behind the walls and the panes. Wind is moving through the leaves. The entire town is a paradise of mulberry trees so that the wind at least may have a hollow for its foot, and the only sound discernible is the on-going soft rooting of all the many lungs. The night isn't all black for the remaining stains of snow (the stripped beards) in the gutters and along the rooftops' slopes throw back the starlight. It is as if, somewhere not far off, there should be bubbling water, perhaps underground. The earth is full of wind.

Now it's lighter and we climb up the slight incline of the street to go break-fast on the patio of one of the big hotels. Your hand clings to mine. Your stride is youthful and vigorous. You've slept well, your eyes are clear, and with every step the long black hair (reminding me so much of a horse's mane) lashes your shoulder. You insist. You want me to relate the story of the horses. Agreed, agreed – but later.

On the stoop some of the other guests are already at table. It is early yet. The square frames even now still show the fine yellow light of muffled electric-ity. We walk down the length of the stoop. In the corner is a Spanish couple – the hidalgo with the grey suit and the cigar and the crossed ankles. Wait for me here then. Let me first go and rinse my fingers because the night was long and my hands are unkempt and oily from all the writing, and the leaves shrill so, exactly like pens proceeding over paper in a scraping way. You order our breakfast meanwhile. I shall take a cappuccino with the croissants. Better to have attempted all things and found them empty than to have tried nothing and leave your life a blank. Did you know that the crescent-shaped early bread originated in Vienna where it is called a *Kipfel* in memory of the Turks who besieged that city? Soon it will be broad daylight.

I am in the tiled bathroom and I lift the hands to my face. The hands smelling vaguely of horse. Water is lapping in the wash-basin. All of this already so long ago. So many years since I've seen you last, since I finally lost you. Whom shall I ever tell my story to? I look in the mirror and am frightened. The long grey hair there, and the terrible thick white face, the blubbery blancmange of the dewlap and the mouth buried in folds, the rough pores of the hide. An ancient dismantling. From face to face. It awaits me.

The Shoes

Late that afternoon we went swimming for the last time in the sea at the bottom of the garden, the slanting rays. Shadows had started fumbling over the land and the sea was perceptibly growing more winy and deeper. The earth is its own impediment to light. In this very blue glow we plashed about until my wife's hair was lank and sluggish like a shoe to the sloe-eyed face, and then we ran back up the garden in our pale bodies. Behind us the sea was churning the gravel, and quickly afterwards darkness.

It was the next day that we departed for our destination: the North. ("The Devil hath established his cities in the North" –St Augustine.) Father, Mother, my wife and I, our dead uncle Don Espejuelo and the warder. We were to drive to the city from where we could take the aeroplane – and onward in two legs, first to a halfway point and then beyond to the true North. Complicated! Cutting up the journey and using two tickets each somehow worked out cheaper. Away from the sea we thus sped, the road winding through the dry hills with the sparse scrub, and in the back of the car our dead uncle Don Espejuelo was coughing dust and shaking his head at the senselessness.

We found the city quite deserted and dark. Even the air terminal was enfolded in darkness as if by heavy drapery and we came upon no other prospective passengers there. Here we were to wait for a while before we picked up our tickets and all the necessary paraphernalia and papers with which to proceed past the customs barrier to the airstrip somewhere outside the limits of the agglomeration. That, I was convinced, would present major problems: the man of customs in his white shorts would leaf through our passports and then poke his head through the rolled-down window to scan the interior of the car and he might just ask a question of our dead uncle Don Espejuelo sitting there as big as life in his dust coat and his dark glasses and surely Don Espejuelo would open his mouth to utter his favourite silly argument – "He is two. Always he is together like wheat transformed. And what is it holds him together? Why, the sandwich spread of the soul to get her. Don't open him up. One-sliced he'll become crumbly and dead: just bread. . . ." – whereupon the perplexed official (not programmed for this type of irregularity) may sharpen his glance and our uncle would vomit his cackling cough and his coat will probably even come awry or flap open to show that underneath it harbours merely dust and then we should be in trouble because it is surely illegal to be gallivanting along the State's roads with a defunct member on the back seat, even though in presence of a warder. . . . "And anyway," Don Espejuelo would compound the official's ire with a bare-toothed grin, "it is anyway to pass from the hardly known to the hardly unknown." Full of disjointed and inappropriate clichés he is, Don Espejuelo. "Point less, hah!"

But for now we went wandering through the murky halls of the air terminal. I thought of buying some reading matter for the flight. At the news stand a magazine named *Times* turned out to be a religious tract. I picked up a newspaper call *The Jewish News* but that proved to be several sheets of advertisements for furniture removers. And the pages were yellow and coated with dust. A little further along the vast mezzanine floor a young lady tried to tempt us with some souvenirs: she wanted to sell my wife a nose-ring of dull silver encrusted with several tiny green emeralds. At this my wife wrinkled her nose and sniffed disdainfully.

Yes, it was time to set out for the airfield. We walked out to the car parked by the kerb. But here Father stopped us. Don Espejuelo, he announced, has gone missing and would have to be found before we may continue. It is not done to discard one's family *en route*. Nobody knows where he's disappeared to, no, not a living soul. And with this he got into the car, adjusted his wide-brimmed hat and smoothed down his double-breasted suit, and drove off with a laugh.

The warder stood in the entrance hall looking down at his shoes with a sorry expression. One black shoe was snub-nosed and high, the other one – black too – was very long and limp and creased. He lifted his mournful gaze to us: no, he felt obliged to declare, Don Espejuelo will never be found, nor will he ever come back. Because he has absconded with the shoes. (Damn.)

Max Sec (Beverly Hills)

1. He gets up after a restless night. Brigadier-General Murphy. Slicks down his yellow hair. Looks in the mirror, into his red-rimmed eyes. Worms the moustache around. He has a secure establishment in his care. All gates mastered, guards posted in watchtowers. Dead areas locked at both ends and key-carrier cooped up within. But safe enough? Those minds, those hearts. What if . . .? Bastards!

So he has a high wall built around the no-go terrain, with TV-controlled steel-plated double gates the only egress. Now it is truly a maximum security. (Young deer let loose to roam over green lawns between wall and fort. He has a weakness for life.)

2. He gets up after the nightmares of half-sleep. What if? One never knows with these traitors and terrorists, these rapists and assassins. HQ was adamant about that: "Let one, just *one* bandit get away and you might as well run with him!" The perspiration is chilly on his back. They are always scheming, these dogs; they have visions of freedom; turn away and they start digging, climbing, feinting, *thinking*, corrupting the boere.

He has the roof torn from the prison to be replaced by a grid of steel, a catwalk permitting the armed guardians to keep a constant eye on their charges. Now, ah, this boop is break-proof.

3. He surfaces gagging from the tortures of sleep. The yellow hair all tousled. Brigadier-General Murphy. Small blood vessels darken his vision. The trembling of his legs. Careful, you may nick yourself with the razor. This damn stubble. My God, what if? It takes just one suicidal escape, *one* only, to have this whole magnificent impregnable maximum-security possy crumble to ridicule.

He has an electronic eye installed in every cell. We shall have surveillance twenty-five hours a day. Snoop lenses sweep the corridors, eliminate the blind angles. Tape recorders are connected to the toilet bowls. From the ramparts he goes to the catwalk. Squints down at the vestiges of humanity below. There's a rash around his neck, just inside the collar, itching terribly. "I want those courtyards covered by wire netting im-me-diate-ly! You think the sly sons-abitches can't scale four metres of sheer wall? And if a helicopter were to – Jesus Christ!"

4. He orders, reviews, refines. Every prisoner must be escorted by a guard-with-dog at all times of the day or the night.

5. No more contact between inmates.

6. The warder-with-dog shall get into the bath with the prisoner. Yes, man, of course the State will issue you with overalls for the purpose!

7. All eating utensils shall henceforth be of plastic. No mirrors anywhere. No exercise outside. (Or inside.) No more smoking. Quiet there! And your grand-mother's cunt!

8. Listen. The dogboer-and-dog shall spend the nights in bed with the con-vict, man on man, a second warder with FN and baton and whistle and walkie-talkie outside the locked, mastered, bolted, padlocked, padlocked, padlocked, steel-reinforced cell door and inside grill. Changing of the shift at midnight.

Ah, but it is good to run a rehabilitation centre fulfilling its first and foremost function: to keep the wards of the State in safe-keeping.

9. The night was an agony. Behind his eyelids, even with orbs staring into the dark, he visualized all the horrors. The headlines. The sanctions. The total breaking. *Today, at noon, an escapee from Maximum Security* . . . Oh sweet dear compassionate cruel merciless God. What if? What the fuckin' hell if, for instance. . . ! He is an old wreck, crushed by responsibility, by the spectre of overthrow.

He has the prisoners, the blind worms, taken out into the central courtyard, stood against a wall, one by one, murmuring, shot.

Now the prisoners are in maximum security, sir.

10. He struggles up, suffocating through layer upon layer of not having slept at all.

The Break

The "Terminus" – so called because it is the worst degree of a series of detention places and for the large majority of those landing there it also means the final point of their peregrination (but the correct name is the Calabozō) – is housed in a tent of enormous proportions. The roof of this tent, one can call it a circus tent, is very high. From up top banners descend, long dark-dyed flags, trapezes on oily ropes, and tatters of another material. The inside space is entirely occupied by cages made of steel bars in which the prisoners are held, two storeys high but without solid floors (everywhere the grid only) so that people can spy on one another from every angle. Between the stacked cages, every stack consists of a block covering nearly 100 x 100 metres, there are streets wide enough for lorries to pass. The streets are slushy with pools of water. High above all this the sombre roof of the tent sings and blows as if it were a membrane moved by breathing, an infundibulum perhaps. It is so high that all sounds caused by it are inaudible. Only rarely a dull ruffle is understood, or a sudden bang. It may be a flock of angels, involved in a quick accident or an altercation – you then think. Nobody underneath this roof, in any event certainly not the prisoners, can know whether it is day or night outside, grey-time or sunshine, summer or winter or autumn. In strategic places along the miry streets poles have been erected, with pale light bulbs burning permanently. But it is always too gloomy to be able to see from one end of the tent to the other.

The lorries come to remove those condemned to die when it is the time to execute them. (In the tent one referred to "prisoners of death" or PODs.) The place of dying is apparently somewhere in the city. On the flat bed of the truck is a steel cage exactly like the units in the tent itself. Armed guards in khaki overalls make the reprobates climb on to the lorry and then into the cage. The prisoners have their wrists handcuffed. While they are being led to the lorry, often with blows and curses, they sing their leave-taking songs. Usually they are already in a trance and the corners of their mouths are stained by a whitish froth. The prisoners remaining behind swing like apes from their own bars to shout good-byes and other encouragements, *hasta la vista compadre, vaya con Dios*!, or to sing in company nearly as defiantly as those being removed. Some just look on with stiff jaws and the knuckles of the hands clenched around the staves white also.

The truck is parked in the alley between Block C and Block D. Prisoner 3926/75 looks down it from his cage, sees how the PODs with great difficulty clamber on to the vehicle until the barred container is filled to bursting. All at once he notices the last passenger of death, shackled like the others: C. He can't believe his own eyes and with the shuddering shock he has to grab hold of the bars to remain standing. Wasn't C in particular one of the privileged class? Surely he was not condemned to die and indeed, according to the rumour running from section to section, was even due for release in a few short weeks! It means therefore that no one can be safe. Or that the selection of executees is arbitrary. South African roulette! Or that the number of detainees is just thinned out from time to time. That all eventually are destined for the strangling cord!

C looks up at him with a pale face, tries to smile one last time and to wave with his entangled hands. The hair falls over his forehead. He is wearing his winter-issue moleskin jacket. 3926/75 hears his call: "You can grab my lunch ration this afternoon, amigo." As one of the last he is helped on to the lorry. The engine snores and the exhaust emits blue fumes. The guards lock the grill with the rattling of keys and key-rings and then get into the cabin with the driver.

3926/75 jerks and tugs at his bars and suddenly notices that the door of his cage gives way, that for some reason it was not closed. The truck has just started moving off. In a flash he is outside his cage, jumping from there into the oozy street, and in a loping run he catches up with the conveyance and climbs up behind the cooped-in prisoners. There he squats down very low, flinging his arms round his knees. If only the warder next to the driver doesn't detect him!

It is a windy day outside with heavy tumbling clouds in the heavens, like an amorphous and inconceivable sea battle. But the passage from eternal twilight in there where he grew old and empty to the penumbra out here is nevertheless blinding. It could be autumn. It would seem that the city is deserted, rocking slightly, or perhaps the route to the abattoir is selected thus with special care. They go rumbling on and he has to lean into the wind so as not to be blown off. Thick and hot tears are squeezed from his eyes.

At the corner of boulevard M and rue S where the traffic lights are, the lorry stops abruptly in front of a Wimpy Bar with glaring neon lights. One of the guards steps down quite unconcernedly, probably to go buy cigarettes or mon-keynuts. 3926/75 jumps off at the back. His knees, cramped from his sitting on his haunches for such a long time, give way under him. But bent over to be inconspicuous he trots at an angle across the boulevard to where he can see the tall trees in the L-gardens groaning in the wind. Then at last (God save our gracious Secretary-General!) he is under the first trees with the lorry-load of

PODs far behind him, and he jogs past the big trunks. The leaves clatter above his head.

When he got thus far he realized – whereto now? – that the story would not work out, that one mustn't cover the ground too rapidly, and he decided to start again from scratch.

The truck with its haulage of alive and hale people who within a few hours will be under the sods, limp and cold already in the kingdom of decay has left now. The sound and the aftersounds of their ultimate dirge have died away. The trembling voice of C too, one of the contingent merely to fill the quota. ("We are all here to complete some or other quota.") Perhaps the vision of their waving chained arms, the staring ecstasy in their eyes, the tight cords of their neck tendons – perhaps that will fade away too. In the huge dark tent the murmuring, sometimes the growling, of convict voices will huff and puff, will be black roses. The yellow light bulbs shake in the wind.

Carefully he opens the gate of his barred cage, casts a quick glance all around to see if anyone paid attention to the squeaks, and then jumps down to the street. Hardly has he hit ground when he scurries with humped back to the wall of the tent where shadows repose in thicker layers. Nobody will take any notice now. He moves away from the principal exit through which the lorry trundled just recently because he knows that this is guarded, all down the narrow alley between the last row of cages and the tent wall. There are prisoners watching him with dull eyes – eyes without the smallest spark of expectation, eyes full of ashes – but it seems as if they don't see him.

Perhaps a quarter of a mile further along he comes across a loose flap in the wall of the tent. He pulls the flap slightly to one side and crawls out. Outside he gets up and starts walking without looking at his footprints, his back still turned to the main entrance where guards dawdle with rifles over their shoulders smoking cigarettes and kick-kicking at the mud with their bootcaps.

The earth-tracks outside are dark and wet. The sombre clouds of the sky are mirrored in the stagnant pools. From wires stretched across the road big limp standards droop, black sheets, frayed lengths of rag: in places one can still discern the bleached writing of some painted slogan. These banners are barely lifted by the wind. They are heavy with dampness. Some reach so far down that the extremities or the seams sweep over his neck and shoulders when he passes by underneath them. Like a cold hand touching his neck. He feels the shivers down his spine. He shudders at the thought and at the touch and senses the contraction of his skin.

When he has progressed further than the length of the tent he sees some back roads forking away from the route he is walking. These back streets are sludgy too, slimy with rubbish and soot swimming on the water. All along the little streets there are inner courts he can look into in passing. This veritable labyrinth is manifestly a continuation of the Department's fief. He knew that the Department's interests were extended over a large terrain around Central with workshops, rubbish heaps, housing for the staff, and probably also vegetable gardens, dance halls and fields for grazing.

In the backyards are labourers with big leather aprons tied around the hips. Some carry spades or pitchforks. He sees smouldering stacks of charred carcasses and he gets a whiff of the pungent and nauseating stench of scorched flesh. A purplish smoke drifts over the wooden partitions between workplaces, curling among the banners and the standards. The workers' faces and forearms are besmirched, black. From time to time soot and ash come sifting down. In other workplaces he sees stacked bones glinting still with humidity after a recent downpour. Or he sees workers (warders perhaps? prisoners?) digging in the earth. In one spot he notices that the aproned people are wielding long whips; he sees the bloodstains on their trouser legs and aprons – as if smeared axes were wiped clean there – and also that the pools of water reflect an oily red colour. He hears inhuman sounds, a cacophony of terror as from the milling-about of the dying who smell the blood, sometimes a raw crescendo and then a fading rattle, but he does not see the origin of these sounds. The workers must observe him going by; they seemingly give it no thought though.

Further than the fenced-in nest of workshops and studios, than the burbling smoke, the shrieks and the bone-scraping aching of power saws, he reaches a point where fields and untilled scrubland gently heave and roll away in the distance. On either side of the road a hedge of brambles. The grass in the fields a dirty green. The inhabited area is already quite far in the background from whence he came, it lies veiled in a thin smokiness. Roads start turning away from him, roads leading to arable lands or sometimes even to clumps of trees which he can see as denser blurs of green on the horizon, and he must decide intuitively like a hunted animal on the right way, or the most convenient one. When he reaches a gap in the hedge he sets off to the right, all along the edge of a field lying fallow. He must try working his way back to the city in a wide, cautious curve, and then to R's house, for that has always been the intention – that he should, if he could make the break, try to reach R's house; the latter would then as go-between effect the contact with his people.

He hears a faint *halloooo* and one or two distant thumps like inflated paper bags being exploded by a fist very far off. He looks up and sees a few persons hardly bigger than the palm of his hand: they are dressed in red jackets, or red shirts maybe, or maybe their torsos are burnt very red from an excessively long exposure to the sun. He sees how they gesticulate and lift long objects to their shoulders: then there are sudden little eruptions of silvery-white smoke. Much closer to him he sees the leaping hither and thither of a hare, elegant to the eye, the zig-zag course and the abrupt changes of direction over shrubs, tufts and stones, the long ears down in the neck like blinkers which have slipped down, the bobbing powder-puff of the tail. He lies low in a hollow in the earth with his nose nestled close to the dirty wet soil. He doesn't hear the hare and he doesn't hear the grassroots either. Nobody will bother about him here. He does hear a vague rumbling which may emanate from tanks being deployed behind a distant hill. There is neither sun nor birds.

In the dog-watch of the night he arrives at R's house on the outskirts of the city. He knocks and the door is opened. R is not at home – or is the old man with the grey crewcut and the heavily framed glasses R after all? In his memory lies a grey desert of empty time-passages, of tastelessness and cottonwool and cardboard. The inhabitants of the house are not surprised to see him. The house consists of a large number of small rooms, all painted white and roughly plastered, and nearly all situated at different levels so that you continually have to climb up a few steps or step down to the next room. The house is full of women and girls in white nightshifts, their eyelids swollen with sleep. Their cheeks have the hue of tomatoes. Must be R's family, he reflects.

He explains that he should like to reach his own people but that the authorities have probably started a manhunt for him by now. R, or the convivial old gentleman who might have been R, his friend from youth, says that there is no hurry and also no need to worry. That much time has evaporated in the meanwhile. That his own wife no longer resides where she used to live before but elsewhere now in an unknown sector of the city, and in any case that she remarried and so she has another family. Also that it will not be necessary for him to apply a disguise, only that he should get rid of his prison garb, but that has already been taken care of, look, here is exactly the right white shorts and here a white shirt for tomorrow, they will fit him. And that they will then put a bicycle at his disposal so that he may go looking for his people somewhere in Market Street it would appear, hard by the yellow cathedral. But for now he must first relax, listen, he should take a bath and then eat something – why not a few peaches? That it is after all still night outdoors and that they are glad to have him there with them.

It is still night outside and wind pushes cool against the walls of the houses, rustles in the papers and the tatters on the street, the dusty branches. He hears the muted rumbling of the city which never really sleeps. He is taken to a small white room where there's a bath. On a chair, next to the bath, there lie a pair of white pants and a white shirt neatly folded. A girl – R's daughter? sister? niece? third wife? – has placed an oil lamp on the table with its dark marble top. He sees their shadows flowing excessively large and grotesque against the white walls. Like fire they move. Now she brings pitchers with steaming hot water which she pours into the ancient bath. He enters the bath. One should not cover the ground too rapidly. She also lifts her nightdress over her head and takes off her glasses. Her breasts are small and crumpled. Without the spectacles her eyes are huge and watery like those of a hare. On her thin thighs small black hairs grow. She gets into the bath with him. Under the water her yellowish body seems to be shivering. The bathroom has no door. He is aware of other figures in their nightclothes in the corridor. And the huff-puffing fluttering of shadows against the wall.

She slides down lower in the bath with her knees pulled up and the small creases of the water over her belly. He pushes her knees apart and covers her body with his. With the fingers of one hand he feels her genital organ which is small and round and stiff under the water. The stone of a fruit without any flesh.

And Move

Do you remember when we were still making memories?

I am human. Or humanoid if you prefer. Subject to the same whims and fancies as you may be. Lazy in a similar way too: the flesh thickens and the mind becomes blunt, the imagination caducous, if you see what I mean. Let me put it another way: that I live like a blind and aged foetus inside the layers of myself, gobbling up whatever experience I find at hand, feeding the caecum (and that that in itself gives carnal satisfaction). I am, I think, (still) bent on gaining *weight* in this charnelhouse so as not to be blown away by the black wind of oblivion. For to live and to feel yourself living you have to jiggle around with D. Death. (Perhaps it is the other way around.) And for sure I am a miserable *petit bourgeois*, an *obyvatel*. Of what possible use or contribution can I be to the revolution anyway? Often the same nightmare recurs: some delegate is dumping a batch of dead horses' heads in my lap and blood and mucus will yet be dribbling from the horrible nostrils and lips to mess up my pants. No, I am too far removed to be (vigorously) of the proletariat.

I have said that I am lazy but it should rather be that I am lying in wait. For what? Ah, for nothing – since I'm not particular. That is exactly it: for nothing. I have thought of that before. Why then communicate? That, I can assure you, is not a matter of choice. Besides – I don't. I digest. Words are winds, obliterating taste. And often I have to assume that I'm still alive. Merely a prolepsis? Even so I shan't be making any hurried attempts to move (even if I could): one shouldn't provoke a prolapsus. It needs something protuberant to get me going if at all; a salient experience. If at all. And then I just leave the acts lying about. Let them grow fat, become facts. *Erst kommt das Fressen und dann kommt die Moral.* I am furthermore, I must tell you fairly, like Procrustes the highwayman who made his victims fit his bed by stretching or lopping them.

This prolegomenon (this proem, yes) is necessary because of what my friends Tuchverderber and Galgenvogel keep saying to me. They don't fancy the way in which I bring up my words (to put it mildly). They carp at my being prolix, verbose. They think that I am putting on. They accuse me of being weighty (which is exactly to the point). They don't comprehend why I procrastinate, why I don't burp and get it over with. (But be careful of the black wind, I feel like telling them.) Of an afternoon we sit chewing the fat and there they are munching their lips and gnashing their gums. "Why dontcha write a simple story?" one of them, either Galgenvogel or Tuchverderber, asks. "Why not 'boy sees gurl, gurl sees boy, boy *likes* gurl, gurl screws boy (or the other way around), alas gurl is already married, boy terminates husband with extreme prejudice, luckily the court finds it legitimate defence and they all live happily ever after'? To what purpose all this hum-hum muck?" One of us refills the little shot-glasses with kümmel (we don't wish to know the sun disappearing). The thin blood from bloated horses' heads has soaked into my trousers. They think I'm writing for obscurity. Just jiggling around with *Kultur*. Little do they know. If at all. Their chins are grey too. Each goitre a gobbling half a gander. Wobbling in earnest indignation. "Ja," I answer, "am I to scribble for the worms?* Would you have me suffer the delusion of a *Weltverbesserungswahn*? To amuse the masses? To be flatulent? (I beg your pardon.) But I'm too fat for that. And D. Death is too thin, too white, too scaly. All the same." All the same what then? A piercing question. "All the same it is a *Kriegspiel*."

I digest these thoughts and counterpoints while I sit in the bus. Perhaps, I reflect, I shall bring them a simple tale after all. It should naturally describe everyday matters in an uncomplicated way. One shouldn't weigh it down with all those utterances of life. For instance, what could be more straightforward than this trip this afternoon? Of course I could introduce a jiggling of beauty here and yonder just for the juice of it – some lacustrine colours perhaps, and a breath of sentiment not too lachrymose. Nothing lacerating however, no – none of that turning inside out or bringing dark mumblings to light.

And really it is quite a clear story. Let me tell it in the past tense and then allow me to go into the future. And move. Merely a prolepsis? But it is the pattern that weaves its tissues which cannot be avoided. (Ah, the layers of blunting and the carnal joys!)

We had a fine afternoon of it together in that big grey building where we used to meet so often. Slowly we lipped and sipped our kümmel and we refrained from observing the sun sinking. Now I really had to leave to rejoin my lady wife. It was cumbersome – my coming out was already a rare occurrence since I didn't move much any more these days. I bade goodbye to my friends Tuchverderber and Galgenvogel. I was inordinately proud of not having made any mention of

Abajo la gusanera!

131

rumours (or fat facts) which had reached my ears lately. Was it Galgenvogel or Tuchverderber who couldn't look me in the eye, who asked no question about my lady wife?

It was late but the day refused to die – just as if it were suspended for an eternity. I wanted to go back to my lady wife. She had been out shopping with Eva and I was thinking that she may get worried upon returning to this unaccustomed absence of mine.

I called my man. He help-handed me into the cart and then set out pulling it. We called him "The Horse" because of the clopping noise he made when trotting. This was due to the heavy and clumsy black boots he wore. He had had polio as a youth and since then the carpus and tarsus were permanently warped and annealed so that he had to go about on his errands with these stiff boots on, keeping the time to himself with rigid wrists. None the less we progressed at a jolly nice pace, jiggling, and I knew that home was only a few canals away from the grey building.

But today he took me back along an unfamiliar route. To tell the truth, it had been such a long time since I'd come out of myself that I no longer recognized the city. (But please don't let me complicate the story.)

Horse was tiring, I could see it by the angle of his grey hat sinking ever deeper between the shoulders. So that I allowed him to convince me that we should take the bus as we neared the station. We got in – Horse with much stomping of shanks, obsequious winking and rubbing of hard hands. Apparently he knew the conductor and the other passengers. Horse and the cart were put in a special compartment rather like a stall separated from the rest of the bus by a steel partition. Against this he proceeded to kick with his clumsy black boots, all the while sniggering and moving his greasy grey fedora backward and forward on his head. He has a grey face with a wobbling chin and the goitre of a cretin. He also drools at the mouth. But this never stopped him from chatting and gossiping – a real flibbertigibbet. Was it not from him I heard the rumours concerning my lady wife and Galgenvogel or Tuchverderber?

The bus, strangely enough, took us right out of town. Horse and the conductor and even my fellow travellers kept on trying to reassure me that this was quite all right, even rather normal. But I didn't remember the city this way at all. I certainly didn't recognize these suburbs and the countryside unfolding – not that I've ever been far enough from my home to know. If at all. But I've always conceived of my home town as flat and shot through with canals running just a little lower than the cobbled streets. Now I saw black hills dotted with sunshine. From time to time the bus stopped and taciturn men with blackened hands and faces half swallowed by the shadows of flat caps got on. These were miners, I was told, and those hills are mine-dumps. What a labyrinth of shafts and corridors and caverns there must be below the surface to excrete all this blackness, I thought. Like thoughts. We also passed places where there were lighter patches not unlike furry growths. I wondered whether these may be flowers – cacti perhaps, or rocks of a vegetable shape? But no, everyone confirmed, they were only the severed heads of horses from the abattoirs and from nearer, I was assured, I would see the blood and mucus still freshly trickling from them, and the scores of busy flies. All the scars. (Or stars.)

But that, I felt, really belonged to another story. And I was quite enjoying the ride despite the unfamiliar proletariat all around me. The day was caught motionless in a decline of dappled lights; distances held the sheen of lacquer rather like the soft sateen of my shirt. *Ja*, I ruminated, this day is finally just like a smile saturated, soaked in sunshine. (But my pants were damp.)

We passed by the lakes. We passed over a bridge with the railway tracks below us. Workers got on and got off. They mumbled and moved their caps with black hands. Horse whinnied and kicked against the steel-plated partition behind which he was standing. We came to a forest. Hills and green trees and the opaque but silver surfaces of water. Porcelain and peppermint and pink. And then behind the tip of the woods the city reappeared.

I knew that this was the same city, I instinctively appropriated the memory of it, and as we entered the first streets I saw in fact that I was now so very nearly home – just approaching it, you know, as it were from behind. I felt quite content. More precisely: I was *heavy* with contentment. Now I should go home, I thought. And forgive my wife my immobility. And perhaps I should go out more often and then reabsorb the familiar from this unexpected angle and show it to her and to my friends Galgenvogel and Tuchverderber too. One could have picnics here. I even felt benign towards The Horse. In truth of course I have the edge over him, I am superior to him – for whereas he hates me I like him. But that has to do with fatness and the blight of a festering class consciousness.

The bus halted. There were now crowds of people milling about in the streets here on the edge of the city. Some girls were dressed in our national costume. It was strange because unannounced and inexplicable. I just couldn't work out what the processions were in aid of. Was this a national holiday then? Or – G. God forbid! – an uprising? revolution? anarchy? Already? (If at all.)

And I found myself as suddenly abandoned in the bus. I called (or burped) for The Horse, but he was no longer in the little stable. So, with great toil and difficulty I managed to alight by myself. People were jostling over one another in the teeming streets. But this must be the same town, I thought: after all I practically know this area and those houses from behind.

In the street I tried to ask my way from a prancing youngster. His teeth flashed. All the people had flashes in their mouths. But neither he nor anyone else among the frenzied bypassers knew any French. A few trees from the nearby forest grew to within the city limits. Under their high canopies the room-like spaces were already dark. Ah, I thought – now the day is finally going.

I felt rather than saw a shuffling of people (skirmishing? dancing? imitating horses?) in a narrow and leafy alley leading off the paved main thoroughfare where the bus was now being rocked by a gaggle of dark-faced juveniles. So I heaved myself over in that direction, feeling true, feeling solid.

When I came near the gesticulating throng gave way (before my weight). Two men crouched in the sudden circle, flecked with patterns of darkness, and they looked at me with saurian eyes, their scaly lips dappled with blood and their grey chins wobbling.

They came to me in a streak of understanding, my two friends: Tuchverderber and Galgenvogel. "Ah," one of them – or it might have been both – breathed, and the other one so rapidly and deftly produced a kukri or a kris – the blade a steely white flash-tongue of all clarity and knowingness and simplicity – jiggling it – that my comprehension froze. And plunged it with a curious little falsetto snigger into the layers of my dumbness. Splitting the blubber, spilling extravagantly the writhing white worms. Death. Yes. D. Death.

(One never digests death my friends.) (If at all.)

Flight Aid

We had lost the sea battle and on rafts or clutching to pickle vats and flotsam we washed up soaked right through on this godforsaken stretch of beach – but our enemies were vengeful, they weren't going to let us get away with our lives. . . . Or, as castaways, expatriates, refugees and at a loss in this strange land, we remained on the lookout towards the sea all the days and all the nights, for where else could our succour come from? and then suddenly we noticed the ships, two, but they could not approach the land for anchorage among the cresting waves. . . . I no longer know, Minnaar, and it is futile that you should keep on questioning me on the how and the why of our being there – it has escaped me as so many other causes did too, the way my words now leave me in the lurch, a runniness. The only clarity is: we were on a sand strip stretching in a half moon around the bay and there was no civilization or settlement or metropolis or dune farm or neon sign or lighthouse or caravan park or life-saver's hut or hamburger stall anywhere near, and we were parched right down to our chapped snail-tongues. The sky was blue. The sea was blue but swollen. Away from the beach, still unfathomably deep in the heaving waters, to port and starboard two ships stood. Three-masters both, and the wind was lavish in the rigging and the sails so that these were bulging like men's fists or like small clouds in the lower sky. Heeling in the water they were, but still they could get no nearer to the land. Nemesis? Deliverance? We (that is Murphy and Don Espejuelo and Breytenbach and I, and our companions – Mooityd, Sweetime, Elefteria, Levedi Tjeling and Marlin Manrob) turned our backs on the thundering ocean slithering over the wet sand and we started searching for direction about us. The long dresses of the women were sodden up to the hips, and clusters of sand grains were glistening in the folds. On the ridge of the nearest high dune an Arab all at once loomed large and after staring for a long moment (at us? at the ships in the bay?) with a hand like a falcon above the eyebrows to protect his eyes from the sun – or was he, because of a sore back, praying on his feet to a Mecca around the curve of the horizon? – after thinking through his eyes for a long while, he waved to us to come closer. Over his white robe in which the wind was trapped like the wings of anxious seagulls he wore a jacket buttoned to the chin and around the head he had wrapped a turban and on his face he had a pointed beard. He thoughtfully fondled the sharpness of the hairy little sword on his chin and carefully and slowly explained to us from deep in his throat that he could, upon request, rapidly accompany us to a place where we might obtain assistance, but only the men would be allowed to come. This after all, was dictated by the customs of Islam. And concerning the women we weren't to worry excessively for they would be safe here during our brief absence. But we had to take our shoes off. With the guide we clambered over the sandhill and sunk to our knees in the shifts and the slides of the surface. Behind the hill we saw the grey sandflats decorated with shadows of all shapes. Like more palpable shadows there were also broad drawers standing upright, half buried in the sand itself, with shiny knobs by which they could be opened upwards. There were five different drawers. The Arab with the burnt-out eyes asked us whether we wished to arrive at our destination quickly or less quickly or less slowly or slowly or in God's own time then. We said: as soon as possible, please. Rather, that was my answer, and I assume the others answered in the same way. Thus he opened the left most "drawer" and we climbed in. And with a giddy speed we tumbled down, transported by a vertical conveyer belt, black and rough like sandpaper, down, down, down, until down below we were spilt head over heels on a square. In the middle of the square was a fountain. Around this square with its fountain there were the fronts of tall buildings – some were even palaces. A crowd of people with smiles wreathed around their mouths strolled up and down and then stopped to listen with cocked heads how the spouting water plunges back with a rinkle-tinkle. It was warm in that place. And it was evening because spray-lights lit up the buildings and shone through the tree of water. I think it must have been in Switzerland. A long long time ago.

The Execution

Quand l'Amour à vos yeux offre un choix agreable,
Jeunes beautés, laissez-vous enflammer:
Moquez-vous d'affecter cet orgueil indomptable,
Dont on vous dit qu'il est beau de s'armer;
Dans l'âge où l'on est aimable,
Rien n'est si beau que d'aimer.
MOLIÈRE

These modern airships, he thinks, are damn well more luxurious and comfortable than the barely flying tin pails of yore. His eyes slide pleasurably over the interior. Nowadays there's even an area, a space reserved in the belly of the body, which has been arranged like a salon, where passengers no longer have to squat like pupils, knees drawn up to the chest, in rows one behind the other, but may lean back peacefully to stretch their legs in armchairs and on sofas, face to face, each with a smile and a cocktail at the lips. ("Cocktail", it is said, originally meant "horsetail", an excited young stallion with the tail groomed and ribbon-interwoven.) There are even mirrors and imitation candlesticks against the sides. Some time ago already it was announced over the squawk-boxes that the aircraft would reach its destination, C——, within a little less than half an hour that the local time is precisely so-and-so and the ground temperature 26°C. The liquid in his glass is a rusty brown and even the two ice cubes, normally naked of any colour, now have very deeply a reddish tinkle. Half an hour and then the touchdown. There's a slight tightness in his throat. Ample time to try and sort out the complications then – for he has no passport. Would it be best to trust in the mercy of the authorities? Across from him in attitudes of well-behaved and very evidently also well-to-do relaxation, sit a group of people with smartly tailored suits and tasteful gowns on their bodies, men and women of diverse ages who, it would appear, form a unit. Then he becomes aware, nearly outside the field of vision of his left eye, of a furtive movement: and not entirely unexpected after all, he realizes within that one moment of realization – one little bud of his attention had been preoccupied for quite some time with this swarthy female of around forty with the sleek black hair, between sips he has been watching her unconsciously, how she keeps shifting about in her seat. Suddenly this woman gets up in a resolute way and she is now moving down the aisle towards the door giving access from the passengers' section to the cockpit (the flywell). That door is painted white. Close to the door, by the first rows of seats, an airgirl is still busy collecting cups and glasses from the travellers, filling up her tray. The fortyish woman, definitely nervous, scratches around in her imitation leather handbag, producing a knife. The knife has the long shimmer of a blade reflecting rolls of light. The hostess's mouth becomes a sucking-black O of terror, she lets slide the tray and both her hands with the deep-red nails fly up to her lips to try and find shelter there, her blond curls are bobbing. It is too far for him and for the fellow fliers in the cabin to overhear the altercation. They all sit bolt-still with nailed shouts. The woman with the knife points at the white door which is half-closed. Then it is as if the plane flutters down, nose first, and the door is slammed close. The blade-lady grabs hold of the door handle and tries to open it, but it is probably locked from the other side. In vain does she push and pull at the door. While tears start running in wet-shiny tracks over cheeks she attacks one of the seats with her hand full of knife, long slits are ripped in the backrest so that the grey stuffing bulges into the open. There is nothing she can do about the situation now. Ichabod, or something like it. The air hostess neatly fetches up her fingers one by one, goes down on her knees, scrapes together the cups and saucers. The passengers relax and pick up their conversations – many, it would seem now, never even noticed the occurrence. He puts away the incident in one of the folds of his memory, so as to be in a position to use it later, and starts tying words with an elderly lady who sits with flabby thighs crossed in the angle of a settee opposite him; the hair a chic blue-grey *coiffure* and flesh-marks over forehead and cheeks, cicatrices maybe of a long-ago accident, or the tattooed imprints of her tribe. He lifts his glass. *¡Salud y cojones!* he thinks, but it wouldn't be fitting to offer this profoundly beneficial wish to a woman; so he settles for a muttered *bis hundertzwanzig*. Yes, the old aunt confirms his remark, they are a tour group of which she is supposed to be the leader, actually a choir. The other members modestly snigger in chorus when they hear her saying this. One is a chap with a very sallow face but cloud-blue eyes – to illustrate he hums a few dark bass notes, as if imitating in song the drone and the purr of the aircraft engines. There are small silvery stains in the black hair above his temples. He is the bass of the company. Well, strictly speaking not yet a properly constituted choir, the elderly soul directing this lot of rich no-goods takes up her talking again: they are all from Nomansland, she confirms with an approving and one could say a congratulatory look at everyone, and they are at present travelling around the world; now and then when they have a free moment (as here) they will form their lips around rounded sounds and allow their vocal cords to tremble, and if they find at the end of their trip that they harmonize and go well together, well, maybe then they will arrive at the decision to form a choral society. Most likely in Johnnysburg. You must feel first, and weigh up, and touch small glasses with the tuning fork. How else does one these days put together a vocal group? In what other way can you get on to the hit parade? Outside the portholes of the aeroplane it is revealed little by little that they are nearing their island destination: a green coral growth in the blue ocean, an atoll – a green pudding on a table covered with blue tablecloth – starts sliding in under the wings of the craft. Slowly they will descend, flaps will be resisting the air. The angles and the peaks of the island capture and reflect blinding knives of light. He removes the dark glasses from his upper pocket, puts them over his eyes.

He dons his dark glasses and the plane lands. A land, any country, is always, when seen from the sky, much greener than when one actually gets there. While dust clouds and the choking shrieks of braking still enclose them in waves, the less green surroundings rush in a smear of speed past the windows. The show is over. The luxury of air-conditioning and saloon cocktails now seems commonplace, dusty, artificial. By the gangway they later walk down to where some small buses are awaiting the arriving passengers on the airstrip, blue blowflies at the exhaust pipes. With feet on the earth the bodies are heftier. Each person settles for the most convenient position to sit or to stand, fingers his tie or inserts the fingers in a shoulder bag. Now it must happen, he thinks. What must be, must be. Not that he is resigned to his lot. He will simply say that he is a political refugee and they will have to comprehend this. Isn't it true, strictly speaking?

He doesn't come with false pretences after all. But will they ever believe him? And if they question his bona fides? To his utter amazement the buses do not stop at the airport building but continue, with neither delay nor control, in the direction of the city. It doesn't mean anything yet, he cautions himself – the problems are just being postponed till later. As soon as they leave the fenced-in area of the airport a rainshower comes (like thwatting grey flags in the rain) to veil the road and the bushes to either side. Behind the rain-flags you vaguely espy the movements of rank tropical plant life; the fleshy leaves, the tendrils and plant-tatters and milky ropes, the ferns and bamboos and palm trees and sugar cane and mango trees and banana plantations – everything heavy and glistening with water. Rain is liquefying silver, it is vanishing colour. They enter the city which seems all deserted. Would it be only because the rain has forced people to stay indoors? But it doesn't look as if the houses are inhabited at all, or could even be used: many are dilapidated with broken roofs, others have their jalousies tightly bolted or grass shoots coming like wrinkles through the window apertures or chinks and slits in the walls. At measured distances, on street corners and at the intersections where the traffic lights are dead and not a single vehicle is to be seen, soldiers with green berets from which the water is pouring are posted. Each soldier has a drooping long red moustache. The moustaches are curly and so long that it appears, when the soldiers worry them with humid fingers, that they may be plaited. The buses traverse the entire city without the voyagers being able to catch by eye a single civilian, private conveyance, tram, trolleybus, chicken, pig or messenger. The tyres hiss with a sweeping sound over the asphalt, a bubbling as of eggs fried in a pan. They are a busload of cooped-up moths. Beyond the built-up zone they again penetrate the worn-out country-side. Here however it has stopped raining, in places maybe no rain at all has fallen, for the leaves are a dusty grey. In cleared areas in the ash-green bush they sometimes pass the ruin of a humble farmstead. Clouds, like the teased stuffing of a chair, curl and roll in all directions. What a dreary day, he thinks, and looks over his fellow passengers, their heads drawn into the shoulders, the wings folded, the antennae thick and without any feeling. They drive ever deeper into the interior, not in the direction of Mesa de Mariel or of Guanabacoa, but along the road past Santiago de las Vegas and Benjucal (with the Cordillera de los Organos to the right) till beyond Batabano where the road bifurcates – to Cajio and Guanimar on the one hand and Rosario and Tasagava on the other. Gradually the road becomes more untraversable because of potholes and gullies and mudpits and the obstacles of larger rocks and tree trunks. After some time the buses stop and they get out, dull and muzzy, to stretch the limbs and reactivate the circulation. The guide – the chauffeur of the first bus, with green beret and a wet red moustache – leads them away from the road through the vegetation to a marshy strip. They slosh through pools of stagnant water until they reach the edge of what appears to be a vast blue lake, certainly less deep than it would seem. Down the length of the watery surface, on high stilts of concrete, runs a modern highway; but this speedway (or what was intended as such) stops not far from where they are placed, high on its foundations, smack in the middle of the pan, as if the construction was abandoned right there. Rusted iron rods which were to reinforce the concrete now protrude everywhere. The road might as well have originated nowhere to reach this spot and remain suspended without destination 'twixt heaven and earth. Now you can see why it is so difficult to effectuate the necessary traffic connections in our country, the guide explains: this water before you has an exceptionally high salt content and contains apart from that a lot of sulphur too (our island is basically vulcanic); it erodes and finally destroys the pillars and the very road surface when it is built too low. And it is nearly impossible to provide for drainage because this water appears so to say overnight and can start welling up in the most unforeseen places and form a dam there. (True, the water must have arrived here rather suddenly, for the pan has no reeds, nor are any birds' nests to be seen.) And there – he points out with an imperious movement of the hand – that there was to be our destination. Across the lake they see, as indicated by the guide, the broken-down walls of a few houses. It is not so much a case of decayed constructions, however, as that of buildings which were never completed. The walls fallen into disrepair are white with a crust of salt right up to the empty window frames. During this explanation his fellow passengers observed everything around them with mouths all black with surprise and interest (and confusion?). One man wanted to take souvenir photos and was furious when it became evident that his spouse had forgotten their camera somewhere – in the bus, the aircraft, or perhaps even in the second drawer from the bottom of the bedside cabinet in the hotel room of the hotel of another country. The fellow with the black face, the blue eyes and the distinguished temples fills his lungs completely with air and then starts to intone with his heavy voice: Bluewater! Bluewa-a-a-ter. . . . Then: It's a first-class day for screwing goats, screwing goats, s-cr-ew-ing g-o-a-t-s!

Think. Such a man, he thinks, it was just such a rare bird with a similar plum-coloured face who at the time became entangled in the merciless coils of being black. How do you know it wasn't the same guy? he asks himself, and removes his dark glasses to better study the basso profundo. Yes, truly, despite the sallow exterior it really is a white man. Because White is *posture*, a norm of civilization. White is the specific arrogance of power. White is certainly as caught as Black by the conditioning and calcification of these relationships. How did Faulkner put it again? "How to God can a black man ask a white man to please not lay down with his black wife? And even if he could ask it, how to God can the white man promise he won't?" True certainly, but equally certain from the mouth of Lucille Clifton:

> *girls*
> *first time a white man*
> *opens his fly*
> *like a good thing*
> *we'll just laugh*
> *laugh real loud my*
> *black women.*

Think. Black, they say, is not human – not yet; it's *kaffir*, they say. The man, that fellow then who may well be the same one here, now, was cultivated and superior and pragmatic (but all abroad, entirely out of his depth) and he walked with wide shoulders and narrow eyes: therefore he must be White, they said; only, the pigmentation of his skin provided him with the ideal camouflage and out of curiosity and impudence he wanted to exploit this. During a police raid on a shebeen – which he frequented anonymously – it was the time of the revolution – he was arrested together with a bunch of genuine Blacks. In the process of sorting out, grading and classifying and partitioning thousands of people each week, a certain amount of confusion and some slip-ups cannot be avoided (made worse by the attempts of the ringleaders and the shrewd ones to obfuscate their true identities). The black White in the twinkling of an eye found himself in a harsh lock-up place, and from there, before you can say "knife", in the death cell as part of a lot of sweating, chanting and feet-stamping black Blacks. You may say that he now ventured into a truly foreign cultural milieu. Also that his eyes were bigger than his stomach. Do you still remember what a row he kicked up, what a fuss he made, how strenuously he protested? Do you still see the flames in his blue eyes? High on the hilltops the fires spark against the moon. While the others sang to the heavens opening up above them, he, squeezed tight against the bars of the cell door, attempted to draw the attention of any passing authority. But nothing could be done to resolve the matter, the moths were blind, water was in the cellars of the houses. Ichabod, or something along those lines. Should one be bothered by the desperate and farfetched babbling of the condemned? It is not just a question of consequences and precedent and perhaps also quotas – there are finally also rules and regulations and a timetable that need to be respected. Struggling and screaming with foam-flecks around the lips, just like the others for that matter, a human being among the Blacks, he went up to the gallows room one morning at daybreak to have his neck stretched. Like a bow tie the rope was tied around his neck. As if for a dinner or a soirée dansante. But the pillory-cord is a pair of scissors snipping off life, he thinks along. You had an acquaintance among the doomed. It gives death another colour, another exultant visage, another smell.

What does this watery surface further remind you of? The stream of his thoughts is fretting the submerged and reticent stones of experience (like a beheaded cock). What does water always bring home to you? Easy, easy now my old one. The cock is in the head. Superlative tail feathers, no? Beautiful the red bubbling at the throat. . . . Remains the problem of your illegal entry, the complications. . . . That Christmas maybe? Remember. He puts his dark glasses back on, hides the eyes behind smoked lenses. It was along the Skeleton Coast and you were in that small coastal town – remember? Everything light and grey, the streets grey, the sky grey, the undefined sidewalks and the bedraggled gardens and the houses grey, and beyond the town the sand and the sea were grey too. A tremendous wind swept over all of this, brought fog-banks and veils of sand. It was cold with a bit gnawing through marrow and bone, a cold you can't keep out of your body, which thoughtlessly and hypothermically takes possession of you in the same way that a thought infiltrates the wind, and without any positive effect you try to ban it. It cannot be chased off. Like ink in blotting paper it sinks into your fibres and the two can no longer be separated, all at once they have always been one. What is a "thought" after all? Isn't it the incredibly complicated combination of partially body-own memories (inalienably part of the biological mechanism, ink in blotting paper, chopped-off head of the cock), and partly of the experiences and remembrances and projections of other creatures, of life – call it "reality" if you wish – of which you yourself are only a minuscule particle? Because you are lived, experienced through the reality, or rather the totality, and it is not *you* who live all raving and jerking. Even when you are isolated from any contact, even if you are without attachments like a dead eye hidden behind blue contact lenses, even then you are "conceived", are you but a crumb of the thoughts of others. . . . The mind is an image of the cosmos, has its gravitational wells, its collapsars. The thought consumes the mind – or can it be the other way around, that the mind, that ever-expanding void, cannibalizes the thought? Without the realization the realizing experience-field does not exist. . . . And every act of taking cognizance has its gravity, its mass in movement, atom and quark. Which swells to a red giant slurping up its environment. Which inevitably must collapse into a white dwarf. Which cools, cools off, becomes colder, denser, blinder, more autistic, a black dwarf. The star is frozen. That's cognition. Black crystal. Ah, which may blow up as supernova, shooting its neutrons at heaven, painting the final extremities in light, rotating deeper: pulsar. The mind goes beyond the thought, the thought wrecks the mind. And everything disappears in the black abyss. Also the black hole. Zero volume. Singularity. Where must it go to? Can "something" be entirely destroyed? Or is it at the same time there again, completely differently the same, as quasar? "Something" must die to exist. . . . The brain, the encephalos, the mind (which is a vibration of perceptions) is a black pool circumscribed by a happening-horizon, an eternity-skyline. You travel, you travel: always you remain the same nothing and never do you return to the original. . . . In this way exactly were you transpersed by the cold. Everywhere about you the layers and crusts of salt, each surface has its edge. As if there had been an ocean which drew back, evaporated, perhaps only became invisible, and deposited this salt all over. But the salt keeps growing, it is crystallized from the wind and the fuming light, crackling, and with the cold rim and rhyme of root-fire it covers everything. The town, that Christmas night, was deserted. Most of the houses were shells only, ruins whistling at the wind. Or otherwise they were uncompleted. It was a luminous night. Although there was no sun and therefore no etched or ironed-out shadows, one could see very clearly and very far. Most definitely the waving fog-clouds brought the light along, and the ugly diamond-fire in the salt crystals. In a side street you came across the parked open-roofed little sports model belonging to Am and Starlet, grey and stain-fiery under its incrustation of salt. You understood that they must be somewhere in town and you took off your rucksack and put it on the back seat of the car. Perhaps you can persuade them to take you with them, away from this region of death, you thought as you continued walking. It was nearly midnight. The wind continued ringing like a soundless bell. Several street blocks along you came across them: Am dressed in an impeccable white tuxedo, of a white which complements his teeth; Starlet had little patches of salt in her hair. They invited you to their home and there was, to the best of your knowledge, not another living soul in town (and not even any dead souls). No, no sweat, it was *selbstverständlich* that you could ride along. With pleasure. It's just that the house had to be put in order before leaving. With Starlet you started washing the floors. In some spots the water flowed several inches deep over the floorboards. You each had a handful of stalks, charcoal sticks, and these you rubbed and rubbed over the floor. The sticks were fragile and the floors extensive – it was a never-ending task. You remember the black finger in the white palm of your hand. Starlet's evening gown was soaked from hem to knees. Then the telephone scattered the silence. It was an urgent call from Johnny-sburg: Am was suddenly recalled, there was some important business which couldn't wait, or he had been elected to play wing in a very important rugby game, or some such event. And then? Ichabod?

Think, think. Because then you found yourself outside the township on the beach. When it was night still you knew of the black depths which cannot be plumbed above the light-sphere of fog-banks, salt-layers, grey streets and decrepit structures. Beyond the settlement it is day however, the darkness becoming light but remaining as far and as deep as ever, and everything just as grey. You are with Ganesh, he with his bleached blue jeans and towel over the shoulder. The beach is all pebble: grey and wet and round. You considered the thought that weird animals may, with the rhythm of the dead moon, have crawled from the sea – fools conditioned by their own procreative instincts – to stupidly come and lay these millions of stillborn stone-eggs. You can hear the sea lapping and flowing against the pebbles – these are only a few metres away but with the pale haze on water and land you cannot see it. You walk along the coastline. After some time you meet on the beach an Indian family who come strolling from the opposite direction. Not a complete family though, just a young girl and her two small brothers. The girl has a small figure and is very white in the face. Her hair is straight and black and her arms and legs covered with little black hairs. Ganesh (with his deep dark voice) and the girl tie a twittering conversation and start walking ahead of the others. She has swinging from the one hand an imitation leather handbag. The two little Hindus stay behind with you. It seems that they are wearing their best going-out outfits: dark blazers and shorts, shirts and black ties. With huge dark eyes they look at you. Their eyes are like oily tie knots. Some little distance further you arrive at a name board, fixed with stones around the base, standing practically in the water. On the board big letters, black originally, but now weathered to grey, probably indicate the name of this place: PASS PORT. (*Spergebiet.*) Grey trails of fog are adrift all over and there is an intense luminosity, a glistening faintness refracted from stone and mistiness and water surface. The light stabs at your eyes and you now regret that your sunglasses remained in your rucksack, perhaps even in another country's hotel's hotel room's bedside cabinet's second drawer from the bottom. At this place there are all around you, in the sea itself, the ruins of houses. From the beach dykes of stones were built, paths leading to the houses; there are also little ponds or dams, maybe used by earlier inhabitants of long ago as vivaria for fish. All grey now, and probably since long fallen into disuse. You and the two little Indians wish to go swimming and you wade into the grey water – which immediately becomes deep. The coast is treacherous. Therefore you decide not to risk it any farther from the side and you shout warnings at the two boys. With quite a lot of difficulty you scramble over the rolling and shifting stones up the bank again. Even though there is no direct sunshine you are rapidly dry. Your body is rough from the salt and it itches terribly. When you lay your hands on the shoulders of the two boys – they entered the water just like that, fully clothed – you feel the rustle under your fingertips of the salty film now causing white blotches on the dark material. They are all fidgety in their clothes. You wish to take their minds off their bodily discomfort and because they are inquisitive also you decide to try reaching one of the houses all along the ridge of a stone dyke. But close up you notice turtles and iguanas in the ooze of the pools, and still others lying motionless in the silver flickering on the banks. Finally you find a path of stacked stones which is not occupied and you walk out to a dwelling fallen in disrepair, about twenty-five yards from the edge, with the two black-eyed brothers hard on your heels. . . .

You opened that white-painted front door and entered a room where, so it seemed, thousands upon thousands of moths were fluttering; as living, caressing, abstract, hairy snowflakes were the wingbeats against your face and bare hands. You advance the hands before, pale as faces, and immediately they are covered by countless little wings. How the hands are shuddering! A light bulb was burning in the room and there were pieces of furniture which didn't look mouldy at all although the floor was at least heel-deep under water. You couldn't detect any switch for the lamp. The moths did not in the least attempt escaping through the open door. When your eyes became used to the gloom, you started deciphering with much effort the inscriptions and bits of writing and graffiti on the walls. Most were German words. In Gothic script. There was, *inter alia*, the fable, reduced to a minimum of words, of the man who had a green parrot chained to him, of how he had intercourse with the parrot, of how it is the bird's ambition to one day hijack an aeroplane. . . . After a while you closed the door of the ruined house behind you and walked back to the beach, away from the room of prayers. Down the beach you saw Ganesh and the girl returning, all along the nibbling of the water. Despite the fact that they weren't touching one another you surmised instinctively that, in the short period they were absent together, a "relationship" had sprung up between them. When they came nearer to where you waited – her sari was draped in an enticing way and stuck to the body to emphasize the meagre curves – she looked at Ganesh with roguish eyes and then – so fast and so small and so intimate was the movement that you had to put your memory to it in order to see it – she wrote a little line over his thigh with one red thumbnail. Then you did understand it all? And now.

Departure

(Rome. He will force his way through the throng in the *palazzo*. His expensive suit of clothes of a natty but sober cut will fit well around the body. The collar and the cuffs of his silvery shirt. The tie hand-knitted. The bronze colour of healthy skin over cheekbones and forehead, and guileless but defiant below the nose the line of a moustache a fragrant thread-worm. In an inner chamber, first there are delicately veined marble pillars defining a sort of atrium and thick bright-coloured hand-woven carpets from Persia over the glossy floor – hunting scenes, timorous love, swans, trees with sun and pomegranates and other birds – journalists will be grouped around a table with a pitch-black wooden top reflecting the light like satin, waiting for him: famous columnists, to start with two from *Le Monde*, *Corriere della Sera*, bourgeois with well-kept pink carcasses, black frockcoats, striped diplomatic trousers, glasses with cautious eyes, bald pates flashing and grey *coiffures*, gold pens, porcelain smiles. He will take his place in a chair with a high carved back at the head of the conference table, distinguished, grey wings above the temples; manicured fingertips a steeple under the chin. "Signore e signori, Messieurs," – his eyes on the dignified but respectful faces around the table, the whole gamut of noses from flat A to F sharp – "comme vous le savez. . . ." Make it known, in fact, yes, that it is his intention to go to Nomansland not only as observer, but to throw in his lot with the guerrilla movement. The people are calling. Injustices crying to high heaven. That it concerns, precisely, messieurs, signore e signori, the age-old contradiction between dreams and action. (A modest little cough.) And can this be overcome? reconciled? mutually complementary? The finer fibres of morality, a clear knowing, investigating, searching. *La condition humaine.* That man carries within him the godliness of neighbourly love. Not in salons and ivory towers will revolutions be made. Purification in the struggle. Self-sacrifice. Freedom! *Liberté!*) One pale hand will be clutched in a fist. Fierce fire in the pupils before the lashes are lowered. Pens scratching over notebook pages. Floop-floop the pages will be turned but polite eyes will not be withdrawn from his facial features. *"Voilà! And therefore must I go!"* There will be some further questions – the economic dimension, the articulation of internal unrest with the tension of international relations, Africa, strategic shifts in the balance of forces, in the light of, cultural survival, and don't you think that? Also at the last moment. But already with a slight bow, gallantly self-controlled but just a touch sardonic, he will be taking leave. A young man, paunchy, with red cheeks and dark hair, will insist keenly. Will then offer to accompany him to the passenger terminus of the airport. Just a few more questions, please. The *grands reporteurs* will object, will try to warn him about the young man. One of the fashionable gentlemen will climb on the table, flap his coat-tails with both hands. Others will be making the movements of puppets, root through the grey hair-do's, crack the eyeglasses, froth on the lips and blubber-sounds of the mouths. He will however withdraw with a smile. With the young man's Volvo will they drive to a tavern on the square opposite the terminus. They will order two dark beers, in thick fluted glasses. The young man will start babbling excitedly. He will be wearing a black leather jacket and his dark hair will be oily, a thick railway-quiff. Seen in close-up his eyeballs will be tainted with a network of red capillaries. His mouth will be weak, with contusions on the lips. If you'd consider contributing to one of our publications, since you will be there anyway. *Streich* or *Streichholz* or some such name the rag will be called. And with a paranoid smile he will make a clean breast of it, that he is in fact an unrepentant Nazi, such is life, no? – partially proud, half-ashamed. Then the young man (young?) will confirm his statement by showing two badges pinned to the reverse of his leather jacket's lapels – the SS-snakes. And in dismay and consternation he will leave the young man there, the wet circles of the beer glasses on the table-top, and rush to the terminus building across the square. It will be a gigantic construction of domes and glass walls held together by steel rafters – a green house for tropical plants of enormous dimensions. The building will be filled with sounds, the murmuring of the many, the clacking of escalators, the echo of loudspeakers, and there will be a fiery wind. Doves freed high under the canopy. In vain will he try, despite the confusion, to reach the right counter. Then he will notice the guards – or are they spies? – centrally positioned at all the nerve-centres of the complex, the smooth jackets with slight bulges under the armpits where the pistols are tucked away, the smooth hair looking like wigs, the smooth faces like rubber toys, the dark glasses as those of blind beggars worn, in fact, to sharpen the vision, the heads smoothly and incessantly swivelling on the necks from left to right and back again to cover the entire view, the hands with the little hairs on the fingers – like well-trained dogs. And he will catch a fright and hurry-scurry be looking for a way out. Outside on the esplanade he will consciously have to refrain from starting to run, so as not to draw attention to his back. There will be a stickiness between collar and neck, and under his arms. He will pick a street leading to a darker, more desolate part of the city. Snow will start falling, in flurries first but then in a steadier way, not stopping, white, small flutters of flesh. His shoes will be soggy and his trouser legs wet from turn-up to knee. He will feel his hands becoming blue, and the shivers down the back and over the thighs, because he won't be wearing an undershirt. The streets will become ever narrower and more empty. But in a small open space, at a crossing, the vague attempt at a garden, now whitely obliterated, a sentence of grass and two or three benches where aged city dwellers can come sit on warmer evenings to breathe through the mouth, he will see a statue. Encircled by a low row of wrought-iron staves. On a cement stand a knight lies on his back, in full dress, the helmet and the armour rusted green. Next to the knight a lion will be resting stretched out on the belly, white snow-dandruff in the brown-yellow fur, with one hefty front paw on top of the knight's tarnished left wrist. The verdigris. The amber-tinted eyes of the lion and the fangs with the colour of snow. The knight's lack-lustre head will be lifted slightly in a futile straining to get up again. In the hollow between helmet and cement already a hand-heap of snow like an inadequate head pillow. On the footpiece all kinds of Latinish words will be chiselled, words like REQUIESCAT and QUAM and UNUM and ET IN ARCADIA EGO and ARS AMANDI and more in the same vein. Until he makes out that it is the monument to a crusader, fallen in action, a certain Helmut Zeller, or was it Zieler? And when he becomes aware of the snowflakes in his hair, the silver droplets being ropes of cold, and cold against the cheeks, and the clamminess soaked through the cloth of the jacket and the wrinkled shirt, the shoulders wet and chilly, then he will walk further. In a poverty-stricken quarter he will enter the vestibule of a dilapidated block of flats, climb up the flight of stairs. There is scarcely any light and outside it is as dark as a hand before the eyes, like a tight run of doves all about the sun. The stairwell will be so full of stale odours, old shoes, potato peels, cabbage leaves, rats' droppings. And unclaimed things underfoot, slippery, pulpy. On the last floor at the end of a corridor with brown walls he will unlock a door, awkward the frozen key between silly fingers, and by the very last lick of light filtering through the *vasistas* he will see lying on the bed by the wall, lying on its side on the bed, bloated and bleached with a naked skin, lying on the bed with the swollen face turned to the doorway, he himself. And over his own corpse, caressing and teeming, already in mouth and nostrils and earholes and in the filmy white eyes, uncountable ants. And how the light captures the waving of the shifting black mass of ants. One blue movement without any sound!)

And Then

It is all really very simple, for it is as it is.
D.E.

When it was still the modern epoch Nefesj decided, with a vague and nearly rancorous feeling of disaffection, to make a god for himself; through all the preceding centuries his predecessors had always favoured some or other deity; sometimes passed the latter on from one generation to the next with instructions and rites and restrictions, sometimes traded it in for a replacement, a fiercer conception, and it was worshipped or at least looked upon as supernatural or paranatural or all-natural – powerful in any event; because there were peaks of culmination and more superficial periods in the intensity of subjugation, also by turns the conceptualization as war god, irenic god, destiny, transmitted aphorism, philosophical axiom, metaphysical jump, or such. But now his historically conditioned immediate ancestors, and so of course he too, had already since quite some time gone without, and started feeling the lack, like a lost soul, it was a lacuna. Somewhere there had to be a principle after all. One should have something above and apart from Nefesj. Senseless sentence.

So he started consulting musty writings as well as diverse manuals and, allowing himself to be guided by a need becoming ever clearer, gradually set out gathering the components of which the necessity for a god would be one. From the nature of the search it had to become a *thing* like any idea taking on shape, but with characteristics ascribed to it which would suspend its essential thing-ness. Another prerequisite of form was that it had to be Nefesj-like: it's a matter of counterpart and short circuit and comprehension. The god had to commence at Nefesj's edge of understanding and contact: a language. Not that it had to *do* anything. First just to be. From being comes doing. Of itself, in due time. (As opposed to man where action precedes being.) And the more incomprehensible the doing, the more powerful it would be. You must incorporate the inexplicability functionally with the idea, in fact you have to create that which you don't understand – otherwise there's neither fun nor development and ultimately no power or exorcism. But the modern epoch was generously endowed with the necessary views to achieve the desired result – much was fabricated and thought out without one being able to foresee the termination, and all the sciences were shot through with emergent references to infinitude, x, unfixed premises, gaps, break-off points, non-elucidated compounds, aimless groping, and the indefinable or unfixable was an integrated formula. Around the not-know the know was illuminated. Without the not-knows there could be no small-know. Simultaneously the techniques were perfected to infinity: a silicon chip could contain a total recall system, computers pointed out their errors to the designers and reprogrammed them, theirs was the procreation of memory, energy sparked off energy without the intervention of mass, there were closed circuits more minute than minus which no instrument could identify or measure and yet with a macro-effect, there were hosts of angels on the needle point. For instance, there were objects which would simply emit beep-beep-beep signals unto eternity.

Nefesj made the god for himself on the absolutely patternless pattern of his mind and put the thing in a room of his house and started adoring it, that is to say – he went to sit in its presence and groped within himself for contact with it. Then time passed and Nefesj started feeling uncomfortable. Some small element, he felt, was missing in the communication. Where the gap should have been there was a hole. It was also as if his god – quite passive there on his-her pedestal, it's true – was sucking from him the words and the thoughts living off the words. He saw clearly that it must be a dimension or a step in the dimension of the relationship between them. He was not sure either that his god didn't have other adherents (after all, he-she talked with the language of mutism) and Nefesj was a jealous creator. He felt the need for an interpreter. And he went forth and let it be known that there existed a vacancy for such an expert.

Then time passed. With the passing of time a man made contact with Nefesj and introduced himself as Brother Galgenvogel. And he claimed that he, Brother Galgenvogel, was indeed a sort of mechanic or technician of religion, a calling which many may look upon as archaic but it is surprising how often his services were still (or again) called for in these modern times. Well, there you have it. He allowed Nefesj to look over the paraphernalia of his craft – charters pertaining to the ritual, regulations and orders, long capes and cowls, pulpit cloths, broad-brimmed hats, cords, collars, candlesticks, incense, little bells, rectories and Cadillacs, and also a manuscript which could render or retrieve the Word and its family – and explained that the utilization of accessories would be defined by the acolyte's individual needs depending on the fee the latter would be willing to fork out. Nefesj didn't appreciate the fact that without a by-your-leave he found himself downgraded within the space of a single paragraph from the position of creator to that of adherent, but he decided that Galgenvogel certainly should know what he is talking about (the first principle being that you must resign yourself to the reference field of the explainer if you want to see the inexplicable explained in the embodiment of an explanation) and thus he did not quibble.

The first principle, Brother Galgenvogel declaimed, is that your god should have a name which nobody must know about for she-he ought not to have a name. The god's name is EN he then alleged, but you who are Nefesj as disciple may not know or mention this. We shall name her-him EN, he furthermore proposed, because then we do not call her-him a god and thus the fact of her-his god-being can be hidden. And if you don't know that she-he is a god you cannot speak ill of her-him. You confirm her-his godliness by calling her-him EN because in so doing you bear witness to the fact that she-he has a secret name which you may not pronounce or take in the mouth. And I, I who am Brother Galgenvogel, Galgenvogel says, I shall be the go-between betwixt thee and EN. Address yourself to me and ask for mediation. I am the mediator.

Then time passed. After a while Galgenvogel proclaimed that the first principle is that I shall reveal to thee through an oracle that you may not enter in the presence of EN, for you may not look upon her-his face. Nefesj said well there's a fine fuck-up for you then because it *has* no face, since actually it is only the inface of . . . of . . . a . . . of EN. But seeing that you now reveal this to me through an oracle I shall accept it because I pay you for it and if I pay you it's because you know what you're talking about in such a way that I don't know what you're talking of. (Isn't it ultimately the first principle?) It's an ill bird that fouls its own nest. And Nefesj withdrew from EN but Galgenvogel called out and warned him to look out as EN had withdrawn himself from Nefesj.

With the passing of time it seemed to Nefesj that he had become unfaithful to EN. What is the use, he enquired, if I am not allowed in the presence of him-her whom I have created and that I therefore forget his-her face and that he-she thus becomes unknowable to me? Because the primal attribute of EN (we may not name the name) is her-his unknowableness, Galgenvogel said. (And isn't it exactly what you wanted? he slyly whispered from behind his hand.) But since you, Nefesj, are weak, and vain and presumptuous (I beg of you: "him-he whom *I* have created!" Hah!), you will once again be allowed into the sanctum; yes, you must have a place where you can isolate yourself and experience the presence of EN, but EN will not be there since the glory is not intended for your eyes and if EN is not there it means that she-he is all over. Trust me; I know what I'm doing; I swear to you by the beard of the eunuch. It's not I (Brother Galgenvogel) saying so but EN speaking *through* me. (Well well now, thinks Nefesj, it's starting to make sense: if he-she is talking with the tongues of Galgenvogel I'm not paying for nothing after all.) And thou shalt be meek, Galgenvogel also admonished. Thou shalt lay down thy will and accept hers-his. It is the first principle. He thereupon admitted Nefesj to the enclosure where the creation had originally been kept and let him perform all manner of actions and there was nothing in the room.

Then time came and went and Nefesj started remembering ever less about EN, of what EN had originally been like or even whether he-she had ever been at all and *what* was he-she before he-she became EN? Or wasn't there ever a beginning? (Because Nefesj had forgotten the beginning and started believing that the beginning had forgotten him: indeed – do I do *it* or does it do an *I*.) Galgenvogel had him convinced that, if he wanted to see a return on his investment, he had to understand that EN had made him (Nefesj) after his likeness;

only, Galgenvogel said, there should be no talk of investment and value – it's commercial. Thus Galgenvogel made for Nefesj an image of EN which he could hang on the wall of the sanctuary lest he forget. And is this what EN looks like? the confused Nefesj asked himself. It is certainly not the way I remember him-her. But how can I remember if I have forgotten? And if I didn't forget why would it be necessary for me to remember? For I do remember that I'd forgotten, yes, precisely that I had forgotten to remember. Still, that reproduction there looks so . . . sick! It is so because it is impossible to create an image of what cannot be imagined, Galgenvogel pointed out. If a true image could be made it would not have been something of which an image could not be made and then it would not have been EN. The first principle, says Galgenvogel, is that EN has no face and that she-he lives *inside* you. Only in this fashion can you hope ever to become EN. And it is the unshakeable desire of creator and creature to be *one*. Doing doing dung.

Then time passed and Galgenvogel came towards Nefesj and said unto him, EN is dead, passed away. What's that? What are you telling me now? the dumb-founded Nefesj wanted to know. What have you done with him-her? Not I, but you, was Galgenvogel's rejoinder. *You* permitted her-him to die for she-he has passed away in *you* after a prolonged sad-sickness. If only she-he had lived in you and had not been turned into just a name without rhyme or reason, she-he would never have gone dead. Now I'm exactly where I was, Nefesj thought, except that in the meantime I must have been elsewhere and now I'm not where I was because something I did not know I had has gone waste in me and there-fore without my realizing it.

And after some time Galgenvogel again approached Nefesj and said, listen, I'm a disenchanted thinker. I have a function in society (and you as society have the duty and the privilege to keep me): namely that it is my task to expose society's myths to public contempt and to demonstrate that they are but figments of your imagination. Take as an example the god idea. It is said that it is dead. Now, if it's dead it could never have existed because that would have been contradictory to the god idea. Similarly to the no-god idea. What you carry around inside you is a dead idea and a dead idea is no idea. Nor could you ever have ideated a god, for the being of divinity is precisely that it is the avatar which ideates *you*. The first principle is that there should be a mystery but it is only in relation to your consciousness that a mystery may exist and make sense. If you cannot think a god it signifies that there is no god which could have thought you and then you would not exist. But seeing that you do exist it may just be that there is indeed a god which conceptualized you. Even that you then passed away in the god and now no longer exist. You see, I'm a creative sceptic and it may therefore just happen that I end up thinking differently about the matter. Or the question. But I now know you could not have ideated a god which is capable of ideating you. It's logical, not so? See here, I also exposed everything clearly in this book *The First Principle* and you may have it at a discount seventy pence only.

Thereafter time passed and without remembering a thing Nefesj went strolling along the river, hands clasped behind the back, in the vicinity of the station over the empty land where the annual carnival and buttocks bazaar take place. There were many distractions and all manner of booths where modern beep-beep contrivances could be admired and others where sausage sandwiches also were for sale. And there was to be seen amongst others a big striped tent with a huge poster proclaiming that one Prof. Galgenvogel daily at such-and-such a time allows to be seen ALL THE MIRACULOUS FABRICATIONS OF

THE ANCIENT WORLD CONCRETIZED admission fee very reasonable. And since it was the time Nefesj bought a ticket and entered the tent and saw a man there with on a table before him vestments, robes, gowns, mitres, strings of beads, incensories, icons, fetishes, prayer wheels, books and all sorts of exotic tools and bric-à-brac. The man was reciting a historical review of the cycle of creation (or "where does the idea of commencement originate from and whence does it proceed if indeed it did originate") and exhibited under glass behind him there were wondrous things indexed on cards identified in Hebrew and Mandarin and Sanskrit and Lap-language and Kitchendutch. One wonderful thing's name (or title? description? serial number?) was EN.

Forefinger

A little knowledge is dangerous;
and how exhilarating to live dangerously!
D.E.

Flashes of light and, prevalent, zones of darkness. A veritable book of darkness, the paler flip of pages being turned. He related of how they had crossed the border into C—— in the dark. (All the while as it were weaving among the words, weaverbirds, experiencing the obstacles, becoming enmeshed, woven into the fabric of sound and its cessation, limitations which are possibilities, hesitantly; lighting up the road to see the darkness.) They must have gone over the line illegally. At the least surreptitiously. On the other side of the barbed wire they stumbled by many people lying in the dark fully clothed in vestments which were as fluttering patches or wads of undarkness. Some of these old ones, he continued, were squatting by the footpath along which they had had to walk. He thought that they must be either drunk or very melancholy. True, some were only gurgling or expectorating. But many were humming. It sounded like humming. Crooning the sad songs in Spanish; more correctly Argentinian – he heard the word "Argentine" caught in the refrain. Soft wind from the nearby marshes rustled the clothes of the bearded old drunkards and their equally ancient female companions. Undigested flowers. Bone-bags spread on the mushy soil, in voluminous skirts and pantaloons. Also the colour of vomit.

The bird had grown accustomed to its cage; outside that captivity it was wing-blind – a state of freedom – its flesh sprung and useless. Thus his hand strangely vulnerable and bald as it perched above the board. Before it came down to coax one of the men into a position of defence or attack, temporarily questioning. As if every move were a murmured *j'adoube*. He was playing white. The forehead was white too.

They had walked on through the night until they came to a hotel. Nearby the hotel there must have been a beach with the constant lap-lapping of water too heavy with the weight of the moon by night and the glare of the sun by day to be still active. And in the several buildings constituting the hotel, he remembered, there was quite a mumbo of mirrors in the halls and down the corridors. He kept on preening, glancing at his vitreous self as he passed by them. Then it would take some time before the images faded from the surfaces. Something to do with the afterglow of fires on the retina. Wet ashes. He was wearing dark glasses and already his eyesight had grown weak. He noticed but always only in the glass, the reflection of an old man with completely white hair and similarly wearing black spectacles. He could see that this old man obviously disapproved of his narcissism, establishing a silence. Yet his behaviour was not self-loving – oh, he was quite vehement about that – but merely the total surprise at meeting his own or supposed likeness again in the light dressed up in a suit now clean-shaven except for the shades. He couldn't be sure that the old fellow was his aged *alter ego*, a *Doppelgänger* preserved in the quicksilver of time. And so he vigorously shook his head denying himself whenever he noticed the old one's reflection at his back. One has to pretend. One has to construct. One has to proceed. (Or complete.) One has to create an image of distance. At default what may pass for objectivity.

He and the woman shared a spacious room with another elderly lady. Quite spry this old lady was. There was the reminiscence of something enticing about her movements: perhaps, he reflected, she had been a voluptuary in her youth. The flesh, of course, tends to sag later on. She had white teeth, or a smile anyway. It was difficult imagining her in the act of osculation. The lips were spread as wide as a purse opened. Maybe the hairy enclosures were too shrivelled to cover the porcelain dentures. The aged female often had a big handbag standing open on the shiny floor. He couldn't withhold himself – he mentioned this rather ruefully – he couldn't refrain from scrabbling around in that handbag when the owner was absent in the shithouse. There were some chopped-up lengths of bamboo in there, short and useless, and many purplish beads. He considered that these constituted the elements of a primitive bead curtain such as one could see forever clacking in poorer houses. Like trying to capture the essence of wind. He also came upon a name tag during one of his secret searches. The old lady was called "Holy Spirit". He said that was what he had read engraved upon the tag. Actually Santa Something or Other which when translated meant "Holy Spirit". The grinning sparrow.

What the room was like? He looked up from the board and away through the barred windows giving on to the day outside. The sky was of the palest bird-breast, flecked with clouds which would absorb the night shortly. Of a similar blue as his eyes, bulging slightly from the sockets, screening the light, and obviously very poor. The pale face growing into the forehead where the light lies.

And the freckles on his hands a kind of concentrated shivering. No, there was little enough to remark upon in the room. It was situated some distance away from the principal complex of buildings. The outside he seemed to remember was decorated down the façade with stucco scrolls and curls. Inside? He turned his wide eyes away from the patches of fading sky framed in the bars, stared down at the squares of the board, some of them occupied and others vibrating, a skein of tension and the many small decisions leading to a further involvement, fumbling. Where does it all lead to? The inside of the room was empty. There was the handbag naturally. Certainly also some scrawled graffiti pertaining to moths. And, it came to him, mirrors in ormolu frames. Also as the swathes of gleaming darkness. Enclaves really.

They had spent the first day flopped very still on the beach. Like seals beached and skinned. A little distance away his old man also reclined on the sand, just fixing him with dark lenses very open and staring and strong. The thing was really to try and trap more than the words only; also the decomposing spaces around them, and their relationships: for words are the husks of dead hindrances. His body was white then and the old man's body was white and flabby in the same way. They had forgotten all about time. The shadows sailing through the sky. He had wanted to ensconce himself in the sand, completed in whiteness. Gulls flipped around the seam of expended wavelets. Eventually, he recounted, the owner of the hotel, a bustling lady of a vulpine appearance – but her hairstyle was too vulgar – had walked down to the beach in her apron and berated them for keeping the personnel in the kitchen waiting. She had used words like "tarde" and "tonto" and "también" upon them. So they had returned and showered until their bodies were tinted a deeper shade of white and then they had walked over to the main building housing the dining room.

There were, he said, trees with preposterously large green leaves making a crackling sound. And the keening of many sad voices singing their sad songs drifted out of the windows in the dusk. It had been a glorious day (with its splotches of darkness) and now it was red and fading. The head waiter with his gules-coloured waistcoat had received them at the door. They entered, he continued, over a polished floor. But inside they were immediately surrounded by a pack of mangy dogs, furiously snarling and barking, so that they were unable to reach their table or even to see the faces of the many diners peering at them through the gloom. All that they noticed in the room filled with shrill noises were the light areas, the clothes of those sitting at the tables. Moths perhaps. Or ashes. Or fingers.

"Naked like a Turkish saint." Desperately mouthing an orison. Putting out the words not sure whether they will please, could bring relief. Like so many votive offerings to the voracious god of silence. A moanologue. Experiencing structure, exploring gaps, fingering strictures, strange wounds, finding the illusion of relationships, fumbling. Slip-finger. Outside the day was constantly falling (with consistency). Pink, and then the first sick mauve. Later even a moon will be fashioned from the ornamental clouds, distilling their brightness. Sucking. The quiver of pain around the mouth.

Yes, he said that at the outset he had been a greenhorn, inexperienced. Technique, as it were, still raw. And the whole set-up was bedevilled by the absolute darkness. He had, he stated, of course pulled his wire many a time before. Beating the meat briskly when it had become unavoidable. To relieve the tension and absorb the illusion. To hover for a brief instant, the duration of a spasm, over the lips of communication. As near as he could come to the Other. Which was the Self. Obscurely. Not much of a lover really. When he had met her and after having exposed himself, that is, after having built up the teetering idea that she might accept or incept him, he had confessed his ignorance of the usages of that proboscis, admitting to the skin of insensitivity preventing him from penetrating knowledge (ignorance is insensitivity at heart) and she had volunteered to put him wise. She was as a sister to him. She knew – had soaked up from previous experience – the knack of stretching the haunches.

But, he repeated, she was adamant that he should not come inside her and laid out to him why this was not to be. Obviously he promised not to. Isn't the woman the all-wise teacher, initiator and priestess of eternity? And fumbled. She was skitterish. Rejected him with a vigorous kick of the hind legs. Eyes like moons. Moans.

Again and again the hand fluttering imperceptibly hung above the pieces. The flank of his attack had been turned, a bishop (*le fou*) sacrificed to no avail. White was in a predicament. The hand had to choose while the forehead caught the light through the barred windows. Stuttering. And becoming enmeshed, woven into the dislocation of parry and thrust and probe, of commitment finally.

So he had promised her that he would obtain some means of prevention. From a medical friend, an old man with white hair and smoked lenses, he managed to procure a contraceptive jelly. Something, apparently a spermicide, which would kill the seeds. Rather like an insect extermination. She, he said, had claimed to know all about the product and the method. And he had remembered about a farm in the North where they could enjoy the desired romantic isolation. It had been his grandfather's, used for growing tobacco, but now it was run by his nephew. His grandfather had died, buried in the mirror. His grandfather had penetrated the soil. Was rotting (in) the dark earth. He recalled the fine tobacco the old man was fond of making for his own consumption: carving up the odd leaves, sprinkling the little curls with rum essence before exposing them in glass jars for three days to the sun.

They had driven to the farm. The nephew wasn't at home. The main building – the master's house – was closed up, but the barn they found unlocked. They went in there. It was utterly dark and she didn't wish him to open any door, afraid that their intimacy might be observed. The empty barn had been used for the storing of tobacco – the enormous crackling leaves becoming wrinkled and veined with controlled decomposition. There was a fine layer of tobacco dust over the floor. He kneeled before her thinking about how his trousers were getting soiled, and she hitched her skirts above the hips. He was to insert the jelly using an instrument somewhat like a small pump with a nozzle. He couldn't quite describe it. Didn't know how to manipulate it. The knees were getting tired. Above all he was afraid of hurting her by introducing the spout too deeply. And didn't dare strike a match for fear of embarrassing them both. Hesitated thus. Fumbled. A bird in the dark having to decide its movements.

Eventually, he said, he felt that the right amount had been injected. Since it was so uncomfortable – unhygienic – consummating the act in the barn, he talked her into rather going down to the dam with him. She was reluctant to be taken outside, had very sensitive buttocks. The soft wind from the nearby marshes was rustling their clothes. The water itself was dead and weighted down. But when they came around the wall by the soft and furry grass they just about stumbled over a black labourer and his companion, naked and glowing, doing that which they themselves had in mind naturally. They would end up lying very still, he thought. He thought he knew.

Night had fallen like a hood. He then noticed, he recounted, lights going on in the central building, the one housing the dining room and kitchen and bedroom. His nephew must have returned from wherever he'd gone to. He led the woman to the house through the darkness. The dogs, he said, the dogs were snarling most viciously around their legs. In the house he asked his nephew for the use of the bedroom. To fuck the lady, he explained. They undressed by the bed in the big dark room. Her handbag on the floor. A vortex of emotions when finally unclothing. Her dress of muslin slightly lighter in the dusk. Discarded wings and sprung muscles. Flashes of light and, prevalent, areas of darkness. An orifice. As if he'd taken narceine. And the smell of vomit. Also her eyes turned up white.

"And then?"

It was, he said, a muddy matter of the vulva. Or valves perhaps.

"I couldn't stay in her. Kept on flip-flopping out. She was too slippery. It was a sticky situation. I had used far too much of the stuff you see. There was no way. The wetness."

(The sadness of his white finger with its stains of smoked tobacco. The sustained shiver. But it was too late: the queen had already been removed and now he was mated. The combination of black knight and black rook was fatal. There was no way out.)

The Redemption of the Image

Once is perversion, twice philosophy.

It rains as if a gigantic watch, a fat onion, had long been clogged, at last burst open, and now may release all its ticks abundantly. Shall we go further? If we have waterboots and raincapes yes. My grandfather carries an onion-shaped watch on a chain in his waistcoat pocket. The watch, just like an onion, has many shells, peels. With his knotted old man's hands dated with brown liver-spots he opens the lids, one after another unto the last one of glass. The glass you mustn't open up otherwise time will run delirious. Quicksilver. Under the glass the flywheels pivot, the cogs circle, the hands comb, the mechanism quirks with the movement of water. My grandfather's watch must be leaking. He doesn't even notice it. His pocket is growing heavier causing his back to bend. "I do wonder what time it is," he says, fumbling his ancient fingers all down the chain. But the hands have become too slippery. When the load becomes unbearable he snaps and he is dead. Tch-tch-tch go the tongues of the family. Some say he died from water on the heart. Others maintain he must have had a poisoned onion. Or simply that his time had come. It is the breaking of the water. His time was done. It became too much. He passed away like showering rain and now there are no more clouds. I peer through the glass caps of his eyes. The frequencies are fixed, the indication of time-passage isolated and breathlessly caught on the bridge between one second and the next. Already gone from the one but never arrived at the non-one. We enclose him in a box, the one lid on the other. Hammer in the nails rhythmically. Fill the box with ticks. We shake the coffin but the guts refuse to get going again. We carry him to earth. Shall we go further? If we have raincapes and waterboots indeed. It is the planting season. There are tears in the eyes of the family as if they'd been peeling onions. Above the huge dark clouds, each with an internal movement, an accumulation – like watches without circumference. I look for an heirloom. What became of the old pocket watch? I return to the hole in the earth, put in the spade: the trough is filled with water. Time has devoured the very mechanism. Wheels and shafts lie under the water like disbanded bones. There must have been cellular decadence, the blue-print is destroyed and now there is licentious procreation, a frenetic vanishing. Dissipation. Onions will do well along here, the earth is nice and sandy. A pity it is so wet. I go looking for an onion. Tie it on a string to my waistcoat pocket because I have no confidence in links. When I hold it to the ear I can hear the ticks. The raven will build a nest of sticks. It is darkly working up for rain. Shall we go further? On the roof the rain comes down tic-tac-toc. Fat, onion-coloured little watches are shattered. Time flows away in water. It's raining like homeless precise delimitations searching for the secure restraint of a timepiece, a grave.

This Little Flea

My acquaintance, Monsieur Keuner, had this little flea. A wonderful little chap not much bigger than a pittance with curly hair and chubby cheeks. To look at you would say just straw and stray, but so full of life and laughter. I got to know them from drinking my first cup of black coffee every morning in the same bistro they stopped at for their *café crème* and *pain beurré* on their way to school. Yes, I envied Monsieur Keuner his flea. And so I cultivated their friendship, hailed them with a bouncing bonjour, laughed with their laughing, nodded with their unimportant projects for the future of the day. Until Monsieur Keuner allowed me occasionally to accompany them part of the way, even to carry and fondle the flea. One day, a Saturday just before school, I invited them to come and see where I live. My flat was on the top floor of an old town house only a few numbers down the same street from the bistro on the corner. One entered through the big porte-cochère giving on to the roughly paved inner courtyard with at the other end the broad staircase leading up to the *étages*. I took them through the green-dark courtyard and at the foot of the stairs I held up the flea in my hand to explain how one climbed and climbed until one reached my front door. Yes, I was tracing all of this with the hope that the flea now laughing in my hand would perhaps remember to come visit me, who knows, all on his own. At that moment the door of the first-floor apartment opened with a black noise and Madame Gasolini appeared on the landing. Ah, the bitch! Always was one, in barren heat, quarrelling, snarling, sniping and snooping. She screamed a stream of words to the effect that she would certainly not allow any flea to enter this building, and many other imprecations. I wanted to stand my ground, should have, felt like telling her to go and have a crap in her best infertile bloomers. But didn't. Madame Gasolini is an imposing woman with very thick lungs. I found myself back with Monsieur Keuner at the street entrance to the building and to my sudden horror realized that I must inadvertently have dropped the flea among the paving stones. I bent over here and stooped there and all to no avail. I even felt with my fingers along the crack until all at once a hairy red spider crawled out and bit me in the index. Monsieur Keuner had two silent thin eyes. The wonderful little flea was lost and just another flea by now. And yet one knew that it was piteously crying out for succour somewhere near at hand. If only one could see as far as one's nose!

Book, a Mirror

Bientôt nous plongerons dans les froides ténèbres . . .
BAUDELAIRE

"During this period the evenings become purple. This phenomenon should probably be ascribed to the fluctuation of seasons – change summed up in a combination of factors: the days longer and ever warmer so that more unused light is left over at the fall of evening; even when day has already died the evening initially has more light and is, apparently, reluctant to confound itself with the pillared portals of darkness; evenings thus have more of a glimmer and the transitions aren't abrupt or clogged; the heat of the elapsed day causes a partial evaporation more visible above the horizons and the resulting condensation becomes a prism and acts as a refractor of the death-flame's longer rays; simultaneously the earth is more powdery day by day and languishing dust clouds, as if the planet were a coach on the dusty road of space, contribute to the manifestation of staining; and the plant life and harvests, both cultivated and indigenous, have just about attained the fullness of their growth, leaves and blades are swollen with sap and the green which will fade a lighter shade as the buds burst forth and the small fruits become fruit, develop flesh and cheek and eyebrow and form around the thought-kernel of the stone, are as yet blue with greenness. All of this taken together and being gathered in a larger totality creates the effect of evenings having for a brief transitional period – between day's sharply outlined depths and night's approach, but also between one season and the next – a purple cape being dragged lightly over the ridges of the amphitheatre. 'Cape' and 'light' – words bringing to mind a bullfight, the 'at five o'clock in the afternoon', the moment of truth during the *faena*, the final *quites* with the sword cloth, the *muleta* which is already impregnated with blood and the rosy froth around the nostrils of the bull being driven back, plod-hoofed now in the *querencia* which no longer offers any protection against the sword-bright piercing of death, the eyes also of a light red colour but already glassy and less mobile, and the matador on his toes, with love and respect and arrogance, he is going to do it from the front in a *recibir*, he takes aim down the silver beam; it brings to mind the dark roaring of the crowd, the handkerchiefs like so many butterflies when darkness descends. But this is no treatise on bullfighting. Hemingway proclaimed: 'The author should tell us only of that part of the external world which the consciousness of the hero perceives in the moment the two coincide.' A symbiosis: the mutually beneficial internal relationship between two organisms of different nature. It is all very well, even though the danger exists that this statement, narrowly interpreted, may lead to a blinkered vision. Isn't the consciousness of the outside world, the non-I, often exactly the explosion point of a boundless stream of associations breaking free in the I? Isn't Lowry's consul closer to reality than Hemingway's Robert Jordan? And the true nature of the observer, that consciousness, cannot be circumscribed by the human mind since that mind knows only of objects: that which I name

'I' is in no sense I. With the best comprehension in the world the self remains merely a little bundle consisting of five tendencies, five skandhas or branches – form, emotions, observing faculties, characteristics and spiritual powers or discrimination, also the idea of the self among others. (There must be a new tearing: the hole-in-the-belly experience of such-ness, *tathatā*, which is the void, *sunyata*, empty of all imaginable things or ideas.) Besides, Hemingway is cheating. It is true that we are being made aware at a given moment, through lean and tense descriptions, of the interpenetrating and mutually complementary protagonist and surroundings, but we become especially attentive to that which is not expressed. And who is the observer? Is the mood in which we are placed or transposed by the description –better still, by the way of describing – experienced by the hero as well? Isn't one of Hemingway's 'manly' attributes really that we are seldom offered a glimpse of the hero's way of consciousness or even his perceptions? Unless the telling is unfolding from the point of view of the first person of course, one can say a personal I. Unfolding like the cape before the nose of the snorting bull. . . . Or should it be argued that Hemingway, in his non-first-person stories, succeeds in creating a certain symbiosis between the invisible narrator (the absent I on the spot) and the indicated third person or hero? Are we therefore served the writer and the writer's writing writhing in the awareness of the penned-down character? Are we led by a ring through the nose? 'You can make an ox of the bull but he still remains a beast. . . .' But this here is not an attempt at polemics, nor an analysis nor even an approach to Papa Hemingway's theories. It is only: a tentative description of the moth chamber which Angelo and his wife, Giovanna Cenami, so much wanted to see. (Concerning the moth chamber more extensively later on.) At the same time the viewing of the moth chamber will give them the chance to spend a few days with Gregor

Samsa and Elefteria. Angelo had already developed guilt feelings concerning the companion of his youth. It is true that he had promised repeatedly to go there on a visit. . . True too that Angelo, pressed by his wide-ranging activities as a writer, only very seldom could find the time-space for going away a few days. And that he shrank from the idea of a trip to the highlands. The heights in more ways than one. But after the telephone conversation with Elefteria of last week a plan will just have to be made. No excuse will let him off the hook concerning his responsibilities to Gregor Samsa. For, according to Elefteria, it is not at all going well with her husband. His work, the demands made upon him – all these, it would seem, are grinding him down. Would it not be possible, Elefteria asked, for Angelo and wife to come spend a day or more with them. . . ."

When he reached this far in his writing he laid down the pen, pushed the note-book away. He removes his thick spectacles and rubs his eyes with the knuckles of his thumbs. He is tired, worn out. Night has long since fallen outside and the wind is playing hide-and-seek with the trees, laughing softly like a servant girl furtively with her lover in the darkened garden. In a moment she will sigh a few times and start biting the air with the small of her back and the lower part of her body thumping and sucking the soft seed bed by the humid hedge. He squints at his watch, brings his wrist right up to the eyes, for without the eyeglasses his vision is weak and blurred and it is only from close up that he can focus. It's true that he feels morally obliged to go and visit Gregor Samsa – old bonds of friendship probably impose it – and half sullenly he remembers that it has been agreed that he and Giovanna Cenami should leave the following day. There is of course the temptation of the strange room. . . . The house also, except for the pool of light over his desk-top, is shrouded in darkness. Just the mirrors glow vaguely as if reflecting something which somewhere gave off some light. He will just have to accommodate himself to the thought of pushing aside his work programme for a few days.

Differential, disc brakes, distributor and contact points, carburettor, gearbox, acceleration pump, de-aerator checked. The glareproof windows defogged. Luggage in the dustfree boot. Fitted into the casing of metal alloys and chromium. Rocking softly on plastic-foam cushions. By the afternoon of the next day Angelo and Giovanna Cenami were on their way. According to Angelo's calculation they should reach their destination towards the hour of dusk. Along the route, climbing and turning, the vegetation gradually became denser; rushing past the car it was often a solid green wall. The trees which exceptionally engage the eye are also stockier of trunk, taller and with leafier crests than those of several hours ago in the lower valleys. After a while it started raining. Like silver wires stretching through the forests on either side, like telephone lines full of dripping sounds, like soft spectacles, like balls which are just contents without any shape against the motor car's windscreen. And when the showers faded away from time to time, the remaining spattering of droplets reminded one of insects, of the inner life of insects. But the reader should keep in mind that this is not a landscape, only words, like a landscape. Angelo remembered again that house which they had bought many years ago somewhere in this area. He was absent, taking part in some seminar, and Giovanna Cenami had to take care of the house-moving all by herself. When he went there for the first time it was on a rainy afternoon much like this one now. The house was situated on a little rise deeper in the forest and quite some way from the tarred road. When he arrived that first evening after several kilometres of sludge, his shiny automobile was splashed with mud. He was upset. The house was still a mess, cardboard boxes and the crates which had contained their furniture scattered all over. Still, when he climbed the steps of the high terrace – somewhat disgusted by the caterpillars of mud clinging to his soles – he was surprised to see how shiny the floors of the corridor and the living room were. There was a sombre glow in the house. Straight-backed leather chairs were grouped provisionally, without any pattern, and there were elegant, long-stemmed candlesticks; so many candlesticks and so many mirrors. Light, which had moved into the house from somewhere, rested with an intimate sparkle on the ribbed silver of the chandeliers and the looking-surfaces of the mirrors. As if the building were full of unworldly but fashionable guests. Do we possess only mirrors and candlesticks? he asked, playfully worried, and his lovely wife came with a tinkle of laughter to be embraced by the reach of his arms. They were young then, carefree, a bow and arrow pointed at life. Later on they sold the house. . . . And the bowstring. . . .

And when they approach the yellow-brick building rain has already died away. As he had foreseen the sun too had started falling behind the horizon, cloudless now and very distant, for they found themselves on the most elevated knoll of the multiple series of hills. In extremely fine fishing nets the raindrops were spun over the dark green lawns, with flowers a startling red and orange caught in the nets. On the terrace of the Director's wing Elefteria waited for them. Heaven a magnificent ink blot, all the tinges of purple and violet, spreading fast to suck up everything. In the wash of twilight Elefteria's white, flowered dress was nearly luminous. Now there remained just a few sunbeams shooting over the ridge of blue shade, low and long and blinding like sword blades, and where they hit the earth with flat edges there was a sprinkling of drops, lilac-coloured and white. The swords were cutting the fishing nets to ribbons. With a travelling bag in the hand Angelo stood looking at the letters, in all the colours of the rainbow, splashed against the wall of the balcony jutting out above the main entrance: THE YELLOW SUBMARINE. A nice name, but is it really fitting for an institution which has such a sombre function? When he sees the iron bars in front of all the windows he tries to shake the shivers from his clothes.

Gregor Samsa was busy somewhere. He had to supervise personally (some responsibilities cannot be delegated) the evening lock-up of prisoners, and had to verify that all are counted, that the count tallies with the morning's total and with the numbers in the books – drudgery, Elefteria hinted. Only in the rooms of the Director's living quarters some last coals of sunlight still flared. And these rooms were incredibly stately with decoration and furniture testifying to wealth and impeccable taste. Thick wool carpets to hush the sound of footfalls. The dying sun shimmered and pulsated in dark wall-hangings, in countless candlesticks with slim silver arms, in rows of mirrors, each in its Venetian baroque frame of old blue and gold, at an angle over low tables massively carved from precious wood and decorated with motifs under chestnut-brown or amber-coloured glass tops, with here and there, discreet but opulent, the flash of an ashtray hewn from jade, an antique silver platter from Samarkand or Fez, Delft porcelain on a shelf or a Greek vase now flowing over with freshly cut snapdragons or bougainvillaea.

They had already lip-tastingly finished the first cocktails, a rusty red liquid since the sun finally withdrew from here too and left behind only a purple bruise, a cool afterburn, when Gregor Samsa turned up. He was glad to see them, so very glad; grasped Angelo's hands in his and squeezed them, but there was an evasive and bashful look in his yellowish eyes. Angelo felt that the hands were cold and clammy. Gregor Samsa sat bolt upright in one of the leather chairs and started talking excitedly, in one flow, about everything, in a disjointed way. At times he interrupted his own jumble of words and, with hands which unconsciously opened and closed over his knees, tilted his head to listen. In the background one could hear uninterruptedly the humming of hundreds of birdies' voices, a warbling and a chirruping. In one wall of the room there was a window reinforced with bars – an abomination in this exquisite space making the harmonious ensemble perverse, obscene. This aperture became ever more conspicuous. Once you've noticed it, it can no longer be ignored. Once you've become aware of the humming of voices, they keep on throbbing in your ears. With the delicate crystal glass still in his hand Angelo finally rose from his chair and sauntered over to the opening. Through the bars (there was no glass in the frame) he looked down upon a large hall lying quite a way lower than the floor of the sitting room towards which the voices rose. Along colourless tables row upon row of prisoners were thronged: the clothes shapeless and of a dull grey material, the heads shaven – he saw the yellowish scalps through the stubble of hair, often fresh scabs or the fainter lines of older injuries, knife wounds, tracks of the ringworm, skin diseases. And all the faces were turned upwards to the window where he stood watching. Some had eyes white with cataracts, sunken in sockets and closed tight, swollen or red from ophthalmia; some eyes were incisively mad, others expressionless as if blind lipoma. And the excretions, the warts and blotches, probably neurofibromatosis. All uttered sounds with pouted lips or with slack and dribbling mouths. The majority had red fists all knobbly and raw before them on the tables, but a few with bent backs clutched their hands (those hurting toys) between the knees or desperately pushed them under the armpits. What does it bring to mind? Bats? On the sidewalk before a pet shop in Paname he once saw an enormous hairy vampire hanging in a cage, a threadbare fox, upside down from nearly human little feet, naked and blinded by the fierce light of day and the screeching and the poisonous fumes of cars caught in the streets. Angelo started noticing the musty body odours filtering into the sophisticated living room, finally not to be evicted by the flower smells or the perfume emanating from the women's little hollows. Why doesn't anyone say something? Obscuring, all of it a glossing over. When he turns around with a sense of loathing his eyes meet the pleading, nearly doglike expression in those of Elefteria. And Gregor Samsa was no longer in his chair. Alone, totally alone, a thought said to him. Like a mirror.

Down the corridor he heard the high anxious voice of Gregor Samsa. There was a small space, long but narrow, rather like a waiting room, with a row of chairs down each wall. (Against one wall there was a painting on the theme of Napoleon leaving Moscow; snow already, and flames lapping at the city walls; the fat little fellow in the big, military grey coat. Facing it exactly there was a framed text; "About thirty years earlier four Frenchmen were eaten to celebrate the Fourteenth of July. They had organized a big fête for the natives to inspire them with a patriotic love for France, when, halfway through the festive proceedings, they were suddenly seized by their ungrateful hosts." Since his student days already Gregor Samsa was a francophile. . . .) He sat in one of the chairs, a rag doll, arms and hands limp over the arm rests, head thrown back. Over his face he had draped a handkerchief. It was as if he had surrendered himself completely to the senseless words which on a poignant note kept bubbling out of him, insatiably. Like a rhetorician having fudged all limitations and parameters. Angelo remained standing in the dark just inside the door with the icy feeling one has when a well-known face is abruptly unmasked, the features distorted and the facial planes undone into something horrible stalking the edges of your awareness, something which yawns and snarls – but he was nevertheless fascinated. Perhaps five minutes went by before there came a break in the monologue. Gregor Samsa pulls the handkerchief away from his face. His face is a filthy mouth, red and wet. Why do you stand there staring at me with an open mouth? he brutally asks Angelo. Haven't you ever seen evening prayers? But when Angelo doesn't react in the least he wipes the sweat from his face with the same handkerchief and continues in a resigned voice: Never mind, you need not be afraid or alarmed, it is all over for the time being – look, I'm absolutely normal.... Please believe me.... Let's go back to the salon.... Forgive me....

In the living room the two unhappy women sat waiting. During Angelo's absence, so they now inform him, a secretary, *deus ex machina*, called to say that he should return to the city, unexpectedly but urgently, for talks with his agent and publishers. Concerning a question which definitely cannot be solved by telephone. Elefteria who had so looked forward to Giovanna Cenami and Angelo's visit, probably with the fond hope that it may in some way be of succour to Gregor Samsa, was clearly upset at this reversal of her projects. With drooping shoulders and downcast eyes Gregor Samsa went to sit in the same chair as before. Apparently the news didn't concern him at all. Only Angelo was briefly and secretly relieved: thank the gods that I need not stay here now, that I have a justified excuse, and there are truly stacks of work and responsibilities.... Why should it be expected of *me* to help him – just because we were friends when young? People change, circumstances don't remain the same, Life unfolds, gets folded, wrinkled.... There is a separation, secretion and segregation sometimes. I do not know this man.... And at the same time he stood wondering in which trouser or jacket pocket Gregor Samsa tucked the handkerchief after using it. He could still see the darker stains caused by the pearling perspiration.

And he knew then that he couldn't leave Gregor Samsa in the lurch, couldn't wipe him off his conscience just like that, not now – and particularly not when thinking of Elefteria. Perhaps, he further reasoned, I can redeem my account-ability by suggesting that Gregor Samsa come with me for a little trip to the city. Should he, or they, say "no", then I'm free after having done my duty. Should he agree, well, it will be good for him to get away from here for a while. And if necessary Giovanna Cenami can remain to keep Elefteria company. Perhaps, he says, Gregor can come with me for a quick there-and-back to the city? At least I'll have a companion for the road and Giovanna Cenami could well stay here in the meantime so that you women may talk your little talks. Ha-ha-ha. Am I right? He turns to Elefteria.

It was decided, with a view to the urgency of his appointment, that he and Gregor Samsa would depart later that same evening so as to be on time the following day in the city. After supper he had a shower and started dressing. Gregor Samsa was ready, stood waiting in the living room, sharply dressed in an expensive summer suit of some light cloth, his damp old-wheat-coloured hair slicked back and his yellow eyes clean and peaceful. (Now that all the decisions have been taken from his hands.) When Giovanna Cenami had felt the quality of Gregor Samsa's tailored suit between the thumbs of her eyes, she convinced Angelo in the guestroom to don his best clothes too, of sayette, and to tie a hand-woven tie of black wool around his neck: a different, more sedate elegance, that of an influential author. It was as if the two women wanted to compete.

The night was tight and still except for the quick quivering of wind in the branches and coppices. Like pilot-lights on high masts were the stars in the blown-clear spaces of heaven, like the mirroring in a dark surface of the rain-eyes on leaves. When they leave the big building is a load of darkness behind them, but they could still perceive the murmuring of many voices beyond the walls – it was as if the whole prison were filled with fast-running water. The headlights of Angelo's Silver Phantom lit up a shallow plane before them, in dust-coloured powder the light-cones for an instant touched the scrubs on either side of the road – the pale plants without chlorophyll, shining – and when later it starts raining again the drops are moths breeding miraculously in the folds of the night, from *Saturniidae* to oleander hawk and *Lophostethus demolini* and *H. osiris* with the sheath like a blade and the death's-heads whose larvae live on the potato, he, *Acherontia atropos* (O river of Hades, O Fate!) who, when fully grown, with his yellow abdomen and stocky proboscis and skull emblem will rob the beehives and utter tiny screams there. . . . Night unfolded. Directly from the front. Gregor Samsa says nothing and his hands are quiet, all trembling gone.

With the climbing of the sun above the ridges they have long since left the wooded area behind them. Not a single cloud in the vicinity. A chain of purplish blue mountains blocked off the horizon in front. Towards nine o'clock they stopped at a filling station. Opposite the road was a motel extending to a café and a supermarket; a little further to the right of the blue asphalt road a town was spread over several hills and in the early morning light, also falling at an angle, the white houses glittered like bottle-shards, so much so that Angelo had to think that these houses were still uncompleted. At a distance beyond these white houses against the slight rise of a further hill with a strip of uninhabited land between the two developments (a no man's land), the first town's sister township commenced, a second half. The first building of this location – it looked like an entry gate or perhaps a tollhouse – was big and yellow but also as if snapped in two, all crumpled and with a hump in the centre: exactly as if it had been hit and summarized by an earthquake. Further back then are strung out the other little houses: small, crooked, poor, and of all the colours of the rainbow. It was very clearly the living area for Coloureds as opposed to the preceding area for Uncoloureds. A pump attendant with a big florid face wiped the last tracks of dust from the Silver Phantom's windscreen with his yellow rag and then planted himself with arms akimbo next to them. With the rag hand he pointed to the shimmering town. Worcester, he said.

Accompanied by the attendant they crossed the road to go and look for breakfast in the roadhouse. They mounted the few steps and pushed open the glass doors. Around smart little tables on high chromed legs several people sat drinking and smoking (although there were no cars parked in front of the motel), mostly farmers from the surrounding fields, with friendly blue-eyed faces and black coats. At the table nearest to the entrance sat a couple, both dressed in Chinese clothes, unaware of the slurping mouths and the looking eyes of the other customers, lost in a game of tiny sticks and cards. Their hands particularly attracted Angelo's attention: flabby, bleached fingers with red tips in which no graphic of mercy could be detected. When Angelo out of curiosity tried to follow the game from close up, the attendant pulled him by the sleeve over to one side and placed a warning finger to his mouth: they are playing "swallow", he explained. Cruel? He repeated the unworded question and winked at Gregor Samsa. Isn't it rather a case of love? And who can stop that? You certainly must know Molière's *La Princesse d'Elide*:

> *Soupirez librement pour un amant fidèle,*
> *Et bravez ceux qui voudraient vous blâmer*
> *Un coeur tendre est aimable, et le nom de cruelle*

N'est pas un nom à se faire estimer:
Dans le temps où l'on est belle,
Rien n'est si beau que d'aimer.

Literature, oh dear – and he shakes his head very primly. Keen apparently
to act as guide and let them see all the advantages of this motel complex, the
attendant invited them to follow him to a large area lying somewhat lower than
the café's floor. They found themselves in a self-service shop with counters and
shelves exhibiting all kinds of toys, condiments, bottles of wine, and especially
motor accessories: from dashpots to piston springs to valves and sparkplugs,
from filters to radios and lubricants. There is also a wheel-shaped bookcase
which can be pivoted. A clerk or salesman presents himself. He wears a neat
and expensive striped suit with a bow tie and a thick black moustache tied like
a supplementary tie under the nose. This is our Travelling Library, all the most
recently published books immediately available – the petrol attendant proudly
whispers in Angelo's ear whilst clutching at his sleeve with a hand rimmed with
black nails. Indeed, the newest editions are there and each volume has a mirror for a cover: one by one the books are pulled with a flash from the shelves by
the agent (or librarian perhaps) and given into Angel's hands with an expectant
smile and a twinkle in the eye above the moustache. There is something by Jorge
Luis Borges; there is a totally unknown long poem by Dostoevsky entitled "The
Kiss" and there is another one dealing with the tactical problems of Bonaparte's
retreat from Moscow; There is the *Popol Vuh*; there is Ludwig Prinn's *De Vermis
Mysteriis* and next to it Abdul Ahazreed's *Necronomicon*; there is *The First Principle*; there is D. Espejuelo's *On the Noble Art of Walking in No Man's Land*; there
is a treatise on the first French motor enthusiasts who traversed the Sahara

from the Algerian coast and far past Pépé de Foucauld's wind-covered grave in Tamanrasset to Timbuktu (that is, those enthusiasts who weren't stuffed into a cooking pot along the way); there is something about popes and something concerning space travel. He takes a thin volume and opens it. Starts reading. "During this period the evenings become purple. This phenomenon should probably be ascribed to the fluctuation of seasons – change summed up in a combination of factors: the days longer and ever warmer so that more unused light is left over at the fall of evening; even when day has already died. . . .

"But this is no treatise on bullfighting. . . ."

He turns the pages, reading a paragraph here and a sentence there. The excellent type page and the neat type font please him: it resembles a carefully penned handwriting.

"It is only: a tentative description of the moth chamber which Angelo and his wife, Giovanna Cenami, so much wanted to see. (Concerning the moth chamber more exte–"

". . . oozing water, salty, and not of the cleanest, of course constituted a major problem which the guardians didn't know how to solve. How water could so constantly penetrate the room, in fact the whole house, was in itself an enigmatic mystery which even the most acute research has not yet been able to elucidate. Although there's water over the surface and although the chairs stand several centimetres deep in water (but the upholstery remains dry) – the moths' appetites don't seem to be stimulated. The question thus arises: how do the moths procreate and what do they live from since the ceiling too is smooth and no one has ever observed them clinging to the walls. For certain these are not the same moths (of the *Sphingidae* family alone several kinds have been identified:

Leucophlebia afra with pink and orange wings, the ochre-coloured *Polyptychus contrarius*, *Sphinx funebris* – several varieties here of, such as *conimacula*, *peneus*, *maculosa* and *ovifera* – the *Atemnora westermanni*, and many more) it was argued at a given time. The answer to this was: (i) that there's no window or aperture through which new arrivals could enter; (ii) that nowhere in the rest of the house and in truth nowhere in the immediate environment have any other moths or even butterflies or dragonflies or wasps or meatflies or suchlike (lepidoptera of whatever nature, be it as eggs, caterpillar, pupa, chrysalis, cocoon or in the final stage as imago) ever been noticed; (iii) that the moths, whenever the door is opened to enter the dark room, have never attempted escaping; and (iv) that, according to the calculations of the supervisors – difficult to be sure, and not scientifically exact – an unchanging number of moths are present. One must make certain that all are counted, that the total tallies with that of the morning and the numbers entered in the book: a drudgery.

"Apart from the mysterious origin (or apparently mysterious, because although the phenomenon has not yet been explained the modern researchers never say die: let's rather state that comprehension is provisionally absent) it is not at all a weird or even a creepy experience to visit this room. Inside there is a gloom of a shade between violet and mimosa which, if one could believe one hypothesis, could be ascribed to the colours of the moths' wings. If this were the case these wings would have to be mirrors* (or like mirrors). In fact

*Note: In the Congo it is the custom among the Bakongo, the Badindo (or Babwende) the Basundi, Babembe and Bateke to make effigies of the ancestors which are kept in memory of the dead or sometimes buried with them; also rougher carved fetish figures intended as concentration points (lightning conductors as it were) for the spirit forces of evil and sickness. These fetishes often have cavities in the bellies– *sometimes covered by mirrors* –where magical things are deposited as "medicine". One of the most common kinds of fetish is covered with nails hammered home by the priest.

the wings (and at times the bodies too) are covered with microscopic scales, together with hair, and these scales are easily rubbed off like coloured dust: the colour of the wings is defined in this way, be it as pigment itself or through the intervention of light in a kind of erosion. Don't handle them: when dead they become extremely fragile. The space is filled with the ceaseless whispering of wingbeats and if the visitor has enough pluck to stop moving and extend his hands and face, he will feel the fluttering touch as leaves of a book full of wind when, let's say, he should one sunny afternoon under a tree touch sleep with his eyelids, like the grazing lip-kisses of a pair of lovers under the hedge. So incessant and unbroken is the muttering and so gratifying the fluttering that the visitor truly loses all sense and knowledge of his own suchness (*quiditas*), decomposes, becomes absorbed in – "

"Tuesday"

So that then, in a weird way – somewhere it was fixed beforehand, but not very clearly so, because reference points fade, memory and anticipation are telescoped, in space the stupefactive mind tumbles with its oceans and its continents and its ice-caps, hypnotically over pole and counter-pole – so that you then obscurely know in advance what is going to happen. The future is unyielding. The dog licks its own sour vomit. When you, dressed in grey just like your fellow failures, ungainly – the clothes fit loosely, too big, the white bodies reserved, reluctant to react to the signals of the will, cold, deadened – when you are permitted to assist at the races in the arena. Together with the supervisors. A forbidden privilege which must be kept secret. The old ruined arena in the hollow of a valley out of sight from the central complex of buildings. And where you may see then how the horses run around in circles, without riders. Or are you seeing bulls? Until they are utterly exhausted. Your friend, the one with the grey hair, the middle-aged one – it is believed that he was the successful manager of a factory in earlier times, long ago – your friend is also with the throng of competitors. You watch him hobbling along, ouch-ouch, desperate and disheartened because of his corns. You know he is encouraging the others to persevere, to fight the senseless battle, and that he himself has no chance at all ever to be the first to stagger across the finishing line. Before your very eyes he is transformed into a black bull with bobbing and ill-fitting shoulders, with swinging lobes of fat. The supervisors cheer with stupid red tongues, shouting raucously at their favourites. When the race is over your friend comes looking for comfort in the rotten paddock. He wants you to congratulate him. He wants you to pretend that he hasn't failed once again, as always. You must kiss him on the salty, sweaty head, between the ears. But it's not sufficient. You must also touch with your lips his slack pink mouth, slippery with phlegm and grume and tears. It nauseates you, but as a compassionate companion in distress you feel obliged to do so. And how the supervisors then celebrate the bets they have won or lost, how they pass the night playing cards in the small wooden structure. Where, if you sit quiet like an unuttered sound and if you don't commit the unforgivable sin of dozing off, no notice will be taken of you. Where you may be tolerated. Grey as the mouse. Don't let the light catch your eyes! And in the morning which is full of autumn you, you and your fellow patients, will be escorted back in a low trailer hooked behind the slow tractor, all along the winding gravel track, up the hill. Right to the central institution at the top where there will not yet be any sign of life. Now you must remain sitting very quietly among the others in your grey clothes. Not be conspicuous. So that the supervisor on the tractor, and the other one who sits in the wagon with his head nodding away the sleep, may forget all about you. Because the tractor continues past the buildings. Goes, creaking, through narrow alleys. Hedges on either side. Other enclosures, gardens, lawns. The green draughtboard. A faint drizzle and pools of mistiness in every fold and hollow of the high landscape of hills. Everything green. Wet right through. Heaven with its grey beard. A watered bleeding. There is light and there is sombreness but there is no sun. Neither reflection nor images nor shadows nor mirrors. Only this rolling land where it is high and chilly. Khepera does not know this kingdom. The earth is barren. The talisman, the dung beetle, is absent. Green and blue. And you with your dull carcass not knowing the differences between memories and projections or imagination. The grey outcrops of your indistinct condition. The nakedness of the mind. We are the rubbish of society, the initiated ones, the self-absorbing brotherhood. We are the zombies. Whence then suddenly these illegal and irrational expectations? Because rising and falling over the curves and the contours of the hills, along narrow paths entirely exposed, peeled, without destination, with wind present everywhere bitingly cold and humid, a wind which should not be there since we lack all directions of the wind – just unlimited space without panoramas – because rising and twisting the road is taking you to that which you remember, or try to conceive of, as the outer gate. Perhaps they will forget you. Perhaps they will unthinkingly pass through the last gate. And you will be *outside*. Where are you then? Far, very far off in the weak blue sky you see someone flying. You see that pale body dangling high, draped over a bar, a trapeze hanging from two kites as blue as blue flags, loftier still behind and in front of him. The flags tell the shivering breaths of the wind. Is it an Icarus? Could it be the son of Daedalus who built the labyrinth? Mew-Man? How sad it all is! This maze has no walls, no corridors or shafts, no cellars or ruins or caves or heartchambers or love. Grey and effaced. The labyrinth of star tracks. The invisible stars. The white net which has dissolved in light, which no longer exists. And there is no sun to scorch the wings, no sea of foam and destruction in which to plunge. There is no feeling in the fingertips. The objective doesn't necessitate a journey. It is a trip without destination. Disconsolate and faint and immobile he hangs from heaven. And drawn against the skyline, on the hill's shoulder, the outer gate. It is a guard post. Small wooden structure. Stored darkness. But there is neither wall nor stockade nor fence that needs watching. Beyond the actual gate of entry – deserted and grey – the path has long since been overgrown and fallen into disuse. And the supervisor of the guard post will emerge even before your slow tractor with the trailer full of grey dopes reaches the dividing line, which cannot be observed, between in and outside. He will come forth and stare at you with a hand above his eyes, and the rifle will be heavy on his shoulder. And sheepishly he will indicate that you must turn back, return, go back to a slightly darker crease in the hill. Through the dew-wet grass he will follow, under the cap lined with fur against the cold his mouth will sag open slightly, and where he walks, where he deposits his traces, the grass blades are darker, snapped, lifeless. And in the slight dip in the bare hillside there will be more soldier-supervisors, with a vehicle parked nearby. In the car a radio will then be playing. A warrant-officer in charge of the supervisors here in this last, scarcely camouflaged ambush before the final gate, will get out of the car. He will not close the door of the vehicle. So that you too will then hear the radio, but there will be no news broadcast over the air, and no announcements will be made. For we are immobilized and forgotten in the coup d'état which is so much older than our most ancient history or fumbling in the past or in the future. Music will flow from the loudspeakers, grey, like heaven and its flier without dimension or reference. The commander will approach his men, there where your trailer with the grey span has been stopped, and you too in the bunch. So that he will then look at your lot in amazement whilst cranking the field telephone in an attempt to communicate with a central control point for further instructions, or to sound an alarm, or to report, or maybe just to hear if there's a respondent on the line. For, with the earpiece pressed to the head – he would have lifted the flap of his fur cap over the ear – and with his carbine on the other, heavier shoulder, also with the mouth hanging open a little and drooling slightly so that the lolling pale red tongue, like that of a bull, may be seen in its cavity, he will say: "And are *you* here too, Turd Breytenbach?" He will talk into the mouth-piece of the instrument but you will know that the contact has not yet been established – only, you won't be sure whether it could ever be done, whether it has ever functioned at all; you will not know whether he's only trying to impress you, or if it's just part of the ritualistic pattern. "But that's dangerous! Do you think then that we can allow *you* just like that, in a greyish way, to leave?" And he will sigh. He will say that it is an emergency situation after all. That he himself cannot make decisions of such portentous importance. Of the far-reaching implications. That it spells big trouble. That there must be a huge fly in the oint-ment somewhere. You will feel grey and deaf and deceased. Your body with its organs and senses and idiotic excretion. Clothes. It is not the gay coat which makes the gentleman. An insensitivity. A dulling. The officer's tongue will fall around limply and a darker liquid will be bothersome in the mouth. He will consult his men while listening to the field telephone for a connection with a deciding core somewhere. When they will ruefully nod their heads. "Not that I think you shouldn't be liberated," he will say. "That is if the decision were to be made by me." And also: "This I can assure you – the President himself often thinks about it. I have heard him, the President, saying on occasion: 'Look, the temptation is strong to just let him go, that is if the decision were to be made by me; I consider it every Tuesday.' I distinctly heard him say 'Tuesday'."

Then and thus you will know that it's Tuesday. As always.

Birds

There was the house of my old father on the outer edge of the town against the first gentle slope, among clusters of reeds trying to frighten away the birds with a pattering of leaves, and other trees with dark green foliage and equally green the splotches and grooves of shadows. Against the plain yellow walls of the upright house, very high veranda in front all along the length of the house, bench behind plants in tins on the stoep, my old father a bit seedy on the bench in the insipid autumn sun. Birds all over, a flock-a-flap of birds, a chirring and a chirping and a cheep-cheeping and a chattering and a chopping of bills and fluted tones; birds in the branches, in the dust baths of the plot of ground, on the roof ridge and the chimneypot, on stoep and windowsills – a constant up and down and fluttering of wings as if old blue bedcovers are ripped in fist-sized strips. Sometimes my father slowly walks home up the hill with on either side of him an attendant in uniform and then his head explodes with light. Just once a year the house is taken over by a league of veteran war criminals, do they stage their annual gathering there. Peep down the trapdoor into the cellar: there they sit around a table stacked high with quicklime bleached bones, the boniness of their skulls in the murky light, the protuberances above the eye-ridges and the lumpy skins over the necks, the purple hollows under the eyes. Do they sit there purling with light-flames in the sockets, caressing with emaciated bird-skeleton hands the musty thighbones and ribcages.

But when it is summer with clouds in procession like carnival floats shinily showering water and other days absolutely blue we are on C's farm among the ultimate hummocks here and lagoons edged with coarse grass and bulrushes there hard by the sea. Do we drive in C's jeep with the flaps against the rain over pasture and fallow land always back to the farmyard. C's head is greyish and bent with compassion for all life. His wife is called Elefteria. Elefteria wears big black farm shoes and she has wrinkles all around the mouth. She feeds the ducks and the Muscovy ducks, the turkeys and the peacocks and the geese and the bantams. She feeds also the sparrows[*] and the robins and the babblers and the shrikes and why not the starlings too. When you are on you best behaviour and ask most sweetly you may, exceptionally, be allowed into the parlour. Come into my parlour, said the flier to the spy. Walk softly-softly, don't make any unconsidered gestures, first stand as still as death. Paintings are hanging behind glass there on the walls. The one picture depicts birds. Now approach on your toes. Look intently, listen well: that painting is a window through which you may have a view of a room full of doves. And then the dove choir starts singing, so that your chest may be filled to the lump in your throat by the dark, poignant, queer song – an enchanting old French freedom anthem. It's Elefteria who trained the birds in this way. What unity! What a union! What a unit! Each dove is capable of one phoneme or sibilant only, but the ensemble is orchestrated to a swelling cantata. And blinded by tears you move along to the kitchen. Meisie, the older daughter, enters from outside with a bundle of wood

[*] "She has found a mare's nest and is laughing over the eggs." Gogol, *Dead Souls*.

and goes to squat against the wall. She is ash coloured, she is an alcoholic, but when you look more closely at her you will notice how attractive she still is and how nicely smooth her thighs for someone who spends the whole day on the land gathering fire sticks. Minnaar, that's the son of C and Elefteria, is a heretic somewhere far away, and a second daughter teaches in Robertson, but Meisie has never been further than the farm. She laughs modestly and more than just a little tipsy. Under her skirt she is naked. And now the doves in flight drag a sparking veil over the loft, and away! C stands on the whitewashed steps, his grey head smoking in the sun. In days of old[*] there were constantly adopted children in his house. Now only one is left (times have changed) – a leprous boy. He comes out, laughs, claps his dull hands with the rose-coloured weals, claps his hands with joy because now that it no longer rains he will be allowed to go for a short ride on one of the many shiny bicycles parked against the wall.

[*] "In the old days women did not smoke." Ibid.

Re: Certain Papers
Left in My Possession

To my Executors

Sirs,

Years ago it was my misfortune to be involved in a rather peculiar situation. A man whom I didn't know – and despite my best efforts I was unable to establish his identity then or since – died. He, however, had somehow left the impression that he knew me quite intimately. After his death – I don't now recall whether it was by his own hand or otherwise, but apparently it took place at a time when he no longer knew who he was, and in a weird place I may tell you – the authorities of the period contacted me in an effort to trace his family or inheritors. Despite the fact that I could be of no help, they subsequently forwarded to me some papers left by the deceased. Among these there was the (uncompleted?) document which I enclose herewith.

You will find scrawled over the top of the first page the rather cryptic message: "To Galgenvogel and Tuchverderber; make no bones about it." I assumed the pages therefore to be addressed to these two gentlemen – or ladies? a couple perhaps? a publishing firm? tailors? – but have never succeeded in reaching them. In later years, of course, the matter slipped my mind entirely. It is only now when I in my turn am about to break through the dark looking-glass – ah, the sweetness of obliteration! – now that I am trying to put some semblance of order in the leftovers of my own life, that I happened once more upon the yellowed fragment.

Could you be so kind as to attempt solving the riddle of its destination? Or else do with it whatever you think fit? Perhaps the best will be to make no bones about it.

Yours etc.,

D.E.

Proposal for a project: The Grave of the Unknown Poet

I propose digging – erecting? – creating – the grave of the Unknown Poet (UP) in Rotterdam. The proposal may also be interpreted as being for a monument or a tomb: personally I prefer a grave, it is still less ostentatious even if it were to be embellished. Naturally the idea is only a basic outline to be built upon or amended by anyone concerned.

The Motivation

Why a grave? The body of the poet is her or his poetry. The corpse of the poet is her or his poetry. The poem is the black skeleton of the poet. It can even be argued that every poem is a grave for the unknowable Poem. . . . The world over the grave is a symbol of man's transit on earth, the last deep footprint, a scratch made in a notebook; the grave – sign of our attachment to our "own" dust; the grave – indication of respect for the ancestors, where we mourn all that is mortal, where we meditate, where we bury and preserve a memory. . . . Often the grave-yard becomes a picnic place. The grave is property at last! but stripped of all sense of ownership: who belongs to what, what to whom? Womb, repository for the quintessence, the mouldering bones. On the one hand truly it's private though chaste – for, as Marvell said: "none I think do there embrace"; but on the other hand it is also a place of integration – the coming together of shadow and flesh. Centre of pilgrimage, of offerings. We go there to rededicate ourselves. We go there to look at the hole in the mirror. We go there for the inspiration which is whole because edged by the sense of time keeping a ticking watch in every cell-rhythm, rhyme, reason! . . . and sweet despair. We go there with flowers for him or for her who has fallen on the battlefield of the white page whilst safeguarding a prized territory or extending a frontier. And there we put our ears to feel the wind darkly blowing through us, rejoicing that there's still something – an I – to lend sound to the wind.

Why for a poet? We all know of examples in the world of the grave for the unknown soldier. Apart from perhaps wishing to piously respect the unknown, these graves speak to us of patriotism, or nationalism, even of praising the military virtues. Are they not also intended to increase the cohesiveness of a nation state? And are they not used sometimes to whitewash the past? The tombstones of history . . . For all soldiers are anonymous. (I'm not speaking of the generals: have you ever come across the grave of the unknown general or the unknown dictator?) Indeed, it is not the soldiers who build cenotaphs or monuments to the unknown number, but the politicians who ever survive indestructibly. At the other end of the scale, but it is really the same end, I've heard of a statue commemorating the anonymous political prisoner. He doesn't need that, and the least we can do for him is to give him the face he struggled for. (Is the anonymous torturer ever celebrated other than by the poisonous stone in his chest?) And Paul has written of a pedestal to the unknown and absent god. . . .

For us it is different. Poets aren't gods, neither are they absent. Poets aren't incarcerated or tortured for their poetry – at least not very often: the powers that be, have been, shall be, prefer to lobotomize their poetry, and it is a more refined form of torture. Poets aren't a nation. Poets aren't a class. Workers do it / students do it / the bourgeois do it / even kings and beggars may do it / so let's do it. . . . Let's talk tough! And yet we are everywhere taking our maggots for a walk. . . .

We are conceiving of a living grave for the poet, be he dead or alive or in limbo. Isn't death only an enjambment of the poetic line? Poets form no ideological group. We are made up of . . . the attempt to make – love poetry, hate poetry, mind poetry, finger poetry, poetry of resistance, poetry of commitment, poetry of the belly-crawl, empty poetry, poetry of poetry: we try to make that from which we're made. And sometimes a little more. Maybe the poet has something of the soldier, the political prisoner, the god – who knows, even the torturer? But he is a human with a drumskin perforated by sounds and sights and feelings. Leaking words. The poet is just a human without a skin. Isn't that why he needs so much paper? Let us make of the grave a sunken garden, a seed bed of . . . agitation for the unknown. That which links us all is exactly the unknown. We are all covered by that absence of skin.

Why for the "unknown" poet? Surely to be known or unknown is entirely relative? Is anyone ever completely unknown? And what is known? Inevitably this may well be so: we don't know of the unknown ones. . . . But beyond that, in every poet there is the poet unknown. And then, even the most known is for a time at least the unknown one. It may be during his body's lifetime and he may be uncovered after its death; more often the known become unknown and one after the demise. The grave is thus for the UP because that is (i) either what we are, (ii) or what we were, (iii) or what we unavoidably shall become, (iv) or finally what we ought to be. The beauty is that one can put in such a grave what one wants and take out what he expects: Sadness. Joy. Even if he only walks by to say:

(t)here
alas
lie
I.

It is moreover the UP who feeds the flames of poetry: in his unknownness and unknowingness he is pure. It will be a grave not merely for Homer and Pushkin and David and Eleitis, but also for Mandelstam and Camões and Lamourt Lasouris and Ivan Ivanovitch; not only for Victor Hugo but also for Villon and Don Espejuelo and Lautréamont and Brecht and Jean Dumond and Ukwezi and Hugo Victor; not just for Mao and Lorca but also for Tu Fu and Li Po and Jane Smith and Titloup and Oma Gumgum. . . . All the unknown from continent to continent. Yes, from our albocentricity nearly everything outside ourselves will be considered "unknown" – not so much from ignorance as a self-induced blindness: "taste" we have, one of the last bastions of colonialism. . . . The UP then is the incalculable and ever-renewing potential. *Alors*: Up the UP!

Why on earth Rotterdam?
Whereas there are a host of reasons for, the most potent one is probably: why not in Rotterdam? True, R'dam is *a* capital for poetry – one doesn't say *the*,

because nothing prevents the scooping out of perfumed graves elsewhere: they tend to multiply anyway: they have a propensity for self-multiplication. But R'dam is neutral (?) whilst being open and attentive to poets with their diseases – and one hopes, poetry – as the efforts of the Rotterdamse Kunststichting have shown. Already they've provided us with some rituals and rites: we came there from afar and also from Amsterdam, some as ambassadors and some as petitioners and some just as posturers or gypsies . . . to declaim our statements from the State of Poetry. To return home with instantly violated treaties and compromises: new poems. Indeed, the Poetry International is our annual Skin Market. . . . We are the halt and the lame come to wait for the angel to move the waters so that we may plunge in and be absolved, cured – cured of our *condition humaine*? Of course, most of us can't swim and there are crocodiles in the pool. . . . Never mind!

Who shall foresee the effect the good yeast of unknown poetry may have on the dour dough of the workbent city of Rotterdam? Imagine the raising in the pans!

Let us come to lay our credentials in the burning grave of the Unknown Poet.

The Project
The location. Will the heavens open? Will one be rewarded with a vision . . . ? Ideally one sees the sepulchre of the UP – anonymous, fictitious? – somewhere on the windblown polders like that of an Ovid . . . on the highest balcony of the tallest skyscraper in town . . . nested and open to the birds in a tree . . . as a foaming white tomb next to an atomic reactor of which it is the offspring and mirror image . . . built into the back wall of a night club. But that means putting a specific or exclusive face on our UP: and although we want to endow him with

a face we want that to reflect every unknown poet, all of us, Jan Alleman. Thus I believe it is best situated in some public enclosure or thoroughfare of R'dam – within the confines of De Doelen – on the Kruisplein – along the Lijnbaan – in such a way that it can become a rallying point easily accessible, a place of pilgrimage where resident and visiting poets may leave their ex-voto.

What should it look like? Let not the heavens decide. Solicit painters and sculptors for ideas. Why not in the form of a competition? There are alternatives. I saw a glass-domed structure (sunken or raised) underneath which all the unknown poems, like insects disposing of words, were exposed; I saw a commemorative statue at the feet of which wreaths were laid with every petal of every flower a poem; I saw an eternal flame periodically rekindled seriously but not solemnly, with decorum and with joy, in which poems can be burned or sublimated; I saw a headstone with some such inscription as:

> *Here lies a body*
> *Eaten by words;*
> *From such earth*
> *Springs poetry!*

And there were the Tibetan prayer flags beating the wind with every flutter of cloth a stanza.

Then I saw the dedication, the ceremony of being confined to Mother Earth in a gaily decorated open coffin, during a Poetry International Festival. Will that coffin, those relics, not be paraded every year on Poetry Day? The bier was filled with poems written specially for the occasion, with manuscripts and volumes of known and unknown writers – and these were periodically removed to be housed in a museum. A band was playing – surely it was the "Rote Fanfare"? And there, among the bearers of pall and slip, were the critics, the historians, the publishers, the recital artists. . . . Because it was a project with branches! During visits by poets from elsewhere and every year during the Poetry International the flame was rekindled. Imagine the funerary orations! Poets known and unknown were encouraged *to continue contributing to the body of the UP*. A periodical containing these verses, called *The Poet Unknown*, was published by the Rotterdamse Kunststichting. The editor was a poet with the illustrious title of Guardian of the Grave of the Unknown Poet, and she or he was a Dutch versifier, at times, for the editorship was held in rotation, relieved by a visiting foreign poet, a poor soul in transit, a temporary resident there perhaps on a scholarship, even invited there especially for that purpose. The poets participating were inducted into The Order of the Poetic Grave, or The Fraternity of Unknown Poets, or simply The Words of the Unknown, perhaps just The Unknown. Each member received a distinctive insignia, a button depicting (I couldn't see so clearly any more) an ardent flame . . . or an image of the statue. . . . And all . . .

And all died happily ever after.

The Hat Which Didn't Make It to Heaven

*A man suffering from premature ejaculation may
not care to be compared to a rapid hamburger eater.*

In the big city there's a small street. In the small street there's an old house. In the old house there are five storeys and a staircase. Three of the storeys are old and two are dated later – that is to say, the one new floor was a stable originally and the other once upon a time a loft. With time they were transformed. Each storey has several rooms large and small. On the fifth floor in a tiny room there's an old man with a flourishing moustache all frayed like a bootlace from too much soup and snuff. The old man flexes his knees as they are becoming very stiff, and worries his moustache from side to side. Then he dons his trousers the way one would mount a horse. Before the mirror on the wall he combs his teeth before plopping them into his mouth. Thereupon he knots his cravat and puts on his waistcoat and inserts two fingers in the waistcoat pocket. In the waistcoat pocket, on a chain, he has a flattish round metal box in which he saves all his remaining time. The little docket has a glass lid so that he may check whether that time is still alive. If he doesn't consume it all, he believes, he won't be able to die. That's why it must be kept alive, because dead time can poison you time and time again. Only then does the old man place the bowler on his pate and exits to stamp down a creakiness in the staircase. The old man goes down the stairwell from the fifth *étage* to the fourth creak-creak-creak ten times creak, and from the fourth to the third creak-creak-creak another ten. Before the door on the third landing he stops. First he removes the bowler from his bald head and places it on the floor by the door. Then he takes his handkerchief from the pocket of his trousers and wipes his hands and replaces the handkerchief and clasps the one hand with the other. He stoops forward slightly, bends his knees a little, props his hands on his thighs in the trouser legs and puts an eye to the keyhole of the door on the third landing. Through the keyhole the old man looks into a room filled with blue light. On the floor of the room there's a carpet. On the carpet a sideboard and a bed. On the sideboard are placed three glass bowls. The first is filled with feathers, the second with nails, the third is full of dust. On the bed lies a woman. The woman is dead. There is lipstick on her lips and also a few flies searching for the sweet breath. The woman's dress is bunched up to just above the hips. Heap hop hip her. Her legs are thick and grey with purple stains. Between the legs, high, there's a wee beard. The old man looks through the keyhole. The old man hems and haws and shifts his dull eye away from the keyhole so that he may put his mouth there. When the old man whispers his whiskers tremble like the shiny laces of a shoe full of corns. Huffapuff, the old man whispers; huffapuff huffapuff. Madam Mafarsikos, it's me again. It is I, Madam Mafarsikos. Huffapuff, Madam. What shall I do? Look, I have a name and a conscience and a soul and a mind and a spirit and a ba and a ka all birds of very different feathers. What shall I do with the parts? Huffapuff, Madam Mafarsikos. And what about the pitter-patter and footfalls and raindrops and the ear socket on the chain from my heart in the waistcoat pocket? So whispers the old man and then he takes away his mouth from the key hole to replace it with an eye to look and see if there be any perceptible reaction. But the old man is very old and most stiff and quite slow and awkward since a long time already. However thin he may pleat the lips around the words and even though he uses a how's-that hand to back up his eye against the light by the keyhole – he is always just too late to observe any results. When his knees start to ache he dries his hands on the handkerchief again, replaces the bowler hat on his naked pate, and treads creak-creak-creak further along the pilgrimage of his ruminations. Every day he comes to wait and watch by the keyhole. Sometimes he also wipes the white keenness of his mouth on the handkerchief. He says huffapuff, Madam Mafarsikos. What must I do and what can I not retain? Anubis, Madam Mafarsikos. Anubis and Isis and Hathor and Min and Set and Amon-Re and Osiris and Khepri dung beetle. Aron and Horus, madam. Geb and Nut and Shu and Thoth and Ptah? Tueris and Ma-at and my loyal Bess. Oh, cemeteries of the hyenas. O devourer of shadows and plunderer of intestines and breaker of bones. Huffapuff, Madam Mafarsikos – huffapuff fuffanuff hemacough! Is the creaking ultimately in the stairs or in my shoe? But I am without blame. . . . The third day he saw that the little beard was growing. The sixth day he saw that the little beard had grown long. On the ninth day he realized that eye and tongue would not suffice, for how would he *hear* the answer? His whole strategy needed to be reconceived from scratch. By the fourteenth day he attempts to whisper through his yellow ear. Oboepoof, Dama Falukamorf. On the seventeenth day the beard is curlicuing over the carpet. The twenty-first day the bowls on the sideboard are swapped around. Comes the twenty-ninth day and the old man knows he is too slow. Searching for answers and observing cause delays: contact is impediment; growth is interception. By the thirty-fifth day the beard reaches the door, a small squadron of dark blood serpentining in the blue. Day thirty-six, the old man's knees are most reluctant and sore. On the thirty-seventh day he opens the door with extreme circumspection. He swallows the keyhole. He wipes the handkerchief on his hands. Down he goes on creaking knees and takes the wee beard in his fingers. Tough stuff, Madam Komafarsi. Lovingly with care he grips the beard and pushes aside his shoelace-shined soup-shined snuff-shined mouth-bemoaning moustache with a shivering sleeve. And the old man starts to climb climb climb climb. He feels the tick-tocket throbbing in the tin in his pocket.

But he forgets the bowler hat on the landing.

Leftovers

In those days many of the inhabitants had already deserted the city. Not a soul dared to be seen along the majestic boulevards which swept through the centre of town. The trees bordering these, accumulating dust, looked as if they had been left behind. Doors and windows were bolted. Balconies overlooking courtyards or street-corners were sightless and the rooms behind them empty too. It hadn't rained for a long time – the daily sky of an indecipherable metallic blue with the organization of stars present and understood though unseen, and at night the moon a soft myopic eye without eyelids – but slime and mud nevertheless oozed everywhere. Some said it must be a vast underground lake forcing itself to the surface through every shaft and cellar and foundation and grave. Others held the cause to be burst mains and cracked sewers. Sabotaged perhaps. It was a time of subterranean modifications. Every pipe jutting from the spongy earth was in reality a periscope, each faucet a listening device. Those who had stayed behind were either too foolhardy or idealistic to leave (and that amounted to the same), or else infirm, soft-minded, left in the lurch without transportation, poor, browbeaten, suicidal, stateless. Some were petty criminals misreading the signs.

Food was practically impossible to come by. In the mornings I sat in my cell scribbling my fibbles, the bits I could remember as if from a lost and aromatic night – about Enfesj and Tuchverderber and Fagotin and Prisoner Hawk and Gregorian Samosa and Savopopo and my wife, Sweetime. Into which night had she disappeared? Outside I could hear the rats rustling. One often saw them, streaked with mud, their unbuttoned eyes, the fangs shimmering. They were everywhere. They were also indestructible. And the range of sounds emitted – the hisses, squawks, sneers, puffs, grunts, screeches, threats! The city was devouring its own innards. The rats, I often imagined, were now usurping the roles of all other animals. Some even walked the dusty trees like birds. If one could only tame them, or cook them adequately. But the power had long since been cut. In fact, we were warned not to attempt using any electric appliances, and there was no timber dry enough for kindling. In the afternoons I took my grandfather to find something to eat, some sustenance, anything to survive on. He was very old and very weak and quite blind. But he'd insist on wearing his spectacles and walking – which meant being walked – as if he could still separate shapes and shades. By wearing glasses he thought people would surmise his eyes still functioned. I took him by the elbow and led him through the alleys of unfrequented sectors of the town. It wouldn't do to be observed anywhere along the dead arteries. We squelched through the mud, my grandfather clutching (pathetically) his sheaf of papers. For, as he used to joke bitterly, we are a line of compulsive scribblers. He wore a waistcoat and a shirt no longer very white, a tie oily with age. We trudged over sticky or slippery surfaces, passing by mouldy hedges, low vegetation already damp as if covered by the juice of the spurge, discoloured façades with cracks widening every day. Working our way secretly to the stadium of grey concrete. In more affluent days, days of pomp and pretence, it was known as the Sport Palace. Now it was merely a huge arena reeking of rot and urine and deceased athletes. But at least it still sported underground spaces resistant to the seeping liquids although greenish fungi splotched the walls. And here the stay-behinds could assemble without being seen. Here too some rations were still to be had. Not much. Doughy bread with a white beard. And grey chunks of horsemeat. The supplies, some averred, came to us (or were left to us) by the grace of the Withdrawn Authorities. And they abjured us not to criticize the set-up for reasons of communal security. Also: if you pretended not to see the food it just might not disappear.

In one respect this area was exceptional. Apart from the ubiquitous rats with their fulvous or blackish coats shiny with dew, there were also thousands of enormous white butterflies fluttering overhead, perching wherever they could with wings a-tremble, clean as unwritten and unthought thoughts. Their darting and hovering a series of sibilant letters.

Going down. Down we went into the cavernous interior. In the good old days some racists had squirted their slogans on the walls of the stairwell. BLACK IS BOUNTEOUS, and THE POPULATION EXPLOSION LIES HENCEFORTH IN THE LAP OF THE BLACKS. Or CAN A MAN TAKE FIRE IN HIS LAP AND NOT BURN HIS THE MUMMY? To which a wit had thoughtlessly added Jung's squib as footnote – FOR WOE OH WOE-EE THE PENIS IS A PHALLIC CYMBOL. But even these were flaking off, being obliterated by the insidious wetness, the caresses of passing butterflies. Our arrival was always raucously cheered and taunted by those already present. In a way those left behind were fond of my grandfather. Wasn't he believed to be the seer? Some were students, young-faced once, gaunt and emaciated now. They sat on the stained concrete steps with sheets of white paper in their hands and these they would fold and refold and then agitate rapidly so that it looked as if each held in the fist one of the big pale insects.

The chorus would continue while we waited for our part of the dwindling daily pittance. Chant: "Mister Meschanin Mister Meschanin" – as my ancestor

218

was called – "when will you let the Saints of Sin come in ah come in." Or again: "Master hey master Do open your heart! Pour to us please Your new work o' fart!" And often one of their number got up and recited, apropos of nothing I always considered: "I have been responsible for three murders – that of Wrench and Pitters and the African."

Gradually the hubbub would die down. My grandfather sitting there unperturbed. Hand him something to eat. We would be handed something to eat, to sustain ourselves with. (The inner man.) Was that not after all the reason for our being there? Grandfather picking at the carrion with bony fingers. And eventually when everything was queer except for the brush of the butterfly multitude's wings and the scurrying of bold rats – shiver-sound of disillusioned ex-students weaving their paper imitations, victims of star-vision – maybe the soundless shifting of water underfoot, inexorable – then my grandfather – and here I should certainly add that he had always abhorred the false-hearted with the prim lips camouflaging primed impurities, the oh- and the so-sayers, the Sunday-sainted scented scavengers – then my black grandfather would lift a manuscript page to the approximate level of his black lenses (which used to embarrass me as I knew his blindness as also his vanity) and declaim in a catacombic voice always the same lines – as if he were addressing the future – the now:

> *The circuses are empty;*
> *There are no more loins about*
> *And e'en the Christians are excreted. . . .*
>
> *I may have emptied my eyes,*
> *But my 'air will grow again*
> *Like chains.*

Know Thyself

There is a man who is very old. He is 46 years old. His hair is thinning and grey-ing above the ears. His nose is high and *shoorp* and the skin over his face is folded carefully. His body is thin in a stiff dark suit. He sits at a table on the first floor. This is where he dines. Light is spread over the table, illuminating the diverse objects on it. (A skein of light holding the disparate together; rubbing out the whatness with too much light.) The kitchen, or perhaps just a workshop, is on the *rez-de-chaussée*. That is where his beloved works. Or that is where his beloved is keeping watch for him. He also has an enemy on the ground floor. The enemy would be named Mr Dove or some such name of a like sound. The very old man decides to kill his enemy before he, the antagonist, has a chance to do him in. He snaps his knotty fingers for the waiter. The waiter appears in the circle of soundlessly reverberating light. The man dips a wrist in a shimmering bowl and extracts a bottle of wine therefrom. He dispatches the waiter downstairs, com-mitting to him the bottle of *vino*, instructing him in a breath-load of mumbled syllables to deliver this here (that there) to Mr 'Ove, with his perishing com-pliments. From the rich man's table. A clatter of plates from down below. The waiter nods, bows, nods, flashes his cuffs, disappears down the steps. Maybe he also smirks. The wine, of course, is poisoned – the move by which the very old man intends to eliminate his adversary. The very old man listens with his hands whorled on the white table. Indistinct utterances float up from below. Then a shrieking which seems to contort the very air as if life-leaving lungs are clutching at noughting. His beloved dies from the poisoned potion. Now, what happened? Did the enemy somehow forestall and thwart his plans? Did his love intercept the gift for some obscure and subtle purpose? Did she assume it was destined for her? Did the waiter misunderstand his message? Is the waiter deaf? Was the waiter not perhaps ordered by his love to bring everything to her first? To protect whom? Did *he* mispronounce, lapsing into metonymy? Did he say anything? Did he really intend? Treachery? Treachery?

The Collapse

... as if from a lost and aromatic night ...
L. LASARUS

In Paname we had the habit – Greg Somesome, Dan Espejuelo and Giovanna Cenami, K and his fiancée, Fagotini, Ganesh at times, Bricole le Tubard and myself – of gathering once a week at the house of Lamourt and his wife, Mooityd. It was no fixed rendezvous; it might have been on a Friday night and on other occasions again a Saturday afternoon or a Sunday when twilight comes shining. Each then brought a bottle of wine, pâté and a cut of cheese, or some or other exotic delicacy originating from a Greek island or the Far East – djalandji dolmas, almond cakes, currants – and Mooityd prepared her fine and nourishing and aromatic dishes. It is a time-slice I often think back on with much pleasure. Later, after Lamourt had practically vanished from the face of the earth and after some of us had become bridle-shy of any association with others (for association of whatever kind is by definition subversive), our little group also disbanded and we were scattered to the four winds of the mirror. In any event, we never formed a "salon" or anything along those lines. But in life, which already is not very long or cheerful, one should honour the good entr'actes as the ant would hide the haystalk in memory of summer, one should cherish them and lay them by as souvenirs the way earth-dwellers of earlier ages always walked with a fragrant fruit, a spice ball, a pomander in the hand – the orange full of cloves which allows it to shrink but prevents it from ever rotting and gives it a lovely odour: to parry the stench of primitive sanitation and decaying cadavers and pornographic manuscripts. Or the pot-pourri, a saucer of flower petals left on a table to ward off the pest-fumes and other plagues blown along by the warm winds from the south. But you must fully realize that this hiatus can only be of brief duration and you must not try and cling to it. You must especially know what I mean. That which is gratifying and civilized you should let run through your fingers just like the bad and the unpleasant. Bread for the fishes. Nothing can be retained. . . .

When it became autumn and winter, of an evening after the meal, we used to sit or recline on pouffes around the fireplace, our hands to the glasses of wine, cigars, coffee, prayer beads. Light from the flames danced over the warm colours of the living room which was entirely wood-panelled, and there were painted wooden shelves carrying Mooityd's knick-knacks and Lasouris's books. Lamourt sat sucking at a pipe in the big wicker chair and Mooityd positioned herself on the goatskin next to the chair, the head on her hands folded over his knees, the glow a darkness pooled in her eyes and her face framed by the long dark hair which had something, the secret something, of that which grows in the night. The night heavy with wind; it chased through the city's streets, tucked at the roof ridges, swept down the façades, grabbed the breath from the chimney-pots – but you couldn't see it: from inside the house the windows were dark mirrors. Sometimes the conversation would drag its silences from mouth to mouth – in fact it would be the mouthification of meagre sound-slips so that you sat listening rather to the smithereening of the flames and the wind than the poor pairing (and paring) of words. But sometimes it occurred that one of those present would half-shut his eyes so that they might glint like strips of silver foil, allow his fingers to fondle the stem of a glass, and then start uncovering. . . .

On one such late winter's evening D.E. recounted to us the following event. It was sharply cold – snow had fallen during the day on the Morainian Mountains and wind had carried the pale freshness of it into the city. We laid another log on the embers to see how sparks shy away from the heat, and all moved closer. (I do not believe in the existence of a soul – yet there comes a time when something inside you moves, moves. . . .)

And D.E. started:

So often one hears a reference to chance or to fate. I wonder. I often ask myself what reality is and if it isn't *everything*, you know, because we are inclined to consider reality with a capital R as a pole, part of a two-step wherein the Other is constituted by irreality. If everything – everything conceivable and inconceivable that ever happened and that can never take place – if it is all reality then it is equally true that it is unreal, or of both "conditions" simultaneously. It follows, not so? Then we can surely say – I'm not trying to put my speculations in a logical order – that all barriers have been lifted. We speak of chance and fate because we cling with constricted buttocks to the conception of time. We have made of time a measuring rod – and that because we experience time as consciousness instead of as a dimension or a thing for instance, or an atavistic instinct we have not yet been able to eliminate through breeding – as the *small awareness* of course, spinning like a moth around the stone of the self; it is a bodily consciousness and as flesh multiplies and ages and very quickly decays, consciousness clinging to that same body inevitably sees time as a passing instant – that is how psychocentric man is – sees it as a passage and a passing, a progression, and we refer to "earlier" and "later". But isn't the small consciousness just a dust mote in the air momentarily irradiated by light or a dance of little flames, "thinking" then that it itself contains and brings forth light? And when light falls elsewhere – does the dust stop existing? Just imagine it falling on a house knocked together of grey planks in another mourner's story? Or on the trembling calves of someone being strung up – where? Woe, woe the old worderer. . . . I believe we shall remain entangled in the riddle's knots until the temple's veil be torn asunder, until we are piloted beyond death-birth – called "life" – and further than *samsara*. I mean – until the tatters of illusion give way before us – the Hindus refer to it as *maya*. Just ask Ganesh, he has Indian friends. It is after all an ancient Vedantaic conception that everything is created out of ignorance, *avidya*, both the goods of the spirit and the body, and indeed by the double process of veiling or *avarana* of the reality, and thence constructing precisely on the basis of that veiling by means of projection, *vikshepa*. . . . This eternal illusion of which we are part and which we always weave further with our consciousness. Until the scales are peeled from our eyes and without beginning or end or limitations we enter the void, *sunyata*. And nothing contains everything. As the old gentleman sighed: "Life is a chasing after fuck all."

Do we live or are we lived? And if we are lived, can we then die? Aren't we just forgotten? But is anything ever forgotten completely? Perhaps it does escape memory *as it was at that time*, the way light caught it then; but somewhere it slid over into something else, did it induce another it, is it at the same time *result* and *cause*. And thus the it did not go lost. Everything continues vibrating and existing simultaneously. If I tell you then that the event which I'm going to depict is taking place now in the tilting of these words! Or that it happened long ago but that you were all present then – you, Greg, with your light hair and your gaiters there by the mirror; you, Mooityd, with your big smooth eye and your flowered dress; you K, with the smell of spoilt horsemeat on your trouser legs; you, Lasouris, with your dressings and your ointments and your armpits; and you, Breytenbach, with your fancy ways; and you, Signora Cenami, with the hot nether parts; and you, Minnaar, old grey one. But that you will only realize it now? And if one of you should write down my words – or rather that which my words became in *your* memory and consciousness, the moth wriggles free and leaves a little hole in the cloth – and carry them forward and transplant them into others which will consume the words and so forth – wouldn't you all have been present in that case? Was I then not, rather, am I *then* not *among* you? It is the ear-blinding of the worderer. The diffusion. And time – let's forget for the time being about convention and conscience – where do we fix it? Isn't it always actual? Those moments when all is said and done are present when I recount them, translate them, just as dot-dot to date as when they will be repeated years hence by one of you and so on et cetera.

Actually I want to describe two incidents for you and at first sight it may well seem that there is no relationship between the two. Yet, when you let your eye penetrate deeply enough, you will see the link somewhere. As you all know, I spent a long stretch in prison. You learn more about measuring there than may be good for your spiritual equilibrium. However it may be, much of that time passed me by. Our word agreements, as you will notice, constitute the structure for our way of seeing itself, so that I must speak of a *time* –like a thing or a dimension for instance – which moves, which is deployed; of an "earlier" and an "afterwards" and a "then". Never mind. I remember that the gaol building was a low, oblong hut. The hut was against the incline of a hillside. At the front, from the side facing downhill, it was two storeys high; at the back of the building the terrain was very steep – higher than the shutters of the second floor where I was kept. It was a small prison, nothing to get excited about. On the ground floor – which received light only from the front – a corridor with rows of cells on either side, but the cells were empty. When Sergeant Roog wanted to talk seriously, to see me eye to eye, he took me to one of the empty cages and then talked long and hissingly right into my face so that I could smell his moustache reeking of onion and egg. Why he found it necessary to take me there I'll never know, since the upper floor, which consisted of one long room, was also uninhabited except for Warder Softly-Softly and the already mentioned Roog (they had to stay with me at all times, day and night) and my wife, Meisie, who was allowed to share my time. We were in a small town on the ocean. The sun shone regularly and the skies above us were open unto infinity but a wind blew daily in large folds. And a haziness at the turning-points of the day, moving, moving. Here the wind blew so boisterously that you could hardly conceive of it blowing anywhere else also: this town with its surroundings must have been its habitat. Or its stoke-hole. From the second-floor windows one could see through gaps between the buildings the stormy sea tossing and turning – with white bonnets being whipped along by the waves as if a whole procession of pioneer women had come to grief there, the waterlogged blue corpses floating under the fluttering dresses.

Our life there wasn't disagreeable. When I say this you can see that I was already . . . free. Sometimes I even thought that the prison must be a holiday camp for warders and that we were there – I at least, for my wife had never been sentenced – just to justify the presence of the guardians: even when on leave there must be detainees to give continuity and steadiness and direction to their existence. And yet they never went walking or swimming or even just shopping or playing the pin-tables; they were loath to leave us alone, and they were at all times strictly according to regulations spit-smoothed and polished in their uniforms. They weren't repressive. Warders will be warders. True, in terms of his arrested development and in order not to lose the grip on his sense of reality, Roog at regular intervals had to bluster and mete out punishment. Softly-Softly was more jovial, devil-may-care. Often we got drunk together, perhaps also to push back the moving fog of ennui.

One evening – it wasn't quite dark yet because there were still a few weak jerks of light coming from the sea – I was again half moved and tipsy. I guffawed in my fist and danced with limp shoes until Softly's red cheeks were stretched and burning with laughter; even Roog's moustache came close to a tremble at one point before rearranging itself in the apposite official crease. A woman dressed in yellow – maybe only a whore, I won't know – came in the half-dusk to a window at the back of the building, looking for trouble. The apertures giving on to the rising hillside had bars in front of them, those in the front had glass panes only as it was too high to jump from there and break your neck. The woman, lustily moving her hips because she knew full well that I couldn't reach her there except through the eye and the imagination – although no force is as ravishing as the imagination – the woman then apparently knew about me – I was reasonably well known at the time since I had once participated in the Olympic Games as yachtsman – and she ostensibly wanted my autograph. It was just tomfoolery and tom-teasing. With more of a to-do than necessary I accepted the strip of paper through the grill in answer to her demand because I really wanted to have her move in such a way as to permit me to peep up her legs inside the yellow dress. Her body was as brown and as blue as the twilight. All of a sudden I heard Meisie calling me to come quickly to the other row of windows above the town and the sea. From the window where she was watching we could look down into a narrow street climbing away from the seafront towards the prison, turning parallel to it just under the walls. In the final wreathing rays of the sun three people moved up the hill: the two brothers Giovanni, motor mechanics working here in Paname in a garage just around the corner from Lamourt's house, and an old gentleman whom both Meisie and I love dearly. The two brothers – the smaller one with the posh swagger who had his manliness ripped away years back in an automobile accident, and the tall one with the crippled knees and the Bob Dylan reddish beard and the crossed blue eyes – were dressed in their khaki outfits, grease stains still clung like shiny bats to the overalls. The elderly gentleman wore dark clothes and his hat of every day. He walked with great difficulty but the other two only sniggered and didn't assist him in any way. The wind was big and thick and dark with colour. Meisie pulled open the window and shouted at him with an excited voice. When he looked up at us she waved and called: "Our best regards at home!" He acknowledged with a nod and struggled on. Wind furled the brim of his hat and slammed our window shut. And the window was dark and glistening as this one here tonight. They were directly below us at the corner of the street and would have been disappearing from our sight within a few seconds when I shouted "Oubaas!" (old master) and tried forcing the window open. But in vain. "Oubaas! Oubaas!" I don't know if he could hear me. When they reached the level area in front of the gaol and started moving away from us, I could see through the glass that he was weeping – and all at once he became very small and old and grey and before my very own shocked eyes his head and shoulders disintegrated, cracked

229

and utterly exploded in grey drops and dollops and splinters as big as seagull-chickens. "Oubaas!" I started bawling, filled with horror and dismay – "Oubaas! Oubaas . . . !" In one dark corner of the room I could see Softly-Softly's cheeks puffing red with laughter. . . .

My second experience. My second experience (yes, fill it up, please) must be fitted into a different time-slot, at other tangent points on earth, and was of a different kind. It was the time of autumn and what I have to relate took place here in Paname and not in Nomansland. Just like that, somewhere on the out-skirts where the limits of the little hamlets which in their own time were quite independent and self-sufficient had long since been wiped out, but it was not yet a very densely built-up area and plots faded here into small farms and then in fallow lands bordering on rubbish dumps, streets degenerated into mud tracks, roads died in the rests of forests. Big City annexes, but cannot always digest. The rainy season was already at hand, the red earth all slush. We were visiting Eva and Noordhoek Hedge in the *pavillon de banlieue* which they had acquired not long before. The house was far from finished even though a local carpenter had been moving heaven and earth over the preceding days. The living room, around the fireplace, was done and had been painted: there was wood panel-ling against the walls, shelves everywhere with knick-knacks and books, easy chairs as for instance wicker seats imported from Thailand, goatskins spread over the floor.

We were due to leave for Burrlin that very same afternoon. To the best of my knowledge Noordhoek Hedge, Eva and Meisie were making all the necessary preparations for the journey; I myself was just pottering about in the wooden annexe to the house and when I started becoming conscious of smothered sounds and a feeble groaning. I at first couldn't make out what was happening. Out of sheer curiosity I walked around the house with in my hand still the pickaxe handle that I had been planing down and with wood shavings clinging to my trouser legs. In the garden path I came across a terrible scene: my wife and my two friends were stretched out on the gravel, clearly dizzy and confused, and on top of them were three youngsters with leather jackets and armed with chains! The attackers knelt over their victims looking hard for soft places to bite and suck at neck and breast – there were blood smears on their teeth and their chins were wet. In the background their companions stood, also armed with chains and evidently just as bloodthirstily hungry. I instantly lost all control over my reactions and started hitting out with the stave. I heard the skulls cracking like dove eggs under my blows. The hangers-on – *cabrones* – turned tail and fled, and I after them as far as the mud and the ooze well past the last houses. There I stopped all out of breath and watched them scattering in all directions, trying to make it to the sanctuary of a copse or a few trees, with red earth on their shoes and their pants.

Back at the house I pulled the still throbbing corpses away from my friends. Noordhoek Hedge had already come to. Together we carried the two women to the living room and made them comfortable by the fireplace, trying to bring them round by wiping their lips and their foreheads and dabbing the blood of their wounds. Their clothes were of course all undone and when they finally regained consciousness they were both very dazed and frightened, but luckily neither of them was seriously injured. Noordhoek Hedge, he knows the surroundings rather well, afterwards told me that they had already during the early part of the afternoon noticed the *loubards* sauntering down the road (a certain Albert and his gang, it would seem), and that they tried protesting when the scoundrels wanted like starved predators to enter the garden, but that they were overwhelmed on the spot and probably only their empty bodies would have been left among the ants and the earthworms had it not been for my providential intervention. Lucky that I could still be there in time.

We summoned the local carpenter to come and knock together some coffins for the crushed assailants – the same guy who had fixed up the living room so nicely. In an incredibly short time he finished the boxes and while we laid out the corpses, each with his own blood-besmirched neckerchief over the face, casked on trestles, he gave the finishing touches to the lids – actually the only task which, in his capacity as craftsman, accorded him any real pleasure. This all took place in the one heated space of the house. Outside a piercing wind had risen up in the meantime – but at least it had the advantage that every single fly, which we were expecting by now around the broken dead flesh, was also blown off course for the time being. It is an ill wind that doesn't blow away flies.

Noordhoek Hedge was showing me his latest masterpiece, a book which he had just finished – for he made it his vocation to take published works (on any subject, but he was particularly fascinated by ontology) and modify them with a fine pen and black ink, sometimes word for word, till a completely new book was created, and always far better than the "original" or the "rough material" as he considered it to be. He was, you might say, stripping the cloak of petrifaction and convention off the work so that the little bones may glisten afresh. I was leafing through this most recent transfiguration and in places I had to catch my breath at the riskiness of some of his ideas – when quite unexpectedly there was the squeaking of the telephone. Very surprised we all looked up – Eva who was busy arranging her little hat (hardly bigger than an apple), because we were expecting to leave a while later, Eva literally remained standing just like that with her hands in her hair – since no one as far as we could tell could have known this number. The apparatus was only recently installed and as far as we were concerned not even connected yet; besides, the intention was to have it registered in the name of Dr Righton Ajax Foroek* exactly to preserve the anonymity and to fool nuisance callers. Noordhoek Hedge got up with the heart's flutter-dance over the brown skin of his skull (under the soft down some crusted blood still pointed a warning finger) and lifted the earpiece off its hook with a long stiff arm as if expecting at any moment to be bitten in the ear. Everyone held their breath; even the carpenter stopped chewing the nails in his mouth and expectantly turned his button-fat eyes to the telephone, hammer and chisel held high in the air.

In this silence we could clearly hear a female voice with a brackish American accent coming over the line – you surely know the sound: like someone playing the cornet without a mouthpiece. "Now y'all jest tell Dawn Espohwaylo that ah know he's leavin' with y'all this afte'noon for Bahlane to attend the Olympic Games. . . ." I just could not believe the unearthly scratching. Who was this woman? How on earth did she know I – we – would be here? Why was she calling about me? How could she know that we'd be leaving that same afternoon for Burrlin (if wind and mud did not render the roads impassable) and indeed because we wanted to attend the regattas of the Games? "An' ah know you're there – you lissen to me, Deedah," the blue-toned voice carried on, "Ah don't an' ah jest couldn't give a . . . a *push* for it!" There was a click followed by everyone's

*The real Dr Foroek (1919-?), also known as Galp Northangle, was the obscure but very unorthodox chess master of whom Alekhine said: "He was the most upsetting opponent it was ever my misfortune to be pitted against."

speechless amazement. My wife, Meisie, turned her eyes with the dark fine targets so suddenly on me that the long black hair moved like a shadow-stain over the lilac-coloured scarf wrapped around the wounds of her neck. Damn! "Who is this woman?" she wanted to know as if she'd taken me red-handed. "Where do you know her from? Why don't you admit that you know her? Was it perhaps an autograph she wanted?" One after another the staccato questions exploded like grapeshot around my ears and my defensive and disclaiming gestures apparently didn't carry the slightest conviction. Wind started huffing stronger outside the dark window panes. In places it was wiping all along the walls but despite the pressure one could see the floppy wings and the little sucking paws of the first flies searching outside over the glass. And soon, led on by the fresh odour, they would find a crack somewhere. Firelight jumped in a reddish glow over the three neckerchiefs so that it looked as if underneath there might be something moving, moving. I could feel the black stuttering in the veins of my neck, and the clamminess between torso and shirt. Around me there was an erosion of light and over a long sad and long distance (behind the wind and behind the present) I heard my tight voice calling: "Oubaas! Ouba-á-á-á-ás!"

Short Story

Once upon a time there was a man by the name of Lukas Percy Vermoken. Well, to be quite honest, he was first a foetus and then a baby and further still a boy before he changed into a man. He was delivered at 01h36 during the early part of the night and already at birth his hands were reddish. For his thirteenth birthday he was given a push bike and his nickname was Small Pears. A ribbon had been knotted around the handlebars of the bicycle. Some years after starting to work as a clerk (in a packing firm), he entered the state of marriage. His wife had one front tooth with a gold filling. The name of his second daughter was Magriet. As a hobby he collected postage stamps which, with reddish fingers, he arranged in albums, under transparent paper, and cats or dogs in the house gave him hay fever. During 1965 he visited, together with his wife and youngest son, the Kruger National Park. On 12 March 1969 he was promoted to assistant manager staff, the adjusted wages retroactive from beginning January. At his retirement he would most surely have received a silver wrist-watch, fittingly inscribed on the back. On holiday with in-laws in Williston he succumbed to cardiac failure. Fried chicken gizzards was one of his favourite dishes. "A silent tear we weep but know you're in God's keep; yeah, we shall ever live with the pain until we one day meet again." Profoundly mourned by Hannetjie, Lukas (Boy), Sunara, Magriet and Freddie (son-in-law), Charles and Elefteria, brothers-in-law and sister. Burial arrangements by Human and Pitt.

A Pattern of Bullets

The Introduction
At last I've found the solution to my problem. Or the excuse for a solution. This morning while brushing my teeth over the basin it suddenly dawned on me – simple: why would it need a so-called explanation or even the appearance of logical probability? And more: a presentation of this lack of reality-like exposition (especially at that important point of articulation in the narrative which is still a dark spot for me) presented precisely by means of this introduction, may perhaps indeed establish for the reader an acceptableness. For me too. And that is after all what it is about. You see, I do not mince matters.

For a long time the unfinished story haunted me. I wanted to be able to complete it because I was keen to fit it in with the other writings, get my characters in perspective, fill my notebook so as to be able to hand it in. One doesn't get any younger. The flesh starts riding you bareback, drags you down towards the sods. In vain! Each time I reached the turning-point of the story – the shooting – how many shots were fired? and what was the relationship between the number of shots and the other premises again? – then I became rigid. The juices dried up. Was it simply a question of the pig-headed un-memory? Or is there a deeper-lying theme which escapes me and am I staring blindly at the variations? Should I arbitrarily have imposed on the course a given turn, thus forcing the whole set-up in another direction? But when you start tinkering with a little nut, apparently innocuous, the whole structure may unexpectedly come crashing around your ears. And in the name of what legality do I deposit my hesitations on any given totality? Until this morning then when I realized that I need not even concoct any credibility in the attempt to disguise my obtuseness or my forgetfulness. As long as I express it clearly right at the outset. I am the writer: I can do what I want!

L.L. told me the story in prison. (L.L., strangely enough, was not his true name – that belonged to a compatriot of his and after the latter's "unexpected" demise, I'm told a violent one at that, in South-West, my narrator claimed it for himself – certainly with obscure criminal designs in mind. Besides, the deceased, who dies intestate, owed my narrator quite a large sum of black money. A teasing question remains with me: if my narrator was (co-)responsible for the untimely disappearance of the original L.L., why then hijack his identity? What kind of identification is that? That it may have an unforeseen and unpleasant sequel he already knew. Shortly before being arrested and sentenced two unknown persons in a motor car tried to force him off the speedway serpentining around the mountainside; during the ensuing mad chase, eventually right into the city, the back window of his car was shot to pieces. After the officers of law and order managed to obstruct their way and had taken them to the police station, it turned out to have been an instance of "mistaken identity": the vengeance had been intended for another L. L. . . . .)

He is a middle-aged Slovak, small of posture with black hair now streaked with grey. He arrived as refugee or displaced person in Nomansland. In his own country – and elsewhere? – he had already at times known the bitter cosmos of concrete and echo-corridors and grills, but then it would seem for more "noble" motives. Nowadays he's just a cheater – a "fraud artist" he calls himself, and moreover one of the aristocracy specializing in the forging of credit cards. You must get to the top of the slippery pole in the best way you can. And he was an obsessive smoker – of private cigarettes if he could get hold of them, if not then hand-rolled pills in any old paper. Often the lighting of the cigarette, the sucking in of the first smoke, went accompanied by a slightly trembling nervousness.

His knowledge of any other tongue bar his own (from which he could quote the most beautiful pornographic verses, popular art, of old boop-bellied Turks in horse cars) was quite picturesquely inadequate. With his tortured words he tried to tell me his story. Not that there's much chance to have a quiet talk in gaol, not when one of the partners is a terrorist, and thus it took several sessions before I could get the thread of it out of him. Perhaps that explains why I lost the track afterwards. I remember (I believe) that he had to repeat portions of it several times. Whether it was the truth that he held up to me I don't know. I pass it on the way I heard it. For what it's worth. In my language.

He has since disappeared. Was discharged and probably sucked up again in the nebulous world of a shadowed existence, perhaps under a new name? And now, often when I think of him – and struggle with the story which for such a long time couldn't be completed – phrases jump to my mind, like: "before I was silver"; or: "and I bit God in the calf". Further:

The Narrative

Sometimes when those birds, the ones you call plovers, fly with their sharpened sounds through the night and when the frogs in the marshes down here start clamouring like demonstrators behind barbed wire, in waves, as if they're the shivering contractions of the moon's skin, the gooseflesh – neither fish nor flesh, amphibian, hermaphroditic, squamous, no recoverable intelligence and yet not just a dull droning, and the moon a smoke, then I shudder to the marrow. Is it because the ancient sounds address themselves to the ancient mindstem, the nerve-tree? Because it takes me back again to the nights I passed in my own country. And seagulls at night also screech a different type of noise – something like a foot in its sock. If feet were to have vocal cords. Can you have the thorax resoled? Nights I'd prefer not to remember. Let them rather sink and disappear in the branches of the pre-intellect. And nights, strangely enough, that I have forgotten entirely. Because memory is a blanket. We also have birds there calling through the night and the sounds are just as inaccessible. Frogs too. And nightingales, these wistful birds you do not know here. I'm now talking of real nightingales, not the Cape kind. There is something wild and inhuman in the night. A nearly prehistoric defencelessness which cannot be covered by reason. Other corridors, other canyons. Moonlight – dead life – it's a totally different dimension. Do you know the Arabs believe you will go mad if you walk under the moon without covering your head? And that they hang out their sheets at night to bleach? The light is silvery, cold but thick. Yet without any weight or substance. On such nights one should hunt the silver fox, when wind pushes tepidly, and you ought to be naked, with dogs to help you – only, the dogs should not have vocal cords. And the splashes under the trees are darker, like pits reflecting the trees. Pools in which the trees are floating. The schemer falls into the pit he digs for another. Not that I'm superstitious or that I'm interested in supernatural manifestations or transactions of the spirit. Although . . . Now listen to this tale – I swear I'm not exaggerating at all. What the meaning behind the events may be, the sense in the being, the explanation to it all, the solution –

that I do not know. But must everything happening always have a reason or an explanation? Take for instance something like a war – the co-operative frenzy and murder. Why? Aren't we often just roaring away in the swamps?

The time of these events, which I try to depict at present, is also long ago already. I was young then and my hair was black. You know by now how I tried to keep body and soul together – I told you all about it the other day: namely by smuggling people across the border. *Also gut*, when I was caught at last they held me as a political prisoner, but actually it had nothing to do with politics. Money has no political or ideological etiquette. When someone contacted me for a border crossing I named my price and if he or she had enough money it was fine, if not, well then it was "hard lines, my friend". Silver always speaks clearly. It wasn't hard work – like black market trading it could be described as a "cottage industry", and many of our people in that zone were involved in it. The border was two or three kilometres up the road from our little town, Osnabrück not far, and Vienna barely 80 kilos away.

An old acquaintance one day turned up at my place, Keuner was his name, and he asked me for money. I was a bit taken aback because K was in the same "trade" as I, just active in another sector, and I well knew that he also dabbled in all sorts of black deals. He should have been making good profits. But who knows – maybe there was a sudden crisis, or an accident. "Sure," I said, "I can advance you something."

"Look, Lamortček," says he, "I don't want to borrow anything from you. Give me 500 kroner and I'll let you have this pistol." And he showed me a 6.35 of Czech fabrication.

"Man, I don't want your gun. You needn't give me a pledge either. I'll lend you 500 kroner and you can pay me back just whenever you feel like it."

"No, No! I told you I don't want a loan. Here, now take this thing. Look, it's just about new, hardly ever been used, in excellent order, I swear. And you can give me whatever you want. Come on!"

So I took the firearm from him. I already had one of my own, a German 9 mill., but it was a big calibre, a Parabellum, and the smaller weapon I could carry more easily on me, even in my inside coat pocket. In a bar or on the street it wouldn't attract any attention, I reckoned.

That's when the strange things started happening to me. At the beginning it didn't really bother me because I've told you, didn't I, that I'm not a man for believing in ghosts or visions. And I'm not a weakling either. First I thought it must just be my nerves giving me a hard time. With my kind of illegal activities one must always be on the look-out and with all that stress you end up being too finely tuned. Like the cocking piece and the trigger of a gun too danger-ously filed down. I thought I just needed to shake off the weird emotions. But I couldn't.

Listen: I'm on the street and suddenly I'm absolutely convinced that I'm being tailed, that someone is right on my heels. I slip around a corner or stop innocently before a display window to look for my shadow, and there's nobody! Or sometimes I return home late through the deserted streets and suddenly I hear crunching footsteps behind me. I jump around and hold my breath: there's nothing, just fog-wraiths perhaps swirling around a lamppost, just old wind-tattered streamers. Sometimes I sense the presence of someone or something, so imposing that I quieten the word-ribbon in my eyes so as to spy about very carefully – useless. Even at home there was no security. A few times I imagined seeing very fleetingly a bearded face peering at me through a window (the way a book character may brusquely become aware of the author), but surely it was god-impossible, I then soothed myself, because my flat was on the second floor of the building without balconies. Once, in a bar, I very strongly felt the "presence" on a sofa next to me and when I looked there was still the imprint in the leather cushion cover where some person had just been sitting and before my very eyes the seat stuffing filled out again. I tell you the short hairs of my neck were on end!

It became so bad that I could no longer trust myself with the gun. One night, it was late and just about no traffic left on the streets – because for purposes of my work I often had to move about when the good law-abiding citizens, the virtuous Zweiks, were already snoring away in their eiderdowns – a young woman as suddenly as a cat appeared from a doorway in front of me on the sidewalk and before I could even think the gat was in my fist ready to blow her to high heavens. Luckily I realized just in time that it was probably a night-walker in a hurry to catch the last tram or train, perhaps with the thighs still clammy. But you must know how dangerous it was – I very nearly wiped her out. And then I would for sure have been in big trouble. I could no longer risk walking the streets with my side-arm and yet I felt I had to, exactly because of the mysterious pursuer or spy.

One of my old mates, Gregor Samsa, was called up for his military service (too stupid to invent, like we did, cripple dependants which would have gotten him a dispensation). Several of us, all old classmates, decided to go and have a decent booze-up for old times' sake, and to see him off properly. It was a weekend and Gregor was due to leave the following Monday night, or maybe the Tuesday morning. Saturday and Sunday we fêted right through. One chap could tickle the piano a bit and we sang and danced and drank like swine. It is with joy that you take leave of your youth, but it also hurts. That is the magic spell – that you can howl from happiness and drunken sadness because everything is so transient, so perishable, without your being capable of understanding it then. Later perhaps yes, and by then you're too cynical for tears. Nevertheless, it's only the present that matters. . . .

Monday I ran into Gregor on the street and he reminded me that I promised to spend tonight, the last night, with him and his girlfriend. All right, all right, I agreed, although I didn't remember a thing about any promises, and we made a date for meeting up again at eight o'clock in the hotel on the old town square. I was restless: I just could not shake off the uncomfortable feeling of "the other person".

The afternoon I went to buy some bullets for the pistol I'd taken over from K. On the black market to be sure, because I naturally have no legal licence for the thing. Such papers one couldn't get hold of very easily by us, and with forgeries you're always taking a risk. And as usual I went to pull off two shots outside town because you can never be too careful with stuff you buy under the counter – sometimes the powder is wet or the cartridges defective. And when you *have* to shoot, you come short.

Towards six o'clock I walk into Gregor again. His girl is with him and they're already on their way to the hotel. He insists that I must join them.

"No, Greguška," I said; "look, we've got an appointment for eight and I shall definitely be there. Count on me. But now I've got to go home first and eat something, you know, then we'll see each other in a little while."

Gregor didn't want to know. I could just as well come for a snack with them in the hotel, he insisted, and like that we're all together, and seeing as how it's going to be the last night . . . The true reason was that he just couldn't face up to the boredom of being for two hours alone with the girl. To say goodbye is galling enough. I, on the other hand, wanted to be by myself a bit, and I was afraid too – of what I can't very well imagine. I explained to him about the unlicensed firearm I carried on me, that I'm a bit apprehensive about perhaps starting to shoot wildly in the drunkenness of seeing him off, and an accident is quicker than a thought.

"Your war games are still ahead!" I teased him.

"Ach man," Gregor laughed, "if that's your only worry! Why don't you just take out the clip and hide it away on your body? Then you can't start throwing lead, however slap-happy you may become. And tomorrow, when you're sober and cooled off, you reload the thing and Franz is your uncle!"

So I had nothing to oppose his argument with. I therefore took the clip from the pistol and tucked it away in a small sewn-on hiding-place in the lining of my pants under the belt. The clip was full – six cartridges. Plus one in the barrel which I removed also. That made seven. I remember I counted them. The discharged pistol I put in my inside pocket.

These precautions turned out to be unnecessary after all as we didn't really get into our stride with the drinks. Probably because we were still saturated from the excesses of the preceding days. We ate, knocked back a few Pilseners, and on top of that several cups of coffee. Drunk I never was.

It was a lovely evening, quiet, not a breath of wind. Bright moon like a clean-washed car in the sky. And the moonshine like dust where the car has been passing. Night birds whistled and trilled. . . . By closing time we got ready to stroll home at a leisurely pace. Our drinking companions of the weekend would never have credited our demure behaviour. In our country the men often have to be chucked out at closing time. But it's not at all like with you people here, even though the police there are armed too. A copper can't just go for his gat there.

You'll never know how many guys I met in the cooler who were there for assaulting an officer! I tell you, the ordinary citizen there very easily gives a policeman a few of the best. And he's not branded for that. As long as you don't get involved in politics!

We were full of good food and good talk and a little melancholy under the moon at the thought of the last embrace. Gregor Samsa was to accompany his girlfriend to her parents' place just out of town; I was to go along till about half-way before turning off to my flat. The streets were empty. Weekdays the workers go to bed early. We sang a little, like

Shine on, shine on harvest moon
Up in the sky–

when suddenly, from nowhere in the street ahead of us a voice started calling.

I shan't remember what the voice shouted; I don't believe it addressed us by name. But we knew it was meant for us. And I, I most definitely knew that this was the secretive presence that had been following me so stubbornly.

Just out of reach in front of us the enticing voice moves. We can't make out anything. Neither light nor movement. Always it keeps taunting us. Does it dare us to come closer?

To the edge of town I walked with Gregor and his girl. There the road splits in two – left to the nearby neighbouring village where her parents have a small plot, right to the broken-down manor house of a ground baron from before the revolution. Just before you get to the ruins and just about bordering on the town there's a reasonably dense forest. In the moonlight the tree-shadows were very dark and solid. The trees floated in the light pools breaking through the foliage. The voice came to a halt in that forest and called out to us to approach.

"Greguška, you take the girl along. I'm going to look who or what's hiding among those trees."

"Are you completely off your bloody rocker, or what?" Gregor wanted to know.

I take the magazine from the small bag under my belt and slip it into my pistol. "I'm armed. There are six bullets in the clip. I count them with my thumb. Plus one which I push into the barrel. That makes seven. I'm not a fuck scared."

"No, you're crazy! How do you know it's not a deliberate trap? Just imagine someone's lying there, waiting for you in the . . . in the . . . the dark, with a machine-gun? What will your little fart-a-puff mean to you then, hey? Don't go, man. Someone is surely trying to lure you out of town to do you in. Leave it alone, I say!" And I consider his words. Could well be he's right. At that time there were indeed all sorts of strange things happening. Particularly the back-and-forth over the border. Americans and Lord knows who all infiltrating people. Underground organizations. Networks. Vendettas. It's true, I could very easily walk straight into a shooting party.

"Turn back and go to bed"– with these words Gregor clinched the argument. "Tomorrow is another day. Why go and risk your skin in something that ten to one doesn't concern you at all?"

I pressed him to my heart and turned back to town.

And now a frightening thing happens, something which freezes my blood like quicksilver in the veins. The unearthly voice who only a while back was still heckling me from the trees is now *in front* of me, between me and the house, and again I'm taunted and beckoned.

Imagine a Middle European town late at night, not a cat on the streets, each house veiled in an isolation which can be called "sleep". Dead silence – and remember, the place is densely populated, all live in town, right on top of one another. You turn down the street where your flat is. Old trees on the sidewalks both sides. Then thunderingly the echoing footsteps. And: a hell explodes. I know about the cracklash of shots, hoarse shouting voices, fire-jets flowering sharply, and powder-stench, and a running, and broken breaths. I know of an agony of fear, an explosion of senses, crescendo, apotheosis. *Break*. And then nothing.

I know nothing more. I woke up on my bed in the flat, quite feverish and completely wet with perspiration. Just in my pants and my shirt. Remember. I tried to remember. Everything was peaceful, beautifully quiet, and it was clear that whatever had happened must have been a denouement, that I'd henceforth be left in peace. I sat up and started looking for the firearm, my hands were still confused. That, the pistol, I discovered hidden under my pillow. I took out the magazine, counted the cartridges. There were two bullets. No more. And yet, of this I was sure: I myself hadn't fired a single shot.

The Explanation

Well, it was a stormy period in the history of my country. In times of changing regimes, when there is a fighting for power, it always goes like that – you will still learn it also. On many a night the silver fox was hunted. Shots were pulled off. There were sometimes raw shrieks in the streets and in the low vegetation by the rivers. The silver reflections of the moon were often disturbed. And when I was arrested one day chance decreed that I be pushed into a cell full of prisoners amongst whom, to my total surprise, Keuner was also. The man caught a fright when he saw me, that was much evident. He was pale around the lips. When he tried lighting a cigarette his hands were nervous so that the little flame shivered.

"*Also*, old K, that pistol of yours that you were so keen to force on to me: let's hear the story!" Thus, more or less, did I address him after we'd gotten the banalities over with.

"D–Do you still have it?"

"No."

"Ah!" He relaxed. And started telling me what had happened at the time. Also that it was never his intention to offload any trouble on to me but that he was so unnerved that he simply *had* to get rid of the thing. (*Ja*, I thought – *cause toujours mon gars!*) It all started after he'd escorted a small group of refugees across the frontier. Four men and a woman. No questions did he ask beforehand. Their reasons were their own business. They had enough money, wanted to get out – the rest was a matter of logistics. Before the crossing he'd asked them to hand over any weapons in their possession to him, K. It was standard procedure – I must remember what it was like? If a border patrol from the other side were to intercept a lot of armed refugees, then the fat would have been in the fire, and the eventuality of a shoot-out on this side was equally an unacceptable proposition or risk for any guide. Only the woman, a particularly attractive lady, had this thing with her: the damned pistol. Everything went off smoothly. Routine nearly. A guide who is worth his pay sees to it. And at the destination, once they were safe, he – K –as was customary, handed the weapon back to her. No, he could keep it, she wouldn't be needing it any more. A little ironic her smile was. Very rapidly she then sketched the history for K, whether he was interested in hearing it or not. She was in fact, she claimed, the wife of a much older senior officer in the political police. But at the same time she was a member of a clandestine resistance group. Did her husband suspect her? Did he know? Perhaps there was another aspect over which she draped a discreet veil – that there was a liaison between her and one of the four students. Maybe the extra-marital

249

relationship was the only point of contact between her and the group. Who would be able to tell? Did her husband intend to manipulate her, use her to infiltrate the illegal organization? And when she learned that the political police were on the point of going into action she outwitted her husband and stole his pistol. As for the rest – about this my colleague K was not very clear. Was the government agent first killed with his own weapon, or did the group just leave? In any event, a curse of revenge was uttered. And the unsuspecting K, back across the border the same night with the stolen shooting-iron, immediately started experiencing the strange persecution which I, later, would in turn get to know. It played havoc with his nerves, made him a wreck. Till it reached the insupportable stage where he no longer could tolerate being the dark instrument for something or someone he could not comprehend. It was then, cowardly, that he "made over" the pistol to me and fled for his life. Apologies, sincere regrets, my old mate, etc. (*Cause toujours mon lapin.*)

This then is the story which I could never really unravel. I must admit that I twisted it a bit here towards the end. It was in fact K who started pumping me about the weapon which he'd sold to me and it was only after I'd informed him about my experiences – and the satisfactory ending – that he enlightened me mouthful by mouthful about the prelude. Truth, after all, has more faces than a polished crystal.

On the Way to Ku

When we were brought here as war prisoners. I can't go on. When we were brought here as prisoners of war it was a journey which stretched over seasons, always through a landscape of mountains, always covered with snow and ice. High, where breath is dry and bitter. Endless distances over glass. On the last rounded summit above the city one wild horse remained etched against the skyline. The troop of horses which followed us all the days of our lives, at a distance, and stopped when you looked back, the breaths lovely warm snorting ribbons, and then sometimes pawed with their forelegs at the ice so that the earth sounded in a hollow resonance, the troop of horses gradually drifted off. (I believe there are among us travellers who sneaked away in the quiet of the night to furtively mount the horses, but I do not know this for sure.) Except for the last one, the one with the ruddy colour of a satsuma and with patches, untamed, high-spirited, who stayed behind on the curve of the white horizon while we moved ever nearer to the city. Until the horse was only a speck on the earth's edge. *And long after the others had continued I still kept looking around.* Thickly swollen with tears my throat was.

We stink. Our bodies stink. The rags on our bodies stink. The animal skins wrapped around our feet stink. In the city we shall get freshly ironed clothes. The building where we are lodged is in an offshoot of the city, an isthmus between white and white of snow. Below the building the street is full of people. There are cinema halls advertising unknown flicks, of romances in distant lands and people with embroidered jackets who can swallow swords and sticks of fire just like that in the open air. There are boutiques and very small shops, some run by orientals selling exotic spices and noodles. Perhaps there are brothels too. But the building in which we are lodged on many floors is solid and new. That is to say it is in the process of being renovated and rebuilt for strewn over the floors inside and piled against the walls are heaps of scrap. *The new rises up amidst the rubble of the old.*

The prisoners of war have new clothes. Lightweight suits. But their faces bear the tracks of neglect. That one with the yellow visage covered by wrinkles and stubble is a famous philosopher. Except (or therefore) that he is also an alcoholic, he says with tears like glad tidings over his cheeks.

Here my wife lived. I roam through the rooms full of accumulated rubbish, from the one room to the next, down stairs and up steps. The floors are freshly laid, the walls strong. Those window sashes she had painted blue so that they may seem like framed entrances to heaven. And this, this unfinished tapestry, she embroidered. Look, it is the repetition of our faces until the mouths together become one black orifice. Far, very far away, in the direction of all our seasons from which we came, on the last crest of the unfolding mountain chain, a wild horse stands silent in the wind. Too far off to be discerned with the naked eye.

But in the snow where we have to work along the other flank of the city's outgrowth there are queer humps under the white matter. We walk with difficulty. We stumble over things. And with the unearthing we see that these are the carcasses of horses, infinite in the distance. How deep down do the dead go? How high? In how many layers? The cadavers are transparent and smooth with the colour of glass. Where blood has not yet coagulated the scratched open surface is slippery. Nothing can freeze here. Although everything is whitened by snow it is not at all cold.

In the white landscape are small groups of brown children. Each little group must imitate the song of a different bird. *Life must be tempted back to earth*. New patterns must define the emptiness. The band who must call up the ducks, stiff upright in the snow, make quick quack sounds. They also have fastened to strings wooden ducks shinily painted and varnished. Like the decoys which hunters of yore deployed in the marshes.

We are the war prisoners. We are the task force. Our duty it is to lay a path of green grass over the snow. So slow, such an infinite time it takes to create the dotted patterns of all the days of our lives. But we know that we have to complete it, green and with a spongy give under the feet, and that we shall go to freedom only along that way. Freedom. Freedom will lie waiting at the end destination of the road we are building and we shall reach it on a Tuesday. And the horse – will the horse still be there?

Shadows Break
through the Mind

In case there's still any doubt in your mind, nothing
short of castration (which arrests hair loss straight away,
but does have other setbacks) can bring back what
nature has taken away.

In all probability it started that time, long hence (although perhaps earlier too) when he strained uphill against the mountain wind. Escorted by two guardians of the morals in camouflage, one at each elbow. They were on their way with him to a place of safekeeping (but that's neither here nor there). And on top of the knob of the incline, behind their backs a promenade along a fretful sea, a rickety house throned. When out of breath but full of wind they swerved left there, here the road runs parallel to the building, he became aware of excited life-signs behind the cloud-mirroring panes of the second storey. This old house is an asylum for the catatonic retarded. Behind one glass panel was the face, a blur as pale as a bat who never sees the sun, of a female with long black hair and oriental cheekbones; and the mouth of the face was opened wide in an outcry, stretched around an exclamation, suffocating, in order to swallow a shout, to force it down. In the next window he saw from the corner of his eye a stocky Black male gesticulating. There was spittle on the Black's chin. Wind crumples sounds. Through the glass, behind the wind, it is as if they were jeering at him. "*Ou haas! Ou haas!*" (Old rabbit! Old rabbit!) That's the way it sounded. Suddenly all of this, the juxtaposition of place and dawn and emotions, suddenly it was all extremely funny and touching and exhilarating. He took off his hat and chucked it in the air so that it took height like a slovenly seagull, his hair exploded in the wind. He is an angel. Tears of exuberance made his cheeks shiny and wet. Lightheadedness took hold of him and he had to give way. He had to make a false step. The urgent realization of the immediate. Now and here for ever, always. ("Easy, easy now my old one", the one conductor exhorted, tightening the grip on his elbow.) But the world is made to stand on its head. Come what may.

Mouse Minnaar one morning took up position in front of the mirror and combed his hair (although perhaps earlier too). He saw that after pulling the comb through his hair-do a tuft remained stuck to the teeth. Never before, as far as he can remember, did he lose as many in only a few movements of the arm. With his hand he smoothed back his quiff from the forehead and to his utmost dismay noticed how much the paler patches above the temples had gained on the hairline, how unexpectedly bat-like his scalp has become. Kindest God. Like ringworm. No doubt any more. (How one misses the doubt once it has disappeared.) He is getting to be big-faced, to lose his finishing touches, to grow past his hair. *Une légère calvitie?* No, a wasteland. It must be because of the worries, he thought. But, for pity's sake, I *have* no more worries. I am safe. Is it the result then of melancholy? Something I must be doing wrong. That something. To have cares is to live inside and outside, to deflect life into reflection so that it is no longer open-minded. To make of life a stick. To stroke the self. Then there is no more life. I must think on nothing. I must find a focal point that I can burn white with undiluted attention. I must fondle the nothing. . . . And from that instant Mouse Minnaar watched his mirror every day: and started worrying so excessively about his diminishing head of hair that quite soon he became completely bald.

Bump in the Night

They drive down the deserted highway, the powerful engine of the Silver Phantom humming, headlights spewing the darkness, probing ahead, illuminating just the immediate ribbon of dusty road, eliminating any sense of the reality of the landscape around them: as if moving down an isthmus of security. Their backs to the North, always with their backs to the North, the North with its horrors and its violence, its uprooting, its desolation; the North always at their backs, the North ever just behind them, dragging their North with them wherever they go, extending it. They have long since become insensible to the dust filtering into the car, caking their nostrils, forming with the perspiration a sediment in the lines of their bodies. In the dark one doesn't write the dust. It is hot. It is always hot. It has always been hot. The land is hot, the road is hot, the stars streaming down the face of the night must be hot – hot and white as headlights moving down highways from a North. Of course it is impossible to escape from the unseen.

Of course it is impossible to escape from the unseen, she thinks. Her thoughts have become jumbled and fragmented with the monotony of trying to escape down the road. We are all just hot and dusty thoughts, she thinks. She thinks: I am a thought thinking itself and not existing when the thinking lapses; Fagotin Fremdkörper steering the car, willing it away from the North, is a thought here in the dark next to me; and all the other itinerants gone ahead of us in their dust, and those who still may escape, may still follow us – they are thoughts too if I bother to think them. She moves over the seat, wants to stretch her limbs in the limited space, doesn't try too hard because always there is the dust in eyelash and armpit and between suspender and stocking. She thinks: we must reach Laputa; ahead must lie Laputa; at the end of the road where night unravels Laputa must be. Safety? Asylum? Exile? Release? Then? No North? The North, the North is moving down in a rush behind the headlamps. She tries to think herself. But she thinks odds and ends of previous thoughts, the crust, flimsy words.

Before leaving the North she had been a courtesan. Many of her race had been courtesans, the unattached ones, the indolent: the country was rich, affairs flourishing, pleasure at a price appreciated though easy enough to come by. Of course the others, the indigenous caste, had been simply whores. But her calling had necessitated a given learning and her craft had similarly been an education. From her aspirants she had taken some words; to these words she tried to fit thoughts. She is tired now. She thinks: fleeing is not the correct environment for feeding the *nous*. She thinks: I must get away, even if only with this taciturn Fagotin Fremdkörper, but how I regret the days which have fallen behind for ever. That is what is known as *laudator temporis acti*. In Italics. And now I am dust. She thinks: I am taking my thinking and myself with me, my Lares and Penates, but my thinking makes of my being a *felo de se*. It is the North. No doubt. It is the heat. It is the night. It is the hope, feigned or real. It is death we flee with, latent, lulling, seemingly innocuous. A passing matelot, for whom she had nearly developed a fancy (wasn't his name Thibon, Gustave?), had told her that one should not run away in order to be free. "If you fly from yourself, your prison will run with you." And since she's not leaving the self behind, she thinks, it must mean that the self is death. It must be the words larded with a strange life. And she thinks: we must get to a latrine soon-soon or my bladder will burst.

She says to Fagotin Fremdkörper that they will have to stop somewhere for there is the need for a crinkle and tinkle, and he answers that it won't be long now, that he knows of a halfway house where they will find all the amenities, refreshment and fuel too, because they cannot continue for much longer like this; and that the place is quite near really, that it is a warm and welcoming joint run by a friendly compatriot, that at least *must* still be so. ("All things have not turned to dust." And: "The alternative is too ghastly to consider.") She attempts to extract conviction from his assertions, she sits up straighter and she reflects that she's conceivably feeling quite feverish from fatigue and perhaps this nice travellers' inn could serve her a cool febrifuge. She thinks: I'll say "f-f-f-ancy that!" And then she thinks further that f's are really funny because they are so ferociously inquisitive, like the heads of wind craning over tall grass. She looks down the beaming blind headlights and decides that she will get out of the car when they reach this haven, what the hell, even if her creased clothes and caked visage are *infra dignitatem*.

But when they reach the service station the buildings and premises are dark. She feels her heart a black word in the throat. Fagotin Fremdkörper doesn't dare use the hooter of the car: the North is still with them and nowhere is safe nowadays. He doesn't have to – a man steps out of one of the dark buildings, cautious. It is the owner, the sympathetic compatriot, morose, with an unkempt moustache. Fagotin Fremdkörper has turned off the engine and they sit immobile in the sudden swishing silence of the immense, dry and glittering night. Yes, but certainly, the innkeeper assures them, they may have some petrol. Although. And he glances around him at the dark as if he suspects informers lurking there. No one is to be trusted any more, he says. I have seen them all pass by. Not many more to come, I should guess. Hard times, hard times. Yes, perhaps I still have a few litres. My last. All taken you know, and never to be replenished. Don't know why I'm still hanging on. He pushes a feeble expectorating sound out into the night: his docile and hollow laugh. But where shall I go? Laputa? I see them come and go, I've seen them going, they are going, it is all gone. But look, he says, I shouldn't be hanging around if I were you, all these informers you know, and he listens, listens in the dark. Let us whisper. No but look, he also says, making a vague movement with a hesitant hand – why, if you're bushed you may stay the night: there are a few other – ah – travellers waiting in their cars back there. Back there must be a parking space behind the barns where landaus and spiders and traps and barouches and calèches and coaches and phaetons and victories and hearses and buggies and ox wagons used to be housed in days of yore when visitors were curious tourists who had to be amused at so much a head. They can hear a rapid soft shuffling sound coming from a darkened barn. S's are snakes. What is that? She asks as she decides to get out and relieve herself words and all.

Out she gets of the car, disturbing dust unseen in the night, and asks: what was that there? The shrouded sound. Squeak of unoiled springs. Then the silence. Fagotin Fremdkörper in the car. The hostelier, turned, cock-eared, taut. Fear.

A moan and they all start running. From the other conveyances people come running. Someone has a torch at hand. Into the barn. Beam picking out spokes, sudden glint of rim, dust, more dust. Furtive movements somewhere. An animal panting. "Quiet!" Listening. More people thronging into the barn. Thoughts, she thinks. Not even words. "Got 'em!" "Damn bastards!" Hysteria there. "Bloody Blacks screwing!" What? Where? Yes, a couple of Blacks it would seem, taking refuge here – having moved in from the North? – but how, afoot? – and softly fornicating in the dusty dark. "Aarrgh!" "Get 'em!" Thrashing, grunting, flesh against wood, panting, bodies in dust. "Out here!" "The beam!" "Put off that light you stupid idiot. Want to attract the others?" "Quiet!" "Quiet, gentlemen!" (Pretension is better than cure.)

The gentlemen are quiet. The sordid and confused movements in the dark. She lets down her panties, squats, relief without thinking, and the hissing sound of it. A form is dragged out. Must be the male, straining against their arms. Kicking of legs. Body against body. Dust unnoticed in the night. A post or some upright part of an ancient vehicle somewhere. A rope. Panting and grunting. The vague shapes silhouetted against the glow of stars. Blows. Thumps. A tightening. Figures moving back, one remaining trussed and twisting. A tightening. Twang of line. A gasp. Silence. No. A gurgle raucous, prolonged, full of spittle, dying away with life. And then, soft at first, but rapidly scaling and soaring through the mark and up into the night: the wild wailing of a woman. Star-sound.

The Self-Death

When it is dark over the small Old-Land town Fagotin Freemkop leaves the boarding house on his way to church. Wing-dark outside, there are no street lamps and starshine doesn't quite penetrate the foliage of the trees lining the street. And it is very hot. The sultry night air is heavily laden with the scents of summer growing – from the mountains come the wet green odour of pines; from the black garden flows the sad but sweet fragrance of gardenias as if the bedsheets of old lovers who had long been separated are now aired over the veranda wall under the cover of night; even the hairy bodies of bats sweep-swooping unexpectedly through the opaqueness smell of wild fruit laid away in the loft, of warm earth. And in front of Pappa Roos's house with its neo-classical portico on columns, lost in the even denser obscurity of the house's shadow in this dark night, a magnolia tree is a mysterious and swooning conflagration: tongues, flames, holiness deep from the earth's womb. Further along the street a cricket scrapes *rip-tip-tip-tip-prie*, only much faster.

And although it is dark, Fagotin knows about the dust all around him; but the dust is warm too, the dust has the aroma of high summer. *Cheet-cheet-cheet-cheet-cheet* goes the spraying nozzle, the rose, of the hose sprinkling its droplets over the library's walled garden. From the other side you can smell the entwined heat and humidity coming towards you. The water becomes perfume. Things unfold.

Diagonally opposite the chunky town hall an invisible voice calls out to him: "And is that you, Fagotin? Will you be on your way to church then?" And when he offers an affirmative answer, the mellifluous notes proceed: "May we share a stretch of the way with you? Ma and Mumford are heading in the same direction. And I . . ."

"Of course! Good evening, madam. Good evening, good evening." An imaginary hat is lifted politely. Ah, but surely this voice he recognizes. M! Upon my word! It goes without saying that the mother and the little brother must be on their way to church where the father is probably already waiting – isn't he, apart from being the school principal, the preacher too? (The old man with the muscular shoulders which he keeps easing, the scowl and the large pale hands made for cigars, but he doesn't smoke.) What would she, M, be doing in town? Fagotin remembers her well. In the dark her silhouette is just a supposed presence, but judging by the soft sounds she must still be walking the same old way – the hips with the loose snaking motion of grab-me-if-you-dare at every step, the back slightly bent, the derrière. . . . In fact she moves, she scoops, like her mother, only with a younger rhythm. And he remembers her dark hair cut short, bobbing when she walks, the long neck, the prominent nose, the mouth as thin as matches in the water and never very loving. Would she still have the same appearance? It's a mumble of years since he last met her. In the dark now the creases of those years are erased. But he did hear somewhere that she was married, to a speculator; that she went to settle up north in the Heartland. He will have to ask her what whim or wind brought her back to the Old-Land.

Behind them he hears the crisping of the gravel and the grit under the soles of M's mother and her little brother. It is so dark that they might as well be on their way to a funeral. And how does he know it's really her mother and her brother? Without him having to poke her with questions, M starts recounting her married life, the problems with her spouse. Whenever Fagotin feels it is expected of him he utters a sympathetic clucking or muttering. But all this unpacking and airing to go over old bloodstains – it embarrasses him. It's a long and melancholy tale of groping, of mutual faltering, of sadness. A mess worthy of Gomorrah in fact. The night is heavy with mild odours, with dust.

Where their road crosses Main Street, on the corner in front of Danie van der Merwe's general store, they tarry a few moments as M announces that she will have to say goodbye here. She will not be accompanying them to church. She doesn't dare, she says. And without even a handshake she turns away from them. At first he still hears her hip-swing walk, the pleats of her skirt opening and closing in the air, and then nothing more. Sees her in the imagination only. Night has swallowed her. A cricket scratches somewhere; it must be way back in the direction of Pappa Roos's house. Blessed cricket underneath the magnolia bush!

Together with the others Fagotin turns left up Main Street. Up on the hill the church bell peals away (in) the dark of night. Like this the night is a sexton and the stars are bells. And suddenly raindrops start plopping around them, weighty and muffled in the dust. Fagotin feels a wet spot on his forehead, becomes aware of darker blotches in the tissue of his jacket. Then he looks up and he sees! He sees high around the town the wonderful mountains, uncertainly at first, then with each drop shock by shock ever more clearly. He stands petrified in the tar road and he looks to the left and to the right and everywhere he sees the contoured mountains. He shouts at the others but he doesn't bother to listen for an answer. With every drop he sees in a more measured way and he realizes now that each temptation withstood and visitation survived brought him closer to this magical gift. (Knowing this, that the trying of his faith worketh patience.) "Do you see it also? Do you also see it?" And he doesn't even listen. Looks around him. Comprehends all at once that the seeing depends on the searchlight of his eyes – that it is light wherever he looks and *where he doesn't look it remains dark!* He sees the summits peaking above the town, the cleanest hues of blue, pink, yellow, green. Sees all those colours distant and vague as if through a layer of ice. It is as though a crust of ice has covered the mountain slopes, right up to the crests, and under the ice insects are scribbling – or is it the shivering of pine trees in the wind? Rain rushes down with the weight of wind. Now he is wet from back to front. And Fagotin goes down on his knees, drooping wet, babbling with deep emotion, bows and kisses the street. Against his lips he feels the blistering ice.

(ii)

The rest I dare not leave to one side. However senseless it may seem here, warmed up afterwards. The possibility offered by the title of the story must be exploited as deeply and thoroughly as possible. A few more connotations should be attached to it. We are moving towards the cut-off. And therefore perhaps the knot of data offered here will be all mixed up. Forgive! I mean, there's hardly any time left to give the information step by step a structure and a direction. As reader you will just have to read a little harder to interpret the signals. (Even so there are projects which have been interrupted and aborted: there is that which I intended writing about the man with the red nose in his breast – and already a black snake in the belly – about how he leans out of the high window to watch the procession, the flags, the rosettes, listening to the slogans, the bands, the marching masses through the streets chanting in unison: "La mort salaud! Le peuple aura ta peau!" – a way of describing the May Day festivities? There might well have been a picturing of the Algiers incident, the stalwart fellow being felled like an ox among all the shoppers on the street, an epileptic fit, and the obscene public mouth of blood. There could have been a transcription of the wandering through the Tangiers Kasbah, of the visit to a *maison close* and about the old whore who has to cleanse her feet after having intercourse with the heathen tourist. And a report that should have been dictated, concerning specific aspects of a bum's existence in Paname, for my old comrade Giovanni Dodd. But this writing is the negative of a skeleton.)

It will not be executed.

First you will hear that Fagotin in earlier times, in years washed by, had a nickname. Tjak. Remember that. One sometimes imagines that you can escape your destination or designation by changing your name. But listen: *the fact that something is fixed in words is no guarantee that it will not take place!*

Of the time before then, when Tjak together with Minnaar lodged in the monastery (or the gaol). Often they were hungry. So that they were only too keen to devour every last crumb of their rations, to slurp the soup with long lips from the tin dishes. The days are like the waves' white break and suck, breaking and sucking white.

They are fetched for an outing by Sergeant Roog and Warder Smokes. It is meant to break the routine. They are fetched for a kind of picnic and Martha and Levedi Tjeling are there too, they are going with, it turns out to be a pleasant trip. Follows a story concerning Martha and L.T., background information, but I don't remember it exactly, and our time is too short, our space too limited.

If there must be a weakness of the intellect, a genetic hitch, which we call "love", then we would consider it sacred, not so? Yes, near the mirror halls they go to sit in fastidious positions on the silver-green grass under the trees. And they pose in such a way as to look like a *Déjeuner sur l'herbe*, after the painting based on Marcantonio Raimondi's *Le jugement de Paris*. But Sergeant Roog is full of fun and games. He disappears. He returns on horseback. The horse has such muscular haunches. The horse sings and no one can detect the sound. The horse rears up on its hind legs and with this the muscles of the haunches are bunched in clearly defined knots. Sergeant Roog has his automatic in his hand. His grip is firm. He shoots. (He is a jealous man. Life treated him shabbily.) He shoots at the large circular targets. He shoots securely, hitting the bull's-eye without having to take aim, and the horse rises up and hits out, hits out at nothing with the pawing front legs. He shoots and tumbles over the precipice, away, totally away, far away.

From here on Minnaar and Levedi Tjeling also disappear from the story since they were never of any importance for its development, except perhaps as wraiths to be addressed, or decorations completing the space of a canvas. It is thus, when you throw off the words, that you become lighter – because you obscure the matter, because the words crawl out of "you", devour the id-entity – under the glass the insects formicate.

Martha takes Tjak to the lobby of the mirror hall. ("I shall come to you again and you will remember . . . my way of walking.") She tells him that it is not going to be difficult. She explains further that the magazine can contain one hundred cartridges. She pulls the trigger, she pulls off shots in the dark to point out to him, Tjak, how easy it is. You must learn to look deeper, under the surface of the present, and what you see and wherever you look will come true, some day, some day, far away. When you see you create and where you don't look it will remain dark, then.

Tjak is in the dark entrance to the hall of mirrors. He dons a satin tuxedo, extremely modish.

> He: The men swimming through the night in dinner
>   jackets like papercups
>   floating on the ocean;
> She: It is not the mysteries that draw the men,
>   but the fear of that great mystery
>   the veiled woman, Isis,
>   mother, whom they fear to be greater than all else.

In a lovable way just about he fires off the rounds into the dark of the mirror-hall. The jets of fire and the terrible boomeranging echoes and jingling and spattering. The white streaks, hard, unique, finger on the future. Silence is an enormous hollow. He switches on the lights and the mirror walls are there in all glory and splendour to millionate the light itself. Tjak has a hand full of smoke. He has also a red flower pinned to the lapel of his dinner-jacket. He walks up to where his representation is standing. Notices the little holes like splintered eyes over the mirror image's tuxedo.

(We must hurry. It is a heartsore ending. This precedes the previous section.)

The Key

They should never have told him about the key. Not that they ever said anything directly. Never that. But Sergeant Roog mentioned to Warder Softly-Softly that painters would soon be coming with a lorry filled with tins of paint to paint the gaol afresh (in cream and army green) and that the key in the door should not be forgotten then it's a potential security risk one never knows. (The door they referred to was that of his cell of course the last in line under the veranda.) And he had heard their words because in the boop one overhears everything even without stretching an ear. As you are blind. Up to now, it must be said, he had never paid any attention to the key. And out of pure curiosity – since he wanted to smell the painters and the shiny lorry surely when the wheels come grating over the gravel – he upped and turned the key in the lock and the door swung open and he put the master complained of in his pocket. And in the courtyard there was no guard on duty everyone gone to watch the painters' brush hands legs apart the cap over one eye thumbs hooked in the belt web. And the outside gate was similarly unguarded. So that he sauntered out whistle-thistle nonchalantly between the lips meaning to just go take a quick peep make a turn and then slip back key in the pocket before they stop forgetting him and the key. At an angle across the Place du Châtré by the bridge against the wind past the

Palais de Justesse on the right the flower market left (where birds in coops are auctioned) another bridge to cross all along the Place Saint-Moche and the boulevard higher somewhat rising away from the Sane. Here it's literally crawling with people. And he locked away all these years in isolation. He is sore thumb out of place here dressed in Khaki. Passes a hand self-effacing over his crew-cut. Must grin then. For nobody's taking any notice at all. Who knows, perhaps prison garb is at present the *dernier cri*. Starts limping because it is as if the key in his pocket is gradually growing heavier. Reflects abruptly then: God, why not just escape? Why not kick out? Yes but for that I need assistance the feet aren't used to freedom. Like a newborn shepherd's babe among butting sheep am I. Turns right by Gilbert Fils's bookshop back towards boulevard Michemain. In a peaceful side street fleetingly eye-cornered he suddenly recognizes his aunt by marriage the late Kuo Dik's widow a few frog-leaps further heavily engaged in whispering. With her myopic little eyes behind thick lenses and the golden eyetooth. How she wipes a small flag of conversation from the mouth with a young man straight-a-back in a dark blue tunic and with smooth black hair blue shining. And then in a clandestine movement passes him something. But for sure! He is certainly the area representative of the Cong, she just paid her contribution. This man he must talk to. Come what may. This man will be able to help him. But not here for all to see in the street. Where unasked-for attention will be as suspicious as the assassin's stiletto. Rather let him carefully keep an eye on the man. Follow. And where *he* enters, knock there. Wherever though goest I go with thee. Present his case. Try to raise sympathy. Solidarity perhaps. The proud young man weaving through the pedestrians making the rue des Cocoles black. He in his wake. But with greater difficulty seeing that the key keeps weighing more. Is it his imagination or is it bigger also? Does the imagination rise? Past the university buildings there are less people. The street now calmer. The houses taller. The asphalt-top bending back towards the river. The houses taller. No people now. Yet. Every ten yards or so on either side of the road on the sidewalk there is half hidden strategically placed in doorway or behind tree a man holding on to the shadows. Each fellow stands quiet but alert with expectations dark glasses over the eyes. Jaws shift rhythmically and an elastic colourlessness is sometimes pulled thread-thin from the mouth regarded dispassionately before being returned to orifice it's the sharpened skepticism finding shape and considered carefully the pop of exploding bubbles brains munched. In coat pockets paperback spy thrillers cum pig-eared manuals. Wide shoulders and bumps under armpits. Must be pistols. Pisstools. Attributes of manliness. Guaranteeing a grip on any reality. What are the security agents looking for here? For him? Why don't they arrest him then? Don't they see how lame he is already with this enormous glowing key in his pocket? Are they waiting for the procession of a statesman to come by? Is it an ambush before the raid? A coup d'état being executed? He senses the focused eyes hand-large holes scorching his khaki jacket. Before him his humped shadow crawling on the back grovelling fawning licking his feet a halting flame teasing his soul. The Cong representative has disappeared ages ago around a corner down a lane underground meeting probably discovered someone on his tail. To his right in the street a wooden door opens. The door is much higher than street level above three steep steps. Against the lowest step leans a tall bicycle. The bike is painted grey but you can clearly see the rust stains coming through a cape of flames *in* the iron. From behind the open door giving on to the highest step a Chinese appears dressed in an army-green uniform. The Chinese wears a pair of knickerbockers and has swathes wound tight about the legs between ankle and knee.

His head is shaven. He keeps his arms straight down his body and bows the torso deep from the hips. There is absolutely no expression on his face and the eyes are part of the face. He hears the windy sound of the political police's moving mouths. Fifteen yards on there is an arcade above the right-hand sidewalk. A big building. A signboard. HOME FOR RETARDED ORPHANS. He struggles to get in under the cool arcade and his one leg has died he drags it along with extreme difficulty his shadow has crawled up the trouser leg the other leg is of necessity. Higher than his head under the shelter is a line of windows. The panes framing a shiny darkness. From which is emitted wild, howling, interminable laughter. "A-a-a-t-l-a-a-a-s-t!" (As a key would crunch in the lock.) (Shame.)

Index

Cher Monsieur Valjean,

I have been requested to finish off these accompanying documents; not to complete them – that, you'll agree, would be unethical – but to book them. This dubious honour befell me basically because I had collected the diverse fragments over several years, and also because I did know or have met some of the memoirists and their companions.

About the background of these people I don't intend or wish to inform you more substantially than they have chosen to do themselves. Why indulge in gossip? Yes, you'll say, but what happened to them afterwards, or what happens now? So before letting you peruse the book in your hands it may be instructive to attempt tracing, however briefly, their subsequent careers. I have since lost contact with all of them: they weren't exactly friends of mine, and thus there was no reason to maintain even the tenuous links of acquaintance. Life is a process of losing contact anyhow. And my information is therefore inevitably based on hearsay.

The one exception is Brother Giovanni who sometimes writes to me from his far – off refuge – not expecting an answer apparently, since he never bothers to cite a return address. Judging from his rambling epistles he seems to be indulging in what used to be known as "life of the soul". (Spiritual fruition to him then!) My own experience is that such a pursuit makes for confused and shallow generalities, that such a pretender must in fact be mildly demented, believing as often as not in beings inhabiting the clouds, in reincarnation or the *Doppelgänger* theory and other weird escapes or escapades. But who am I to judge? Perhaps a mental or physical defect forced him to withdraw from the bustle of our materialist environment – and I seem to remember that he was anyway much influenced in that direction by his friend Mr Thelonius Monk. If that is the existence he desires (allegedly of no-desire!), so be it. We are all failures at something or other. Nothing wrong with his sentiments though. Here, see for yourself, from a recent letter.

> I salute you. I am your friend, and my love for you goes deep. There's nothing I can give you which you have not got: but there is much, very much, that while I cannot give it, you can take. No heaven can come to us unless our hearts find rest in today – No peace lies in the future which is not hidden in this precious instant. Take peace!

Another I did stay close to – this will surprise you – is Patanjali. In fact I have him here with me. We actually work together, with Rab too, for the Cirque d'Hiver. Talent will out in the long run.

Then of course, why hide it? – there's Levedi Tjeling. I love her as one would love a singing bird in the cage of the heart, and I have always done so. I love particularly the knobbles of her spine. But *she*, alas, has remained as elusive as ever. I can only guess at her whereabouts. Reading some of these pieces you may well come away with the impression that she was romantically linked to Minnaar.

Not so! Minnaar was a much over-estimated mouse – don't you ever believe that myth of the supposed potency of the blacks. It will only be wishful thinking on your part. I even once taunted him to his face with the epithet "Lousy Lover". I tell you, virility is the most subtle and final mask of death!*

I'm digressing, forgive me. Still, as I say, Levedi Tjeling is the one closest to me and yet I know not where or when or even how to find her.

Samsa has gone into literature. He's let himself be used as a "symbol" by the practitioners of *belles-lettres*. K is acting as his agent – I have read his claims that Samsa's experiences or antecedents constitute "an original angle from which to view reality". Whatever *that* may signify.

Nefesj, with his reputation of a dandy, a dabbler (in the occult too), an amateur, Nefesj surprisingly turned out to be one tough cookie. He asserts his gayness publicly – belatedly: in our world it's no feat, surely, to join the majority; and as publicly took as "concubine" young Boy. I believe he treats him very harshly, like a slave or a trained animal really. On weekends, so they say, he's fond of taking Boy to the woods around the city where he has him dodging the trees and sprinting across the glades, completely naked. And all this while Nefesj sits morosely huddled in his car, fumbling a news-sheet, puffing a cigar. How the hypersensitive philosopher has perished . . . or flowered. . . . Who can tell if Boy enjoys the life of kept appendix or not? He has never yet been known to utter a sound. At home (the eccentric old Egyptian gentleman, called Horse, with the toothless shuffle, still looks after their needs in the luxurious flat on the fifth floor), I believe, Boy passes the time surrounded by mirrors, voluptuously

---

*". . . one of the heresiarchs of Uqbar had declared that mirrors and copulation are abominable, because they increase the number of men." *The Anglo-American Cyclopedia*.

studying the wrinkle and sag and bald patches of his thickening, ageing body. Nefesj has been heard to remark bitterly: "He's in such an indecent hurry for bugger all."

Tuchverderber is employed in the rag trade in America. Eva owns, and guides along, an art gallery in Amsterdam. There is the concentration of inner space. Galgenvogel is reputed to be running dagga on a grand scale. Ms Cenami got married to someone in Flanders and is no doubt having it off at any time of the day or night whilst miraculously retaining still her virginal airs.

Braytenbach came to a sticky end. Or so it would seem. There's somewhat of a mystery there. It appears that he turned up in Paname out of the blue and that he there one day approached a lady (on a public thoroughfare) insisting that he was her husband returned from nowhere in Niemandsland, claiming that he's been looking for her and persistently addressing her as "Mooityd". (She didn't know him from anywhere, was either divorced or a *vieille fille*.) They say that he was so obviously distressed, and so pathetically recalling incident upon incident, creating pell-mell a rickety structure of supposedly shared memories and impossible imaginings, that the strange lady was ultimately moved to play along. She must have had a white heart. Was it pity she took upon him then? Perhaps she thought that he was obfuscated by amnesia or some other (temporary) delusion. Anyway, he was quite a harmless old maniac with the most ridiculous fancies and conceits. And so – you won't credit this – they started living together. She donning completely the life of Mooityd, as reflected in his fire and nostalgia, if indeed such a person ever existed. Well, in due time Braytenbach died the death, in the end claiming and maybe believing that he had been a poet, and innocent (his deathwords: "Not guilty, your Honour" – which indicates how Calvinist he must have been), and the lady, by now passably Mooityd, even grieving over the deceased, wrote off to the authorities in Niemandsland enquiring about the dead's previous life. She needed to fill in the few minor gaps of her own newly inherited old life. They responded (after the normal bureaucratic foul-ups, because things move by channels) that yes, ah, indeed they were in possession of records pertaining to a certain Brethenbach who, so *he* claimed, had been united in the state of matrimony to one Mayted. This subject had spent many years in safe custody, subsequently absented himself illegally and unlawfully even, gone (by all accounts) to Cuba, returned rebuffed, was freshly apprehended . . . and was eventually obliterated whilst still serving his time, by general debility and the rot of said time. Now the interesting part is that these events (sentence, escape, blue, re-sentence, death) all took place while the imposter was already living the life of Breathenbach . . . in Paname. And the question arises: who were these people? I leave it to you.

Ganesh was executed, legally chopped that is, in Pirax – what for I don't know – where, so it is rumoured, he entertained his fellow cons on the sweetest singing of slightly off-colour ditties, until the very end. Another unsuspected talent left unexplored and gone up the spout. A macabre twist to his demise – one hesitates to mention it even, can only hope it's unfounded – is that, so it is believed and thus is it whispered, the head was severed from the body and further that that head was embalmed, stuffed even (by a taxidermist?), and is now prized by some police museum somewhere, shown only to the most senior visitors.

Galp has disappeared from circulation; completely so. Nobody I know knows him. Sorry. Percy Vermoken, I see in the *Mother City News*, was recently promoted to an executive position in the firm he works for and is quite understandably no longer active as a trade unionist. C. Murphy, Eugene Marais's guide in the bundu, is reported to be employed as an immigration official at one of our border posts. Brink is back teaching at his old university, finally cured of the attacks he suffered from.

Don Espejuelo? I knew you'd want to hear about him sooner or later. But honestly, I know next to nothing of him. And to be frank, I prefer it thus: I'm more than half sure he's mixed up in some murky clandestinity, be it as snooper or spook or militant, perhaps even as an undercover agent for the Anoms. To which I must add that it won't surprise me in the least were he to be unmasked as the biggest fake yet. What a devious fellow he is, planting little secrets in any sandy plot at hand. And irrigating it with a smirk or two. How did he get to frequent the others in the first place? Perhaps the best would be for you to get hold of his book, *On the Noble Art of Walking in No Man's Land* (translated into Afrikaans, I'm assured, as *Die Oupe Lyf*). Maybe the answers are there for all to see.

My mission is hereby completed. Now it is for you to take it further, to decide what you wish to do with the evidence, if anything.

True, over the several years I knew them I did develop a sympathy for some of them. They often reminded me of coolies, the word originating, as you know, from *ku-li*, literally meaning "eating-bitterness-people".

Or maybe – let me leave you with this thought – an apt description of them in their futile movements hither (slither) and forth over the page would be, as Graham Greene wrote in *The Power and the Glory*:

Something resembling God dangled from the gibbet or went into odd attitudes before the bullet in a prison yard or contorted itself like a camel in the attitude of sex.

Again: don't expect me to know what you are to do with this information, or with these writings. Perhaps the best would be to do whatever you think fit. And in any case to make no bones about it.

Veuillez agréer, cher Monsieur Valjean, l'expression de mes sentiments les plus distingués.

Juan T. Bird
Mouroir, 1975-1982

Hoe sterven es met mi gheboren.
Maerlant

Shiki soku ze ku, ku soku ze shiki.